Midnight without a Moon

LINDA WILLIAMS JACKSON

Midnight without a moon

HOUGHTON MIFFLIN HARCOURT
BOSTON NEW YORK

Copyright © 2017 by Linda Williams Jackson

All rights reserved. For information about permission to reproduce selections from this book, write to Permissions, Houghton Mifflin Harcourt Publishing Company, 3 Park Avenue, 19th Floor, New York, New York 10016.

www.hmhco.com

The text was set in Fairfield.
Hand-lettering and art by Sarah L. Coleman
Book design by Sharismar Rodriguez

Library of Congress Cataloging-in-Publication Data is available.
ISBN: 978-0-544-78510-6

Manufactured in the United States of America
DOC 10 9 8 7 6 5 4 3 2 1
4500636216

This book is dedicated to:
My husband—Jeff—for always believing.

My children— Olivia, Chloe, and
Benjamin—for almost *always* listening.

My mom—Ernestine Scott Williams
(May 18, 1928–April 26, 2011)—
for always showing, and not just telling.

And to my longtime writing buddy—Alice Faye
Duncan Thompson—for always cheering.

STILLWATER, MISSISSIPPI

1955

July

Chapter One

SATURDAY, JULY 23

Papa used to say I had a memory like an elephant's. According to him, an elephant never forgets. I'm not sure how my self-educated, tenant-farming grandfather knew what an elephant's memory was like, but he sure was right about mine. Most folks didn't believe me, but I could remember all the way back from when I was only a year and a half old, when my brother Fred Lee was born. That was June 1943.

I remember Mama stretched out on the bed, flat on her back, her body stiff like a board.

A blue and white patchwork quilt covered the bed.

Sweat covered Mama.

What I thought was a watermelon tucked beneath her faded yellow dress looked as if it had sucked all the fat from her spindly arms and legs and placed it in her stomach. Since her lips were so dry and crusty, I thought the watermelon had sucked all the life from her face, too.

With her head swaying from side to side, Mama moaned and whispered, "Y'all, hurr'up and fetch Miss Addie."

My grandmother, Ma Pearl, standing as tall as a mountain, her thick arms crossed over her heavy bosom, shushed
Mama from the doorway. "Hush, chile," she said. "Save yo'
strength for pushing."

Other than the tiny room reeking of mothballs and rubbing alcohol, that's all I remember, because Ma Pearl shooed
me to the front porch to watch for the toothless, bent-to-the-
ground Miss Addie. After Miss Addie came hobbling along
on that crooked stick she called a cane, I wasn't allowed back
into the house. But even from the porch I could hear Mama
screaming. I thought the watermelon was eating her.

That night, I cried when I couldn't sleep with Mama. She
had the watermelon wrapped in a blanket and wedged against
her bosom. From that day on, whenever I wanted her to hold
me, she held that watermelon instead. I was convinced she
loved the watermelon more than she loved me.

Twelve years and one month after listening to Mama give
birth to what I thought was a watermelon, I was halfway
through my six-mile trek to Miss Addie's—not to fetch her
for Mama, but to deliver eggs to her from Ma Pearl—when I
heard a pickup rattling up the road, crunching rocks behind
me.

Without looking, I knew the pickup belonged to Ricky
Turner. And without a doubt, I knew Ricky was looking for
trouble. He had a reputation for trying to run over colored

folks just because he had a notion. He'd chased a nine-year-old boy named Obadiah Malone straight into the woods and all the way to Stillwater Lake with that rusted-out piece of junk only a few days before. So when the rock crunching grew louder and the engine clanking more intense, I flew one way and the egg crate another as I dove toward the grass. Not a second later, the pickup rumbled by, pelting me with rocks as I crouched near a tree. The eggs I was to deliver to Miss Addie lay scattered on the road, cracked, ready to sizzle in the midday heat.

As the truck rattled up the road, Ricky and his buddies leaned out the windows. They guffawed and hollered obscenities at me. Without thinking, I ran to the middle of the road, picked up the biggest rock I could find, and slung it at the disappearing truck.

That was a mistake.

I don't know how they saw me. But when the truck stopped, I froze.

Ricky shifted in reverse.

In a cloud of dust, the truck roared back my way.

I scrambled toward the grass.

When the truck stopped right in front of me, my heart sputtered worse than the pickup's engine.

Ricky poked his angry red face out the window and yelled, "Gal, don't you know better'n to chuck a rock at a gentleman's truck?" His face tightened like a fist as he released a stream of tobacco juice from his twisted mouth.

I wiped the brown spit from my legs and tried to stare at the ground like I knew I should. But I couldn't take my eyes off Ricky's scowling face. He snorted and spat again. This time at the ground.

"You could've broke my back winder," he said. "Now, how you 'spect to pay for that?"

For the record, the back window of his dented-up Chevy was already cracked six ways. But my stomach was twisted in so many knots that I couldn't have uttered that response even if I'd wanted to. Besides, three other boys sat crammed in the cab of that pickup. I recognized only one by name. Jimmy Robinson. The youngest son of the man whose place we lived on. And even *I* had sense enough to know that his fourteen-year-old self had no business riding around with the likes of twenty-year-old Ricky.

A freckled boy with a thin mustache and sweated-out orange hair leaned across Ricky. A grin revealed his tobacco-yellowed teeth. "What's the matter, darkie?" he asked. "Cat got your tongue?"

Ma Pearl always said that one day my foolish tongue would get me into trouble. Without my permission, it poked itself right out of my mouth to assure the freckled boy that the cat didn't have it. I bit it. But not before the freckled boy noticed.

He frowned, then leaned over and felt around on the floor of the pickup. When his hand came up, it held a beer bottle filled with black liquid.

"Uppity nigra!" he yelled, and hurled the bottle toward my head.

I ducked as it whistled past me and crashed against a tree.

Tobacco juice spewed in every direction.

The quartet in the pickup hooted, and Ricky gunned the engine. "Next time it'll be a bullet, you coon!" he shouted over the clanking.

Shaking like a beanstalk in a windstorm, I huddled near that tree until the sound of the pickup disappeared. When I was sure they wouldn't return, I grabbed my egg crate from the side of the road and scampered home. Miss Addie would have to make do without eggs this month, as I wasn't about to make a second trip and take a chance on Ricky returning for more of his devilment.

Folks said that Ricky wouldn't actually run over anybody. He just liked to give colored folks a good scare so we'd remember our place. Well, he'd given me, Rose Lee Carter, a pretty good scare. I vowed to never walk alone again, especially on a Saturday, when fools like him had just bloated their bellies with beer.

I'd been surprised to see Jimmy Robinson riding around with the likes of Ricky. His folks were what Ma Pearl labeled "good white peoples." And he always seemed friendly when I went to the Robinsons' house with Ma Pearl while she worked. He had once even been friends with Fred Lee, back when we were real little. He used to come over and play all the time. But at around age nine or so, Jimmy cut Fred Lee off like a bad ear of corn, barely even speaking to him anymore. As I passed their house, standing stately and white among the brown and green of their vast pecan grove, I couldn't help but wonder what his mama thought of him running around with a peckerwood like Ricky Turner.

Unlike the Robinsons' grand house, our unpainted house —with the two front doors and the rusted tin roof—paled gray against the lush green of the long rows of cotton in the surrounding fields. But as I kicked up dust along the path to the weatherworn front porch, I was happy to see Mr. Pete's shiny black car parked in the yard, adding a bit of sunshine to the scene.

Mr. Pete was my mama's husband, and he had only recently bought himself a shiny new car. A DeSoto is what he called it. That car seemed as long as a train and was niftier than any fifty-dollar suit. No one in Stillwater had ever seen anything like it. And seeing that none of the white folks in Stillwater—other than Mr. Robinson—even owned a car that fancy, Papa, my grandfather, said that Mr. Pete could get himself killed just by driving the darn thing.

Whether it was a danger for him to drive or not, my heart leaped with joy every time I heard Mr. Pete's car pull into the yard. That Saturday, I was surprised to see his car waiting when I got back. We didn't see Mama often, and we weren't expecting to see her for another two weeks.

As soon as I reached the ancient oak in the front yard, Mr. Pete's children, Sugar and Li' Man, bolted out of the screen door from the parlor. They moved so fast that their little feet barely touched the porch before they bounced down the front steps.

Sugar, her two braids flying high behind her, crashed right into me. It was the second time my egg crate went flying out of my hand that day.

Li' Man came right behind her. His crash sent us all to the ground.

Both of them sat on top of me, grinning.

"Aunt Rose! Guess what!" Sugar said, her eyes shining brighter than a noonday sun.

"First, y'all get up off of me," I said. "Then I'll guess."

They both scrambled up, but not before Sugar hugged my neck and kissed me on the cheek.

Sugar was seven and Li' Man six. They were Mr. Pete's children with his wife who died before he married Mama. Their real names were Callie Jean and Christopher Joe. It was Mama who started calling them Sugar and Li' Man. It was also Mama who insisted that they refer to me and Fred Lee as Aunt Rose and Uncle Fred. I thought the idea was stupid. But Mama and Mr. Pete thought it was cute.

I pushed myself off the ground and dusted my dress. Sugar picked up my egg crate and hugged it to her chest. I was so happy to see them that I almost stopped worrying about that trouble with Ricky. Besides, nothing was bruised but my pride, and I was already used to folks beating away at that.

"Okay, now y'all tell me what's going on," I said as we headed toward the steps.

Sugar shook her head. "Nuh-uh. You gotta guess."

Because she was grinning so, I squinted at her and asked, "You lose another tooth?"

She giggled and said, "Nah, that ain't it."

Before I could guess again, Li' Man blurted out, "We finn'a go to Chi-caaaa-go."

Sugar's bright smile dimmed quicker than a candle with a short wick. She slammed the egg crate to the ground and stalked off, yelling, "Li' Man, you jest spoiled the surprise!" She stomped back up the steps and stormed across the porch. When she snatched open the screen door and yelled, "Papaaa! Li' Man jest spoiled my surprise to Aunt Rose," Li' Man's eyes bucked bigger than the moon. When the screen door slammed shut, he charged up the steps and raced into the house, ready to defend himself. He knew better than anyone that Sugar was as rotten as a bushel of bad apples, and it wouldn't take much of her whining for Mr. Pete, or even Mama, to take a switch to him.

But I stood at the front steps, too stunned to move.

Chicago.

Colored folks didn't go to Chicago to visit. Colored folks went to Chicago to live. In the last few years it seemed everybody had been leaving. Folks were fleeing Mississippi so fast it was like birds flying south for the winter, except they were going north, or out west to California. "Migrating" is what my seventh-grade teacher, Miss Johnson, called it. "A great colored migration," she'd said. "Like a flock of black birds." Except, unlike birds who returned in the spring, these folks rarely came back.

I picked up my egg crate and tossed it across the porch. Plunking myself down on the top step, I glowered at Mr. Pete's big black car—the car that would take my mama to Chicago. Li' Man had said "we," and of course that had to include Mama. She was Mr. Pete's wife. But I already knew it didn't include me and Fred Lee, because it never did. We were Mama's children, but we had never been invited to be a part of her new family. Nor had we ever set foot in their house. It was bad enough we never saw our daddy, Johnny Lee Banks, even though he lived right there in Stillwater. Now we would never know when we'd see our mama's face, either. Some folks who'd migrated up north made the South an annual visit. Others, it seemed, never came back. Seeing how they rarely came to see us anyhow, I wasn't so sure in which category Mama and Mr. Pete would fit.

I was seven when Mama left us the first time. Six years had passed, but they felt as fresh as six months. At the time, Sugar was a year old and Li' Man was still a lap baby. Their mama's heart simply gave out, folks said, and Mr. Pete found a replacement so quickly that it seemed as if he held the funeral for his first wife and the courthouse wedding to his second wife on the same day. And it didn't seem to bother him one bit that Mama already had me and Fred Lee but had never married our daddy.

Folks said that Mr. Pete was interested in only one thing —a pretty face. And that, Mama certainly had. I remember how she stood before Ma Pearl's dresser mirror that chilly March morning and smeared red lipstick on her pouting lips. Among the dullness of Ma Pearl's bedroom, she looked out of place wearing a silky beige dress trimmed in lace. So I asked her, "Where you goin', Mama?"

She grinned and said, "Rose Lee, honey, yo' mama 'bout to marry a fine man. And I'm go'n take care o' his babies for him."

"What about me and Fred Lee? Ain't we yo' babies?"

Mama giggled like a silly schoolgirl. "You and Fret'Lee big now," she said, waving her hand at me. "Callie and Christopher is the babies. Besides, y'all got Papa and Ma Pearl. Callie and Christopher don't have a soul but Pete. And Pete ain't got time to raise no babies," she said, smiling. "He got all that land to farm."

"Can me and Fred Lee come too?"

"Nuh-uh," Mama said, frowning, as she leaned toward her reflection. "Two babies is more'n enough for me to care for."

After making sure that she was as lovely as a spring morning, she bent down and placed her soft hands on my shoulders. Kissing my forehead, she said, "You be a good girl for Ma Pearl and Papa. Don't make Ma Pearl have to whup you."

That was the last thing she said to me before she became a mama to Sugar and Li' Man and a memory to me and Fred Lee.

When the screen door to the parlor creaked open that Saturday, I jumped. But I didn't turn around.

"Sister?" Mama called softly.

Reluctantly, I turned and faced her.

Mama was tall, shapely, caramel complexioned, and movie-star beautiful. Except for the height, I looked nothing like her. I was string-bean skinny and as black as the ace of spades, as Ma Pearl liked to say. In her crisp green dress, Mama looked fancier than some of the ladies in Mrs. Robinson's fashion magazines. As pretty as an angel, some folks said. Even the afternoon sun seemed to form a halo around her freshly pressed and curled hair.

But according to Ma Pearl, her daughter was definitely no angel. Having had me at fifteen and Fred Lee at sixteen, Mama was what the old folks labeled "ruint". And Ma Pearl never let me forget it. She was so strict on me that I was allowed around only two boys—Fred Lee and Hallelujah Jenkins, the preacher's boy.

Mama smoothed a curl from her pretty face and said, "Sister, why you ack'n shameface?"

She'd begun calling me Sister when I was ten, and calling Fred Lee Brother when he was nine. We hated those pet names more than we hated the old-folksy names, Aunt Rose and Uncle Fred.

I shielded my face from the sun with my hand. "I ain't acting shameface," I said, squinting at Mama. "I just don't wanna come in right now."

With a wide grin plastered on her face, Mama gestured

toward the door. "Well, you better git on in here and say bye to us 'fore we leave."

I cringed. Those were the exact words she'd used the day she pranced off to the courthouse in Greenwood and married Mr. Pete. I had stayed awake all that night, lying in the bed we shared, worried. Waiting for her to come home. Of course, she never did. Now she was heading to Chicago, and she'd probably never come back from there, either.

Instead of following her through that squeaking screen door, I wanted badly to make a run out back to the toilet to settle my gurgling stomach. Plus, with Ma Pearl's cheerful chatter flowing from the parlor, I knew I didn't want to go in there and watch her awe over Mama's new family as if they were a collection of Mrs. Robinson's fine china.

Yet somehow I managed to stand and stumble toward the screen door. Then I stopped, my stomach flipping, my heart pounding, as I hesitated before Mama.

She smiled. Her brown eyes, warm, glowing like a welcome fire on a cold night, beckoned me, as always, to do what I didn't want to do. But before I took two steps inside the parlor, Ma Pearl, with her ample frame crammed in the chair right next to the door, took one look at me and frowned. "Gal, what the heck jest happened to you?"

Chapter Two

SATURDAY, JULY 23

THE CHATTERING STOPPED. AND EVERYONE — MR. Pete, Sugar, Li' Man, Fred Lee, Papa, and Mama — all stared at me. They knew Ma Pearl wasn't one to reckon with. She'd as soon give any one of her fourteen grandchildren a taste of the backside of her hand if we just smiled too long.

"Why is you so dirty?" she demanded.

When my eyes shifted to my stained beige dress, hand-crafted by Ma Pearl herself from old croker sacks that had once held flour, my mouth fell into an O. The tobacco splashes on my legs were the ones I felt when Ricky spat at me. The splotches on my dress — from the bottle hitting the tree — were the ones that caught me by surprise.

I reshaped my mouth to explain, but the look on Ma Pearl's fleshy face made the incident with Ricky feel about as scary as a church picnic. If she was that upset about my dress, I knew she wouldn't take lightly to those cracked eggs frying on the side of the road.

With no other options, I smoothed down my soiled dress

and muttered, "I accidentally fell when Sugar and Li' Man ran out to meet me."

When Ma Pearl's nostrils flared, I braced myself for a scolding.

Luckily, Sugar pointed at Li' Man and said, "He did it."

Not so lucky for Li' Man.

Mr. Pete squinted at him.

Li' Man fidgeted.

Sugar smiled.

Mr. Pete, a huge man with heavy hands and an even heavier voice, creased his forehead and said, "Christopher Joe, apologize to your Aunt Rose. You got her dress all dirty."

Li' Man dropped his head to his chest and muttered, "Sorry."

Before I could defend him, Ma Pearl cut me off. "Go take off that nasty dress." She pointed toward the porch. "Don't come in here. Go through the front room."

Humiliated, I backed out of the parlor doorway, took three steps across the porch, and entered the house through the front room as I had been commanded. I hurried to the back of the house, to the bedroom I shared with my fifteen-year-old cousin Queen, to change into clothing more suitable for entrance into Ma Pearl's parlor.

The parlor was a space she reserved for special people,

like Mr. Pete — or for herself and Queen, her favorite grand-child, when they wanted to sit and listen to their daily radio programs. The parlor also held Ma Pearl's good furniture: the worn powder blue sofa, settee, and chairs that were no lon-ger welcome in Mrs. Robinson's parlor. As a matter of fact, everything in Ma Pearl's parlor, from the sofa to a pair of melted-down white candles, all came from the Robinsons' grand white house up the road.

Papa always said, "Don't never turn down nothing the white folks gives you. And make sure they sees you using it."

Ma Pearl should have turned down those outdated Sears and Roebuck catalogs she kept stacked in the corner, col-lecting dust. The only use we got from them was flipping through the pages, dreaming of things we'd never own.

By the time I found another homemade dress to slip over my head and returned to the parlor, the chatter had returned as well. Like a bird in the early morning darkness, Ma Pearl twittered incessantly about the dangers of living in the city. She had been listening to radio programs about crime in big cities like Chicago and Saint Louis, and she wanted to im-press Mr. Pete with what she thought she knew about living up north.

Papa, his expression serious as always, sat in one of the powder blue chairs next to the window. He wore his

Saturday-going-to-town clothes—creased khakis and a starched white shirt—for the occasion. His black pipe, filled with Prince Albert tobacco, but never lit, rested between his lips.

Though tall, Papa was not a hulk of a man the way Ma Pearl was an amazon of a woman. Farm work kept him slim. Also, unlike Ma Pearl, he was not impressed with Mr. Pete. As "ruint" as Mama was, he was not fond of her being married to a man who, at forty-nine, was closer to Papa's fifty-nine years than Mama's twenty-eight, regardless of how much land he farmed.

Even though I had changed into a clean dress, I hesitated to enter the parlor. With Ma Pearl and Papa being the only two privy to Mama's visit—and obviously to her northern migration—their appearance almost matched the crispness of the Chicago-bound family. Plus, I hadn't thought to wet a rag and wipe the dust from my ankles and feet. I was about to turn around and head back to my room before Ma Pearl noticed and gave me another scolding, but when Mama saw me lingering in the doorway between the parlor and the front room, she invited me to join her. She patted the spot next to her on the settee and said, "Come set beside me, Sister."

As soon as I sat next to Mama (and scooted my feet as far under the settee as possible), Sugar left her spot next to Mr.

Pete on the sofa and wedged herself between us. "I wanna set beside you too," she said, glancing up, grinning at Mama. When Mama smiled her consent, I scooted over and made room for Sugar. If Mama had waited a bit to nickname her the way she did me and Fred Lee, perhaps she could have named her Salt instead, seeing that sometimes she could be just as salty as she was sweet.

Mr. Pete smiled at Fred Lee, who stood rather than sat. "Me and Christopher Joe don't bite," he said.

Fred Lee, leaning against the wall, his arms crossed over his chest, his eyes cast to the floor, ignored Mr. Pete. I could tell he was as angry as I was that Mama was leaving for Chicago.

Fred Lee was tall like Mama. As a matter of fact, even at age twelve, he was almost as tall as the burly Mr. Pete, without the bulk. But we both, according to Ma Pearl, looked like our daddy, Johnny Lee Banks. She also claimed that's where Fred Lee got his "slow wits." Of course, I could confirm neither, seeing I had never met the man myself, even though he lived right there in Stillwater with his wife and children.

When Fred Lee didn't answer him, Mr. Pete turned back to Ma Pearl to continue exchanging notes on city life. As he bragged about the things they would do once they got to Chicago, Papa took his pipe from his mouth and regarded him curiously. Leaning back in his chair, Papa crossed his right foot over his left knee and interrupted the conversation. "What kinda work you say you got up there again, Pete?"

Mr. Pete sat straighter. "I got a position with Armour and Company," he said proudly. "The meat factory."

Papa furrowed his brow. "They 'low coloreds to handle meat up there in them factories?"

"I won't be handling meat," Mr. Pete said matter-of-factly. "I'll be making soap."

"Soap?" Papa said, uncrossing his legs. "At a meat house?"

Mr. Pete tilted his head to the side. "You never heard of *Dial* soap, Mr. Carter?"

"I makes my own soap, Pete. No need to concern myself with the store-bought kind."

Mr. Pete jerked back, his face flustered. "You never heard the radio advertisements?"

Papa placed the pipe back in his mouth. He shook his head and pretended to puff as he uttered, "Nope."

"Can't believe you never heard the advertisements," Mr. Pete said, his voice low.

After a moment of silent staring, his expression bewildered, Mr. Pete cleared his throat and said, *"'Aren't you glad you use Dial? Don't you wish everybody did?'"*

I suppressed a chuckle. But Ma Pearl, with a grin as wide as the room, couldn't contain her enthusiasm. "Oooh, Pete," she said, clasping her hands like a child before a candy counter, "you sound jest like the man doing the abertising on the radio."

Mr. Pete beamed like a lighthouse.

Papa, still not impressed, countered, "Don't much listen to the radio, Pete. So I reckon I ain't never heard of a meat house making soap."

"Aw shoot, Paul," Ma Pearl said. "Ain't no different than the rough lye soap you makes from the hog fat."

Papa rubbed his chin, pondering. "I reckon it ain't."

As Mr. Pete, Ma Pearl, and Mama prattled on about Armour and Company, Chicago, and their shiny new apartment awaiting them on the South Side, Papa continued to regard Mr. Pete with a furrowed brow. "Pete," he said finally, his forehead wrinkled, his pipe dangling from his hand, "you sold all that land and bought a fancy car just so you could drive up to the city to make soap?"

Mr. Pete's expression soured. "Mr. Carter," he said, his voice booming, "a Negro can own all the land in Mississippi and still be treated worse than a hog. I can't even register to vote in this county without the threat of being gunned down on the courthouse steps." He placed his arm around Li' Man's shoulders and pulled him close. "I didn't sell my land to buy a car," he said, staring intently at Papa. "I sold my land to buy an opportunity. A future for my children."

"Well, making soap still don't sound like a proper way to make a living to me," said Papa.

Mr. Pete shook his head. "I don't want this kind of life for Callie and Christopher." He gestured toward the open window, suggesting the cotton fields beyond it. "They deserve better."

"Better than what?" asked Papa, his brows raised.

Mama interjected. "They got real good schools up there," she said. She smiled awkwardly and tugged at one of Sugar's long braids. "Our babies can even go to the same school as white children if they want."

Good schools for Sugar and Li' Man, huh? With white children. Well, what about me and Fred Lee? Don't we deserve good schools too instead of that haunted school for coloreds where everything in it is junk the white folks didn't want in their children's schools anymore?

When I was little, watching Mama pamper Sugar and Li' Man, I used to think that maybe if I had light skin and long hair like Sugar's, she would love me that way too, maybe even let me live with them. And the same for Fred Lee, except his hair would be curly and coal black like Li' Man's. So every night after I finished reciting the Lord's Prayer to Ma Pearl, I prayed earnestly, "Jesus, please let me wake up in the morning with bright skin and long hair like Sugar's." But every morning I woke with the same chocolate complexion and short, nappy hair I had the day Mama left.

I finally gave up on the prayer after two years and two seriously callused knees.

Now all I wanted was to scream at Mama and shake her till her head rattled. But of course I didn't. I didn't say a word as she and Mr. Pete sang the glories of their new life up north. And neither did Fred Lee. He was as silent as a stump.

When Mama got ready to leave, she hugged me and kissed my cheek. She smiled at Ma Pearl and said, "Take good care of my babies, now." When she tried to hug Fred Lee, he pulled away.

"I'll write soon as we get settled," she said. Surprisingly, her voice held a slight quiver.

As Ma Pearl and Papa walked the Chicago-bound family to their train of a car, Fred Lee, with his shoulders hunched and his fists clenched, left the house and headed to God only knew where.

Me? I collapsed in the chair next to the window and peeled back the curtain, my heart breaking when I peered out. Piling into that shiny black car, smiling, Mama and her family looked so happy, as if they had stepped off the pages of one of those Sears and Roebuck catalogs in the corner. And I would've torn off my right arm to join them if I could have. I spent six years wishing I could be a part of her and

Mr. Pete's family. Now they were heading to Chicago, leaving my life and Fred Lee's for good.

I tried to hold back. I had promised myself I would never cry over Mama again. But I couldn't stop the flood. Tears gushed out before I knew it, racing down my cheeks, rushing over my trembling lips. I hugged my knees to my chest, dropped my head, and sobbed into the folds of my dress, welcoming the tears, urging them to hurry, to flush the pain from my heart. I sat there trembling and sobbing, burying my face in my dress, wanting to block out the world, until the sound of slamming car doors jolted me to my senses.

My tightening chest reminded me that I couldn't bear another chastisement from Ma Pearl for wearing that tear-soaked dress in her pristine parlor. I gave my face a final swipe, sprang from the chair, and fled to the back room to release my tears in private.

Chapter Three

MONDAY, JULY 25

BEFORE OUR OLD ROOSTER, SLICK CHARLIE, EVEN had time to crow, Ma Pearl called my name from the doorway of the bedroom. "Rose Lee," she said. "Git up, gal."

I didn't move. Monday meant laundry, cooking, and cleaning. And that was all before noon. After that, I had to go to the field. Besides, with Mama gone, the heaviness in my heart had radiated down to the rest of my body, paralyzing my arms and legs. When Mama was a car ride away in Greenwood, I knew I would occasionally see her when she felt the need to have Mr. Pete drop her off for a visit on a Saturday afternoon. But with her all the way up in Chicago, I'd be lucky to see her once a year, when all the other northern Negroes paid the South a visit. If she ever decided to come back, that is.

"Rose Lee," Ma Pearl said again. As long as her voice remained low enough so she would wake only me and not Queen, I pretended to be asleep. But when she leaned inside that sheet-covered doorframe and said, "Gal, git up. You going to the field this morning," I shot up faster than a stalk of corn in the middle of July. Laundry, cooking, and cleaning were bad, but going to the field all day was worse.

I didn't bother putting my housecoat on over my thin nightgown or even rubbing the crust from my tired eyes. I dashed out of that room and chased Ma Pearl through the house, asking, "How come I gotta go to the field this morning, Ma Pearl?"

I stumbled through the moonlight of Fred Lee's room, on through the darkness of Ma Pearl and Papa's room, all the way to the soft glow of the kerosene-lit front room. The floorboards of our old house creaked with every step.

For a big woman, my grandma sure could move fast. I panted as I tried to keep up. By the time we reached the kitchen, I was sweating. And it didn't help one bit that our old woodstove in the corner was lit up like a campfire.

Ma Pearl lumbered over to the icebox and pulled out a bowl of butter. A basket of fresh eggs from the henhouse waited on the table while the nutty aroma of coffee percolated in the pot. Without even a glance at me, she finally answered my question. "Albert and his boys cain't make it today."

I shaped my mouth to protest, but she cut me off. "Don't complain."

When she sealed her words with a steely-eyed look, I plopped down on the rickety bench next to the window and yanked back the faded yellow curtain. It was still black outside. The only indication of morning was a pink haze lingering over the horizon at the end of the long rows of cotton. The yellow glow in the barn meant that Papa was already in there preparing for a long, hot day. I yawned and wondered why I was up before Fred Lee, seeing that he had to go to the field as soon as the sun came up too.

On a normal Monday, before I worked like a slave in the house, I would go out to milk Ellie while Queen lay around somewhere curled in a ball, pretending she had the monthly cramps. I let the curtain fall and peered at Ma Pearl. "Is Queen go'n milk Ellie this morning?" I asked.

With her face in a tight frown, Ma Pearl dipped flour from the croker sack with a tin can and poured it into her sifter. She held the sifter over her scratched-up mixing bowl and cranked the handle. Like a soft dusting of fresh snow, flour flowed into the bowl. When she was good and ready, Ma Pearl paused, pursed her lips, and glared at me. "You know that gal cain't tell a tit from a tat," she said. "You go'n milk Ellie. You got time."

Like a small child, I crossed my arms and pouted. I couldn't believe I would have to go to the field all day *and* still be expected to work around the house. With the help of Mr. Albert Jackson, who lived a few miles down the road from us, and his two sons, Levi and Fischer (Fish for short), I at least got a break from the field two mornings a week.

"What happened to Mr. Albert 'n'em? How come they can't come today?" I asked.

Ma Pearl's pudgy fingers pinched the butter into the flour. While she worked at the mixture until it resembled yellow cornmeal, her eyebrows knit into a deeper frown. "I said they cain't come."

"But Levi already took off early on Friday," I complained.

Ma Pearl's face hardened. "Stay outta grown folks' bizness."

Well, it *was* my business if I had to go out there to that hot cotton field and do the work of three men, one full-grown and two almost grown. But I couldn't say that to Ma Pearl. She would've slapped me clear on into July of 1956.

She wobbled over to the icebox and pulled out a quart-size bottle of buttermilk. With a heavy sigh, she lumbered back to the table and slowly poured the buttermilk straight from the bottle into the mixture of flour and crumbled butter. While turning the stiff mixture with a fork, she mumbled under her breath, "Anna Mae and Pete did right leaving this dirn place. Nothing here but a bunch a trouble."

I tilted my head to the side. "Ma Pearl—"

She scowled.

I sealed my lips.

With her forehead creased, Ma Pearl went back to work on the biscuits.

She shook extra tablespoons of flour into the sticky mixture as she began half singing, half moaning, "Stay outta grown folks' bizness," as if it were a real song. "All these dirn chi'rens jest oughta stay outta grown folks' bizness."

While her fingers shaped the sticky batter into dough, her made-up lyrics morphed into the humming of a real song. *"'Why should I feel discouraged,'"* she sang quietly, *"'and why should the shadows come? Why should my heart be lonely, and long for heav'n and home?'"*

Something was wrong. Mr. Albert Jackson and Levi and Fish never missed a full day of work. And Ma Pearl never bothered with Gospel music unless it was Wednesday or Sunday, church days. Otherwise, she swayed and snapped her fingers to the blues.

I pulled back the curtain and stared into the early morning darkness again. As the sun peeked over the horizon, promising another blazing hot day, Slick Charlie finally got his lazy self up and crowed. I dropped the curtain and stared down at a crack in the floorboards as I listened to Ma Pearl's chanting, *"Jesus is my portion. A constant friend is he. His eye is on the sparrow, and I know he watches me.'"*

Her singing annoyed me. I was thirteen, not three. If something had happened to Mr. Albert and his sons, I was old enough to know about it. I studied Ma Pearl's face for answers as she worked the big ball of dough. She rolled and patted, stretched and pulled, concentrating, as if that beige lump were the most important thing in her life at the moment.

I tried one more time. Taking a deep breath and letting it out, I quickly asked, "How come Mr. Albert ain't coming?"

Ma Pearl's hand paused midpat. She glanced at me but didn't say a word. She sighed and began patting the dough again. "Colored folks just oughta stay in their place. It'd keep us all outta a whole lotta trouble. One Negro do something, white folks get mad at everybody."

I rubbed goose bumps from my arms even though it was probably a hundred and ten degrees in the kitchen with that stove burning. Mr. Albert didn't seem to be the kind of Negro who would get in trouble with the whites. To my knowledge, he had always stayed in his place, just like Papa. Just like white folks like Ricky Turner warned us to do when he chased us off the road with his pickup. Then I had the nerve to challenge him by tossing a rock his way *and* by poking my tongue out at him. I couldn't help but wonder what Ma Pearl would have thought of that.

Cautiously I asked, "Did Mr. Albert do something? Is he in trouble?"

Ma Pearl ignored my question. "Fetch me that rolling pin from the safe."

As I got up to get the rolling pin, she spoke under her

breath. "These young folks don't know noth'n. Go'n get us all kil't. Running round here talking 'bout the right to vote."

Young folks? Levi or Fish. But right to vote? That would be Mr. Albert. He was the only one old enough to vote. Now I was even more confused. Could Mr. Albert even read? And surely he wouldn't do anything to stir up trouble with whites in Stillwater.

My heart pounded as I opened the door of the gleaming white cabinet where we kept things we didn't want the rats to feast on during the night. Just two months before, back in May, a preacher named Reverend George Lee had been killed for helping colored folks register to vote. I prayed that nothing like that had happened to Mr. Albert.

"A Negro ain't got the right to do nothing 'cept live free and die," Ma Pearl said.

Live free? When we couldn't even walk up the road without being chased down by a peckerwood in a pickup? I didn't realize my hand was shaking until I reached up to the middle shelf for the rolling pin and knocked over a Mason jar full of last winter's pear preserves. Like dominoes, that jar knocked over another jar, and that one, another. All three of them rolled out of the cabinet and crashed to the floor.

"Gal, watch what you doing!"

"Ma Pearl—" I started, but didn't finish. It wouldn't do any good. I could tell from those lines in her forehead that she didn't want any apology I had to offer. Plus, I knew it wasn't just those fallen preserves and the sticky mess they made that had her in a huff.

I handed her the rolling pin and sighed. "I'll clean it up."

Ma Pearl groaned. "I'll clean it up myself. You just go'n in there and git yo'self ready to work. I didn't git you up early jest to sit round here and run yo' mouth. You got a long day ahead. Now git. You know how slow you is."

"Yes, ma'am," I said.

"And wake Fret'Lee, too." She sighed and pursed her lips. "Try not to wake up Queen. She didn't sleep good last night."

When I was halfway out the door, she stopped me. "Go'n empt' that slop jar too," she said, turning up her nose. "That thing stank worse then skunk spray. You and Queen piss through the night more'n anybody I know."

You mean Queen pisses through the night more than anybody you know, I wanted to say. *I sleep through the night because you work me like a donkey all day.*

But I was smart enough not to talk back to Ma Pearl. Like I said, there was no sense in arriving in 1956 before the rest of the world got there. So I kept my mouth shut as I went on to the back room to fetch the slop jar and take it out to the toilet to pour out the queen's pee.

Chapter Four

MONDAY, JULY 25

Here's how I figure things happened earlier that Monday morning before the sun ever rose over Stillwater, Mississippi:

God called his faithful angel Gabriel to his big shiny throne and said, "Gabe, I have a special job for you today."

Gabriel honored his boss with a bow and said, "Master, whatever you wish is my command."

Then God said, "Take a great big bucket and fly over to the sun. Fill that bucket with as much heat as it will hold; then go down to Stillwater, Mississippi, and pour it over a girl named Rose Lee Carter. Then bake her. Bake her real good, until she learns not to complain so much."

And I know old Gabe did just what God ordered, because by midmorning I was so hot I could hardly breathe. That sun beat down on me like I owed it money from six years back. Sweat dripped in my eyes so bad that I couldn't tell cotton from weeds, and I know I was chopping down both.

But even with my impending heat stroke, I felt I had a right to complain just a little bit after what Ma Pearl did that

morning. Before I could get my clothes on good, she was calling me to get to the barn to milk Ellie while Queen slept.
And it didn't help one bit that that cantankerous cow (Ellie,
not Queen) wouldn't cooperate. Milk squirted everywhere
except the darned bucket.

Queen claimed she'd been cramping all night and hadn't
slept a wink. It's a wonder she didn't bleed to death as much
as she had the cramps. Queen was two years older than
me. Well, almost three, seeing she would turn sixteen that
October. And like me and Fred Lee, she lived with Ma Pearl
and Papa instead of with her mama, my aunt Clara Jean, and
her family. That's because Uncle Ollie, Aunt Clara Jean's
husband, wasn't Queen's daddy, like Mr. Pete wasn't mine.
Matter of fact, Queen didn't even know who her daddy was.
Nobody did, except Aunt Clara Jean, of course. And Aunt
Clara Jean never would tell a soul who Queen's daddy was.

Folks said he was white. And that wasn't too hard to believe, seeing that Queen was light enough to pass for white
herself if she'd wanted to, *and* seeing that her long hair never
needed the heat of a straightening comb. Plenty of folks in
our family were yellow, but Queen was different. And with
the way she never lifted a finger to even wash a plate, she
acted like she was white too.

Folks said that when Queen was born, Ma Pearl took to
her like ants to a picnic. They said she snatched that newborn

baby from Aunt Clara Jean's bosom and claimed her like a hard-earned prize. That's because Ma Pearl favored pretty. And to Ma Pearl, light equaled pretty, even if the person was as ugly as a moose.

Folks said that when I first came out of Mama, my skin was as pink as a flower. Mama said she took one look at me and declared, "I'm go'n call you Rose, 'cause you so pretty like one." But Ma Pearl said, "Don't set yo' hopes high for that child, Anna Mae. Look at them ears. They as black as tar. By this time next year, that lil' gal go'n be blacker than midnight without a moon, just like her daddy."

Of course Ma Pearl was right. Before my first birthday rolled around, on February 4, 1943, I was as black as a cup of Maxwell House without a hint of milk. And according to Aunt Clara Jean, I was the ugliest little something Stillwater, Mississippi, had ever seen.

Of course, my dark skin is what sentenced me to the field. "Queen too light to be out there in that heat," Ma Pearl always claimed. But like Goldilocks's claim about Baby Bear's porridge, my dark complexion was just right.

As I gripped the hoe between my callused palms and stared down at what seemed like a mile-long row of cotton, I wanted to cry. Thanks to Mr. Albert and sons, I now had to suffer at least four full days in the field instead of three.

I usually didn't go to the field on Monday and Thursday

mornings, the days Ma Pearl worked for Mrs. Robinson. While she kept their house, I kept ours. And Queen, even though she was almost sixteen and pretty much grown, did nothing—except sit around and read magazines that Mrs. Robinson had tossed out.

But I guess I should've considered myself lucky. Most colored folks didn't have it nearly as good as we did. Since Papa was one of the best farmers in the Delta, Mr. Robinson put him in charge of his cotton. Other colored folks who lived on plantations had to deal with straw bosses like Ricky Turner's evil daddy. And some of them were, as Ma Pearl put it, "the most low-downed white mens you ever did see."

I looked up and saw that Papa and Fred Lee had left me way behind. They always did. I was a slow chopper. Ma Pearl said I had my head in the clouds, daydreaming. And she was right. I was always dreaming about the day I could have a house like Mrs. Robinson's, with a maid to clean up after me, a cook to prepare all my meals, and a substitute mama to change my baby's diapers simply because I couldn't take the smell.

Actually, I decided I would have a house better than Mrs. Robinson's, and it certainly wouldn't be in Mississippi. It would be in Chicago. Because no matter what it took, I was going there one day, just like Mama and all the rest of them.

In Chicago I'd go to the finest school they had—a school

where coloreds and whites went together. No white school with good stuff and a colored school with a bunch of old stuff. And we'd all use the same bathrooms and drink from the same water fountains, too.

Then I'd graduate from that school and go to a fine college, a college where only the smartest people could go. I'd study to be a doctor, like my friend Hallelujah wanted to be; then we could both be rich like that colored doctor he told me about who lived in Mound Bayou. After I became a doctor and made a lot of money, I'd come back down to Mississippi and buy Papa a brand-new car, one better than Mr. Pete's. And I'd teach him how to drive it. Next, I'd buy him a big white house just like Mr. Robinson's, and I might let Ma Pearl live there with him. Then again, I might not.

Those were my plans. Chicago. College. And caring for my family.

Daydreaming—it's how I survived that dusty cotton field.

"Rosa Lee!" a second-soprano voice called.

Before I even turned, I knew I would find Hallelujah Jenkins standing at the edge of the field, waving at me.

Nobody called me Rosa but him. "A pretty name for a pretty girl," he'd said.

"A preacher's son ought not to tell lies," I'd said back.

Besides, who else would've been calling my name from the edge of a cotton field midmorning instead of working in one? I glanced up at the sky. The sun was between nine and ten o'clock. Every Negro I knew, other than Queen, was somewhere working, either in a white man's field or in a white woman's house.

Hallelujah Jenkins was the most privileged colored boy in Leflore County, Mississippi. Slightly chubby and not so athletic, he always wore starched shirts, creased slacks, funny-looking suspenders, and brown penny loafers, even in hundred-degree weather, just like his daddy, Reverend Clyde B. Jenkins the Second. And he was constantly pushing his thick black glasses up the bridge of his pudgy nose.

Hallelujah was actually Clyde B. Jenkins the Third. But everybody called him Hallelujah. When he was eighteen months old, that was the first word out of his mouth, at a funeral, no less.

Hallelujah even dressed nice when he helped us out in the field on occasion. And trust me, those occasions were few and far between, as the old folks used to say. Ma Pearl said he was too delicate for farm work. But Papa said it was a sign that Hallelujah would be a man of books and not of brawn. "A learned man like his daddy," Papa said.

"Erudite" is the word my seventh-grade teacher, Miss Johnson, would use to describe him.

Hallelujah was a strange kind of fellow, but he was also my best friend. And when I saw him that morning, I remembered it was his birthday. He was finally fourteen. "Fourteen going on forty," as Papa would say. But to Hallelujah, fourteen seemed to be the magic age when he thought Queen — the girl he claimed he would one day marry — would finally pay attention to him. Guess he forgot that she would keep having birthdays too.

Like me, Hallelujah didn't have a mama. Well, I had one. She just didn't act like one. But Hallelujah already had three mamas in his brief lifetime. Hallelujah's first mama, his real mama, died when he was four, his second mama when he was eight, and his third mama when he was twelve.

It's true. They all died four years apart. Folks said Reverend Jenkins killed them. They said he bored them to death when he forced them to listen to his sermons all week before he put his congregants to sleep with them on Sundays. Rumor had it he was on the lookout for wife number four. Too bad every woman in Leflore County did her best to avoid even shaking the poor man's hand on Sunday morning, in case there was any truth about his sermons boring his deceased wives to death.

Hallelujah trudged on up the row toward me, his penny loafers collecting dust along the way. It was so hot that even he wore a wide-brimmed straw hat to hide his face from the sun, when a fedora usually graced his head.

"How come you didn't grab a hoe?" I asked him. "Can't you see I need some help?"

Hallelujah shook his head. "Can't. Preacher let me stop by for only a minute."

"What? Long enough to eat some of Ma Pearl's cooking?"

Normally, Hallelujah would've laughed. But that day he didn't. He didn't even smile.

"Happy birthday," I called, hoping to at least conjure a lip curl.

But Hallelujah's expression remained stoic. With a wave of his hand, he gave me a dry "Thanks."

I leaned on the heavy hoe and wiped sweat from my face with my sleeve. When Hallelujah got closer, I could see that his eyes were red, as if he'd been crying.

"What's wrong?" I asked.

Hallelujah tilted his head sideways. "Didn't you hear?"

"Hear what?"

"About Levi."

My legs went weak.

I knew something bad had happened.

With Ma Pearl acting jittery that morning and Papa being quieter than usual, I knew something had happened that they didn't want me to know about it. Mr. Albert, Levi, and Fish had been working with us in Mr. Robinson's fields for as long as I could remember, and they had never missed a day of work.

My top lip felt numb when I spoke. "S-something happened to Levi?"

Hallelujah removed his glasses and wiped them with a handkerchief from his shirt pocket. Before he put his glasses back on, anxiety shone in his eyes. "Rosa Lee," he said, his voice shaking, his eyes tearing up, "Levi's dead."

My knees buckled. If it hadn't been for the hoe, I would've crumbled to the ground.

Black, pulsating dots flashed around me as Hallelujah's next words floated to my ears: "pickup . . . shotgun . . . head . . ." Dead.

The black dots multiplied as the earth spun beneath my feet. Nausea rose in my stomach, and every drop of biscuits and eggs I'd eaten that morning threatened to come back up.

Dropping the hoe, I grabbed my stomach and bolted from the field.

As I stumbled clumsily between the dusty rows of green cotton leaves, I couldn't help but resent them. Levi Jackson, a fine young man, had spent most of his life tending to that field, bringing that cotton to life every summer. Now he no longer had his.

I wanted to scream. I wanted to scream until my anguish was heard all over Stillwater—all over Mississippi—all the way to Chicago, straight to my mama's ears. I don't know why, but I hated her at that moment. I hated her more than the nameless face that had shot Levi Jackson for no good reason.

But I couldn't scream. I couldn't open my mouth and take a chance on throwing up and killing any of Mr. Robinson's precious cotton.

By the time I reached the edge of the field, my stomach lurched. Racing past the chickens scratching in the yard, I dashed toward the toilet, heaving the whole time.

I'm not sure why I ran to the toilet, knowing its stench would only make me gag more. When I reached it, I ran behind it, my body lurching forward, spewing the last of my breakfast toward the ground.

Hallelujah banged on the door of the toilet. "Rosa Lee, you okay?"

"I'm back here," I called weakly, all my strength now a yellow puddle on the ground.

Rubbing goose bumps from my arms, I came from behind the toilet and headed up the path to the backyard. Hallelujah trailed behind me. When I reached the yard, I hugged my arms around my stomach and doubled over. A sick moan followed.

Hallelujah put his arms around my shoulders and ushered me to the back porch. When my body dropped on it like a sack of overgrown potatoes, I pressed my face in my palms and screamed. I screamed until my stomach hurt.

I shouted into my palms. "Why, Hallelujah? Why?"

"He registered to vote," Hallelujah said, his voice hoarse. "And they killed him."

I raised my face from my palms and wiped away tears with my sleeve. "Levi wasn't old enough to vote," I said angrily.

Hallelujah removed his glasses and wiped tears from his own face. "He turned twenty-one last Thursday," he said. "Went to the courthouse and registered the next day."

"Levi left the field early on Friday," I said, my voice choking. "Said he had something important to do."

Hallelujah stood right beside me, but his words seemed distant as he detailed the little he knew of Levi's murder. My mind was on Levi and what a fine young man everybody said he was. So all I heard from Hallelujah's rant was "forced off the road" and "shot in the head."

I could see Levi's dark brown face as if he were standing right in front of me. It hadn't been a week ago that I heard him brag to his younger brother Fish that this would be his last summer "chopping some white man's cotton." He was the first person in his family of eight boys to graduate from high school and attend college. After his first-grade teacher declared him brilliant, his parents scratched and scrimped for nearly twelve years in order to send him. In the summer, he came home and chopped cotton to help out, with the promise that when he graduated, he would get a good job and move his parents off Mr. Robinson's place. That September would have been the beginning of his last year at the colored college Alcorn. And it was all for nothing. Levi was dead. Gunned down like a hunted animal.

"Something needs to be done about folks being killed for registering to vote," I said, my teeth clenched. "First Reverend Lee in Belzoni, and only two months later Levi?"

Hallelujah wiped his face with his handkerchief, then put his glasses back on. He laughed, but it wasn't a happy laugh. "White folks won't do a thing to another white for killing a Negro," he said, pushing his glasses up the bridge of his nose as he stared out toward the cotton field, where Papa and Fred Lee were mere dots on the horizon. "They won't even do anything if a Negro kills a Negro. A Negro ain't worth a wooden nickel to them. Kill one, another one'll be born the next day to take his place." He took his glasses off again and wiped his eyes.

Hallelujah plopped down on the porch beside me. We both stared out at the chickens clucking aimlessly around the yard. Slick Charlie, our only rooster, stood guard at the door of the henhouse, as if to say *You hens better stay out there in the yard where you belong. Stay out there till your work is done.*

When the screen door burst open, I jumped so hard I almost fell off the porch.

Queen stormed out the door. It was well past nine o'clock, and she still wore rollers in her hair. Her pointy nose stuck up in the air, as if she smelled something foul. She pinned her hazel eyes on me and Hallelujah and said, "Y'all cut out all that racket. I'm trying to sleep." A copy of *Redbook* magazine hung from her hand.

Hallelujah tipped his hat. "Morn'n, Queen," he said. "Didn't mean to wake you."

Queen ignored Hallelujah as if he were a leaf on a tree. Instead, she glowered at me. "Can y'all hold down the noise?"

"Queen, Levi Jackson got shot last night," I said.

Queen shrugged. "Niggas get shot round here all the time."

Hallelujah stared at Queen, his eyes narrowed. "Levi's dead, Queen," he said sternly. "They say some white men in a pickup forced him off the road and shot him in the head."

For a brief moment, shame crossed Queen's face. Then, as quickly as that moment came, it vanished. Queen turned up her nose and said, "I knew that uppity nigga would get hisself killed one day." She stormed back into the house, allowing the screen door to slam shut behind her.

Hallelujah and I stared at the door in silence.

A few seconds later, I sighed and shoved myself off the

porch. "I've gotta get back to the field," I said. "Ma Pearl will beat the black off me this evening if she finds out I've been sitting around talking to you instead of working like I'm supposed to."

"Preacher'll be back shortly to pick me up," Hallelujah said. "I'll just head on up the road and meet him."

"No!" I said, grabbing his arm.

Hallelujah flinched with surprise.

I quickly moved my hand and said, "Don't walk down the road by yourself."

Hallelujah stared at me, confused. "I meet Preacher along the road all the time."

I told him about my encounter with Ricky Turner.

He slumped back down on the porch. "I'll wait for Preacher," he said.

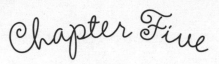

Chapter Five

THAT MORNING, MR. ALBERT WAS RIGHT BACK IN Mr. Robinson's cotton field with sixteen-year-old Fish and one of his younger sons, Adam, barely ten. Adam would replace Levi.

Mr. Albert's three older sons had left, one by one, for Detroit six years prior. Like Mr. Pete, they had packed up their young families and fled the dirt clods of the Delta as soon as they saved up enough money to start a new life someplace else.

Nobody talked about Levi, at least not in my hearing, anyway. Ma Pearl and Papa acted as if their words might get picked up by the wind and carried over to Mr. Robinson's ears if they said anything about the shooting. Hallelujah had said that folks acted the same way when Reverend George Lee was shot in Belzoni back in May. Some, he said, even claimed it was the preacher's own fault that he was killed. "If he'da just took his name off them voting records like the white folks told him," he'd heard a woman at church whisper, "he wouldn'ta got hisself kil't."

I was glad when I saw Reverend Jenkins's brown Buick stirring up dust along the edge of the field, as I was sure Hallelujah would have some news about Levi.

When Hallelujah jumped out, Reverend Jenkins—his thick glasses glaring in the sunlight—said something to him, probably instructing him to mind his manners. Then he waved and drove off. He honked and waved at Papa at the far end of the field as the tires of his Buick crunched rocks on the road.

I paused (not that I was doing much work anyway) and leaned against the hoe. "Hey," I said, waving at Hallelujah before he even reached me.

Hallelujah smiled and waved back. It was good to see him smile again. But as hot as it was out there—and I mean heat that wrapped its arms around me like a long-lost relative giving a hug—that boy was wearing his dark brown fedora instead of a straw hat.

"What you trying to do," I said as he got closer, "get black like me? You gonna burn up in this heat."

Hallelujah touched the tip of his hat and grinned. "The blacker the berry, the sweeter the juice."

"Who told you that lie?"

"Read it in a book," he said.

I chuckled and started chopping again. "Even the devil got sense 'nuff to wear a straw hat in this heat."

Hallelujah followed me as I crept along the row. Again, he didn't bother to stop by the barn and pick up a hoe to help out. But there really wasn't much to chop, seeing that Papa knew how to take good care of cotton. We didn't have many weeds, like I'd heard about in some fields. But I was still slow. Even little Adam could outchop me.

I was dressed in Fred Lee's too-big overalls and his long-sleeved shirt, and it took a lot of effort for me to walk up and down quarter-of-a-mile-long rows of cotton in the suffocating heat for five hours straight. I stopped for a water break at the end of every row. It's a good thing I worked under Papa's supervision instead of a white supervisor like Ricky Turner's evil pappy.

"What's your business today?" I asked Hallelujah.

Hallelujah shrugged. "Preacher let me take a break from the store. 'A couple hours only,' he said."

"You helping Miss Bertha today?"

Hallelujah nodded. "Yep."

"And you need a break already," I teased him.

Hallelujah grinned and pretended to wipe sweat from his brow. His aunt, Bertha Jenkins, owned a small grocery store —the only Negro-owned business in Stillwater. Even though she sold mostly staples, like flour, cornmeal, and sugar, white folks still weren't too happy about her store, seeing that it took business away from theirs. It had been broken into more times than anybody cared to count. She could barely keep her shelves stocked. The police dismissed the vandalism as "coloreds destroying their own property to try to make God-fearing white folks look bad." But we all knew who was really trying to sabotage Miss Bertha's business.

"So, what's Miss Sweet cooking today?"

No matter how many times I heard it, I just couldn't get used to people calling Ma Pearl "Miss Sweet." She was about as sweet as a slice of lemon soaked in vinegar. Her real name, of course, was Pearl, but I couldn't see how that one fit her either, seeing that a pearl is usually a thing of beauty.

I squinted at Hallelujah. "It's Tuesday. Not Sunday. What else she go'n cook besides beans?"

"What kind?"

I shrugged. "Pinto, I reckon."

"That's good enough for me," Hallelujah said. "Beats the air soup I would've eaten."

I teased him. "So you really stopped by to get fed, huh?"

He patted his thick middle and said, "Yep."

I glanced down the row to make sure I was still far away from Papa, as he and Fred Lee were coming back down the row toward me. "Heard anything about Levi?" I asked under my breath.

Hallelujah stuffed his hands into his pockets. "Preacher's getting the NAACP involved."

Spit caught in my throat, and I almost choked. I stopped chopping and placed a finger to my lips to shush Hallelujah. "Not so loud," I said, my eyes darting toward Papa.

NAACP—Ma Pearl said if I ever uttered those letters in her house, it would take a year to wash the taste of lye soap from my mouth. The letters stood for National Association for the Advancement of Colored People. And according to Hallelujah, the group was trying to do just that: help colored people advance. "To help our people find their way out of these cotton fields," I once heard Reverend Jenkins say.

Reverend Jenkins was involved in the group. Secretly, of course. So Hallelujah knew all about it, had even been to some meetings. I knew nothing, except what I got from him or from the discarded pages of the *Clarion-Ledger* newspaper, which I sneaked and read while out in the toilet. The *Clarion-Ledger* was the largest white-owned newspaper in Mississippi, and it was the Robinsons' favorite. What it reported about the NAACP was that it was nothing more than a bunch of northern Negro agitators coming to the South to incite good colored people to stir up trouble with whites.

And Ma Pearl agreed.

"The Robinsons is good white peoples," she said. "So we ought not 'sociate with Negroes who stir up trouble."

She said we were lucky. Mr. Robinson let us keep hogs,

chickens, and a cow on his place when other landowners wouldn't. Most coloreds had to buy overpriced meat, eggs, and milk from the white stores because Miss Bertha didn't have the means to keep such things at her store. Or they had to just do without. So we should've been grateful for Mr. Robinson's generosity, especially with the way he kept our house furnished, always allowing Mrs. Robinson to buy items she'd soon tire of and then pass them on to Ma Pearl.

Even Mr. Robinson himself had said he'd run any Negroes off his place if they caused trouble. "Any nigra bold enough to drink that poison the NAACP is pouring out is bold enough to find another place to stay," he'd said. "Including you, Paul," he told Papa. And Ma Pearl was taking no chances on getting "thowed off" Mr. Robinson's land.

The only thing I was grateful for was having a friend like Hallelujah, whose papa wasn't afraid of white folks — or at least knew how to sneak around them. If Ma Pearl and my own grandpa wouldn't tell me anything, Hallelujah sure would. My thirsty ears drank up that "poison" as quickly as he could pour it out.

"Preacher said they'd try to get Medgar Evers to come this way and see if he can get the sheriff to do something," he said.

"Medgar Evers?" My heart pounded. Medgar Evers was

a big name in the NAACP, from what I'd heard. Field secretary. I wasn't sure what that meant, but I knew Ma Pearl would've scourged me if she'd known I was learning such things from Hallelujah.

I started chopping again, in case Ma Pearl decided to spy on me from the kitchen window. Sweat poured down the sides of my face, and I wiped it with my sleeve. "Didn't Medgar Evers go down to Belzoni when Reverend Lee got killed?" I asked. "Nothing happened then. Nobody got arrested. Didn't even make the papers," I said.

Hallelujah corrected me. "It didn't make the white papers. Plenty of colored papers like the *Defender* reported it. And *Jet*, of course."

"That contraband?" I said, teasing.

Hallelujah laughed. The first time he brought over a copy of *Jet* magazine, Ma Pearl caught a glimpse of it while we sat in the kitchen flipping through it. Unfortunately, all she saw was the shapely, bathing-suit-clad model in the centerfold. She yanked the magazine out of Hallelujah's hand, flipped through it herself, and immediately judged it preachy and pompous. "A bunch a high-class northern Negroes trying to make everybody else feel bad 'bout how they lives," she said. She tossed the magazine back to Hallelujah with, "Preacher oughta be 'shamed of hisself letting you read that trash full o' half-nekked womens."

She never said that the fashion magazines Queen got from Mrs. Robinson were trash. Yet they too held plenty of pictures of bathing-suit-clad beauties, except they were white.

I shivered, even though sweat poured down my sides under my two layers of clothing. It scared me that the only newspapers and magazines I read were the ones the Robinsons read—the safe papers—the papers that didn't report the story about a preacher being gunned down for registering himself and others to vote.

I learned from Hallelujah that Reverend George Lee had been shot in the head while driving his car. He ran off the road and crashed, dying before he made it to the hospital. Nobody was arrested. Just like probably nobody would be arrested for Levi's murder, either.

"What are they so afraid of, Hallelujah?"

"Nobody wants to die, Rosa Lee," Hallelujah said quietly.

"I don't mean colored folks. I mean white folks. Why are *they* so afraid? Why are they killing people just because they want to vote?"

Hallelujah furrowed his brow. "Rosa Lee," he said, "with the privilege to vote—to choose—we can change things, even put our own people in power."

"You know how crazy you sound? Colored folks can't even own a store round here without white folks sabotaging it.

Can you imagine a Negro running for office?" I removed my hat from my head and fanned myself. "He'd have a bullet in his head before his name got on the ballot good."

Shielding his face from the sun with his hand, Hallelujah pondered what I had just said. He was always thinking, always digging deep into that reservoir of information he had gleaned from the magazines and newspapers he frequently read. I knew he'd come up with an answer to any challenge I might present. Sure enough, after a moment he pointed at me and said one word: "Kansas."

I questioned him with my tilted head and raised brows.

"Brown versus the Board of Education," he said. "Topeka, Kansas."

I shrugged.

"The Supreme Court declared segregation unconstitutional," Hallelujah said, smiling. "No more separate-but-equal. White folks *have* to let colored children go to school with white children in that state now."

I still didn't understand.

Hallelujah squinted. "Don't you see, Rosa? Now that we have the power to vote, we. can make that happen in Mississippi, too."

Hallelujah's words took a moment to soak through my heat-damaged head. But when they did, I dropped the hoe and doubled over. I thought I would die laughing. This time I knew Hallelujah had gone too far with his crazy thinking. Whites and coloreds at the same schools in Mississippi? Never in a million years.

Chapter Six

TUESDAY, JULY 26

When the sun began inching its way toward noon, Hallelujah folded his arms and said, "Ain't it about quitting time?"

"C'mon," I told him. "I'm 'bout to die out here even if it ain't. I'm so thirsty my mouth feels like it's stuffed with cotton." I dragged my hoe back along the row, too tired to pick it up. "If we walk real slow," I said, "it'll be close enough to twelve by the time we reach the house. And maybe Ma Pearl won't be cross with me for leaving the field a few minutes early."

When we reached our grassless backyard, the first thing we saw was Slick Charlie chasing three hens toward the hen-house. Hallelujah laughed. "Ain't them hens got sense enough to run in opposite directions?"

"I think they like being chased by Slick Charlie," I said, nudging him in the side. "Kinda like how Queen likes being chased by you."

Hallelujah took off his hat and fanned himself. With his light brown complexion, I could see a hint of pink spread across his cheeks. "Humph," he said. "I ain't stud'n Queen. If Queen had any sense, she'd be chasing me." He snapped his suspenders and said, "I'm a man who's going places."

"One, you ain't a man," I told him. "And two, the only place you're going is to Ma Pearl's kitchen to eat up her food."

Hallelujah tucked his hat under his arm and broke into a strut. "I'm going up north like everybody else," he said. "Except I'm going to Ohio. Columbus. Because it was named after the fellow who discovered this country."

I spat a dry spit and said, "You ain't going nowhere." But I didn't mean it. I'd never heard of any Negro going to Ohio. But if Hallelujah said he was going, then he probably was. The Jenkinses always did things differently from other colored folks. And Hallelujah was forever plotting to be the first Negro to do this or the first Negro to be that. I just hoped he didn't leave before I figured out a way to get to Chicago. There was no way I could survive the dusty Delta without him.

In the middle of all that heat, a breeze picked up. The threadbare sheets and pillowcases Ma Pearl had hung on the line that morning flapped and snapped in the wind. It made me think maybe God was smiling at me instead of frowning. And maybe he'd send old Gabe down with a few clouds and some wind for the afternoon chopping time.

When we climbed the steps to the back porch, the scent

of pinto beans hit my nose. I should've been tired of beans, seeing that we ate them nearly every day, but Ma Pearl didn't fix beans the way other folks fixed them. She simmered hers with tomatoes, brown sugar, onions, and green peppers because that's how Mrs. Robinson liked them. She had seen the recipe in *Better Homes and Gardens* and had Ma Pearl fix her beans that way ever since.

After washing my hands with the lye soap in the basin of water sitting on the porch, I hurried and kicked off my dusty shoes and left them at the back door. Hallelujah did the same. As soon as we walked through the screen door and saw Queen sitting at the table, I swear I heard Hallelujah's knees knock together. He stammered when he spoke. "A-afternoon, Queen. Y-you look lovely today."

Queen, with her straight black hair pulled high in a ponytail like some movie star, didn't even acknowledge Hallelujah. She sat at the table with one dainty hand wrapped around a Mason jar filled with iced tea and the other flipping through a Sears and Roebuck catalog, as if she had money.

Her sleeveless red and white checkered dress clung to her curves like gold on a ring. And she wore enough rouge and red lipstick to put a harlot to shame. If I had dressed like that, Ma Pearl would've laid an egg.

When Hallelujah spoke to her a second time, she stopped

midflip and turned up her nose. She stood, sneered, and said, "Go to hell, Clyde Bernard Jenkins *the Turd*."

Satisfied that she had sufficiently insulted Hallelujah, she picked up her iced tea, snatched up the catalog, and switched on out of the kitchen, that smirk still plastered on her ugly face.

Hallelujah shrugged as if he didn't care, but I saw that hint of red come back to his cheeks. I felt heat rise in my own face too. It made me want to slap Queen straight on into the next week. Just because she was almost sixteen didn't mean she could damn the preacher's son to hell and call him a turd.

Queen didn't return to the kitchen until all of us field hands — me, Fred Lee, Mr. Albert, Fish, and Adam — had washed up and were seated at the table. Her face was pinched up worse than the edge of a pie crust as she sat on the bench next to the open window. Ma Pearl never let anybody else sit away from the table.

When Papa came in and took his place at the head of the table, he smiled and asked Hallelujah, "How's Preacher?"

"Just fine, Mr. Carter," Hallelujah answered.

Papa reached for the jug and poured himself some tea. "Gettin' his sermon ready for Sunday?" he asked.

Hallelujah nodded. "Yes, sir."

Papa squinted at him. "It any good?"

Hallelujah fidgeted for a moment, then lowered his eyes and muttered, "It's a real killer, sir."

We all laughed, even Mr. Albert, Fish, and Adam, despite the grief that hung on their faces like veils.

Amid the laughter, Ma Pearl brought a huge pot of beans and set it in the middle of the table. Whatever we didn't eat at dinnertime, we'd have again for supper that evening.

When Ma Pearl took the top off the pot, the first thing I saw were little slimy pods of green floating on top. Before I knew it, I gasped and opened my big mouth. "Ma Pearl, you put *okra* in the beans?" I crossed my arms and huffed. "You know I hate okra."

When Ma Pearl frowned, I knew what was coming next. I cringed and felt the sting before her heavy hand even reached my face. *Whap!*

I tumbled backwards, toppled the chair, and landed on the wood floor.

Ma Pearl stormed to the other side of the table and stood directly over me. Glaring down, she crossed her arms over her generous bosom and said, "Beggars shouldn't be so choosy."

With both palms soothing my stinging face, I muttered a choked, "Sorry, Ma Pearl."

Tears raced down my face as I slowly rose from my sprawled position on the floor. I wanted to get up and run, but Ma Pearl might've thrown a skillet at my head if I had left that kitchen.

As I righted my chair and sat, I didn't dare look up. I knew everybody at that table shared my shame. They clamped their mouths shut and stared at their hands.

But Queen? Without even looking, I knew her lips were curled up in a grin.

Ma Pearl finally dropped her hands to her sides and stomped back over to the stove. She snatched up a pan of cornbread and threw it on the table with a clank. "If you don't like my cooking," she said, scowling, "try catching a train to Chicago and see what yo' mammy got on the stove."

I wiped my face with my shirtsleeve and choked back fresh tears.

"Rose Lee," Papa said gently.

I didn't answer him, and I wouldn't look up.

Papa's voice was stern but kind. "Rose Lee," he said, "when you lay down on your bed last night, was your belly crying for food?"

I muttered, "No, sir."

"Then thank the good Lord for this food. Not everybody in this world has some."

"Yes, sir," I mumbled. I bowed my head and said as quietly as possible, "God in heaven, thank you for this food. Please let it satisfy my belly so I won't go hungry. Amen."

Except for Ma Pearl's angry breathing, the kitchen was silent. Tears blurred my vision, but I could see well enough to swallow my shame, pick up my plate, and ladle a good helping of beans onto it. To appease Ma Pearl, I made sure I included one, and only one, pod of slimy green okra. I just prayed they were all gone from that miserable pot come suppertime that evening.

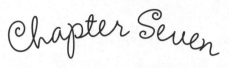

Chapter Seven

SATURDAY, JULY 30

I WAS TEN YEARS OLD WHEN I ATTENDED MY FIRST funeral. It was the funeral of what I thought was a very old woman. She had long white hair surrounding a wrinkled black face, and the undertaker had shaped that face into an awful frown. The woman's name was Mrs. Vergene Miller, and she left behind thirteen children, all full grown. And with the way the undertaker had molded that frown on her face, I couldn't help but wonder if she ruled her children with an iron fist, the way Ma Pearl ruled hers.

But what stood out most and made me remember Miss Vergene's funeral was not her white hair or her frowning face; it was her thirteen children and the way those children, especially her eight sons, wept and wailed and fell out on the floor in a dead faint as they cried out for their mama.

Before that day, I had never seen men cry. And every time they cried out "Maa-maa," I cried too, because I knew what it was like not being able to see your mama every day. I cried so hard that I had bruises under my eyes for seven days.

So that Saturday morning, as I sat packed in a pew at

Little Ebenezer Baptist Church, I stared at the black casket that held Levi Jackson's dead body and I didn't even try to hold back my tears. Every time one of Mr. Albert's sons cried out, "Lord, why they kill my brother?" I thought about Fred Lee and how I would wail too if somebody killed him.

The air was putrid with perfume and perspiration. All around me, people fell backwards on the wooden pews, wailing and weeping. Levi's mama, Mrs. Flo-Etta Jackson, or Miss Etta, as everyone called her, stood at the end of my pew. She wore her white usher's uniform and her thick-soled white shoes. As head of the ushers' board, she took her job seriously, standing at her post even at the funeral of one of her own. Nevertheless, tears rolled down her round cheeks and onto the collar of her white dress as she used one hand to fan mourners and the other to distribute tissues, not bothering to wipe her own tears, even though they flowed heavily enough to flood the church floorboards.

"Gawd has called one of his angels home," the flat-nosed Reverend E. D. Blake bellowed from the pulpit. "Too soon, some might say. But Gawd says right on time. For his ways are not our ways, and his thoughts not our thoughts."

Tearful "amens" rose from the congregation, as if what Reverend Blake had said was the truth. I shouldn't have been surprised to hear such nonsense coming from him. He, like

Papa and Mr. Albert, was the kind of Negro who stayed in his place, which was probably why Mr. Albert chose to have Levi's funeral at Little Ebenezer Baptist Church rather than at our church, Greater Mount Zion Missionary Baptist Church. He knew that Reverend Jenkins wouldn't have been afraid to speak the truth about how Levi died.

God didn't call Levi home, I wanted to shout at Reverend Blake. *A white man's bullet did.* But I couldn't shout that any more than I could shout "Hallelujah!"—because there was no proof that it was a white man's bullet that killed Levi. Only the word of disgruntled Negroes who, according to a group called the White Citizens' Council, wanted to stir up trouble in Mississippi.

I'd heard of the White Citizens' Council from Hallelujah, but three days after Levi's death I got the chance to hear from them with my own ears. That Wednesday, Ma Pearl sent me to Mrs. Robinson's to pick up a bag of her older son Sam's old clothes for Fred Lee. I was supposed to go by at twelve, during my break. Instead I left the field early and went by around a quarter before noon. Four cars were parked in front of the Robinsons' house. All four of them belonged not to Mr. Robinson but to other white landowners and business-men. While I waited at the back door, I heard Mr. Robinson and the other men, who were sitting in the dining room and ranting about what the Citizens' Council must do to protect the rights of white folks. And one of those things was not to let that group, the National Association for the "Agitation" of Colored People—the NAACP—contaminate the good colored citizens of Leflore County. When Mrs. Robinson returned with the bag of clothes and realized I could hear everything being said in the dining room, her face turned as red as a tomato. She practically shoved me out the door after handing me the clothes.

So I was not surprised when the NAACP tried to get involved after Levi's death and Mr. Albert told them to let it be. "The boy's already dead," he said. "Stirring up trouble for other Negroes won't bring him back."

Just thinking about it made me shiver. For if it had been Fred Lee lying in that casket dressed in a cheap brown suit donated by Mr. Robinson himself, Papa might've said the same thing.

"Peace over power" is what he always said.

"How can a man have peace if the fear of death is always at his back?" I asked him.

He said he'd learned to do like Paul the Apostle and be content in whatever state he was in.

I'll be content, I said to myself, *when the state I'm in is no longer Mississippi.*

After someone died, it normally took colored folks a good two weeks before they had a funeral, seeing how they had to gather up enough money to pay the undertaker and everybody else. But Levi's funeral happened quickly, in less than a week, as Mr. Robinson paid for the funeral.

I was already annoyed by the way folks acted as if Levi had simply died in his sleep, but when Louvenia Smith, also known as Miss Doll, began belting out "Swing Low, Sweet Chariot," I became even more annoyed. A self-appointed funeral singer (and Ma Pearl's personal friend), she sang a solo at every funeral she attended, whether the family asked her to or not. Back in her younger days, she had been a great singer, I was told. Now she was way past her prime, and her voice had faded significantly, but the kind folks in Stillwater didn't have the heart to tell her so.

"'I looked over Jordan,'" she croaked, *"'and what did I see?'"* She moaned. *"'A band of angels comin' after me . . .'"*

And with that, Miss Etta hit the floor with a thud.

A gasp escaped from the crowd, followed by a hush, as Sister Jenny Louise Harris stopped banging on her out-of-tune piano.

Within seconds, Miss Etta was surrounded by a flurry of white uniforms.

"Scoot over!" a male usher ordered our row.

We practically piled on top of one another as we moved over to make room. On the count of three, four ushers hoisted Miss Etta up and onto the pew. The pew creaked.

Did I mention that Miss Etta was about the size of Ma Pearl?

Chapter Eight

SHE KNEW DIRN WELL SHE COULDN'T SERVE AT HER own boy's fune'," Ma Pearl said as she dropped large spoons of chicken dressing on plates as mourners passed through the assembly line in Miss Etta's cramped kitchen. Once served, most of them headed straight on out the back door to feast under the shade trees as they fanned away flies. I was surprised they held the repast at the Jacksons' anyway, seeing that theirs was one of the smallest and most dilapidated houses on Mr. Robinson's land. But it seemed that all the colored people in Stillwater and the other small communities in Leflore County were assembled there that day.

As usual during a repast, each family had brought their own plates, cups, and utensils, along with a large pot or pan of some food item to share with everyone else. Ma Pearl had brought a pan of dressing and a pan of fried chicken.

Miss Doll—who was anything but—frowned as she slapped creamed potatoes next to the chicken dressing. "If it'd been my boy," she said, "they wouldn'ta been able to keep me outta that casket. Shame how they ack'n like nothing happened. Like that boy just died from somp'n natra." She tapped the spoon against the side of the pan to rid it of stuck-on potatoes. "Wadn't his time," she said, shaking her head. "I don't care what Rev'ren Blake say. Wadn't his time."

I stood beside them, as silent as a stump as I made sure that each person in the line received one, and only one, piece of Ma Pearl's famous fried chicken.

"Humph," Ma Pearl said. "That boy was a fool. That's what got him kil't."

Miss Doll's face tightened. "They didn't hafta shoot him. Coulda jest warned him like they did Say-rah's boy. You see how he got on outta here the next day. Caught the first bus to Memphis."

Ma Pearl snorted. "Memphis ain't no better. They kil-lin' niggas up there, too." She gave me an evil look and said, "I bet' not catch one of mine going down to the courthouse talk'n 'bout vot'n. They wouldn't hafta wor' 'bout the white man. I'd kill 'em with my own two hands."

Miss Doll dipped the spoon into the mountain of pota-toes and scooped up a helping. "I still don't like how they ack like the boy just died from somp'n natra. He was shot," she said bluntly. "How else they 'splain the bullet hole in his head?"

"If you ast me," Ma Pearl said, "he already had a hole in his head. A *whole* lotta stupid."

Miss Doll chortled. "Sweet, you sho' is crazy."

"Not half as crazy as these young folks," Ma Pearl said. "I ain't too happy 'bout the way things is myself. But they better than they used to be. And they sho' ain't worth gittin' shot over."

Miss Doll sighed. "Nah, they ain't," she said, shaking her head. "They sho' ain't."

Ma Pearl groaned. "My name ain't Jesus, and I ain't 'bout to be nobody's sacrificial lamb and find myself hanging from no dirn tree."

I doubt there's a tree limb in all of Mississippi strong enough to hold you, I said to myself.

"What's so funny?" Ma Pearl said when she caught me grinning.

I shook my head. "Nothing."

"Then wipe that grin off yo' face, 'fore I do it for you," she said. "You jest left a fune', not a dirn wedding."

I pressed my lips together and concentrated on the chicken. But out of the corner of my eye, I caught a glimpse of Miss Doll. She, too, was trying hard not to grin. I could only wonder what she might have been thinking.

"Psst," came a soft voice from the back door. I turned and saw Hallelujah beckoning me with his finger.

"Can you come outside for a minute?" he whispered.

I poked a chicken thigh with a fork and slid it onto the

next person's plate. The chicken pan was still half full, so I asked Miss Doll to cover for me while I talked to Hallelujah.

As we slipped out the back door, my nose rejoiced. I was glad to be out of the Jackson house, which always smelled like day-old cabbage and musty feet.

Unlike our house, the Jacksons' house was surrounded by trees instead of cotton fields. As the yard was congested with people picnicking on blankets in the shade, Hallelujah and I went for a walk in the wooded area out back.

Mr. Robinson, it seemed, owned half the land in Stillwater, plus land dotted throughout the county. What he didn't use for farming, he built shanties on and rented them to colored people at exorbitant rates. His wooded land, he used for lumbering. There were plenty of stumps in these woods, where trees had lost their lives for the shacks Mr. Robinson built.

We walked away from the house until we could no longer hear the whispered chatter of voices—some mournful, some confused, but all angry, either at the white men who killed Levi or at Levi himself for getting killed.

We sat together on a wide stump, and Hallelujah placed a newspaper on my lap.

When I saw the picture and the headline, I screamed and flung the paper as far away from me as I could. My stomach did somersaults as Hallelujah retrieved the paper from the trunk of a nearby tree.

He thrust the paper into my face and said in the deepest voice he could muster, "Read it!"

"No!" I said, shielding my eyes with my hands. My body trembled, and sweat poured down my sides. I didn't have to see the paper again. Its headline, PREACHER'S MOUTH SHOT OFF, would be seared in my mind forever, along with the gruesome picture of Reverend George W. Lee with his face sewn up like Frankenstein.

As if loaded down by a heavy weight, Hallelujah dropped his body next to me on the stump. He sighed loudly and said, "I promised Preacher I'd never show you this." He paused and stared back at the cluster of mourners congregated around the Jacksons' yard. "But after seeing how people reacted about Levi's death, like it's not a big deal, I had to share it with somebody." He extended the paper toward me. "You need to know the truth, Rosa."

My stomach churned, but I took the paper hesitantly. I glanced at the headline again. PREACHER'S MOUTH SHOT OFF, TONGUE SHOT INTO, ALLEGEDLY, BY WHITE MEN. Across the top of the page read *Southern Mediator Journal*. I had never heard of the paper.

"A Negro paper?" I asked.

Hallelujah nodded. "Yes. Arkansas. Little Rock."

He pointed at the top of the paper, where it read, "The South's Progressive Negro Weekly. Little Rock, Arkansas." Hallelujah took a deep breath, then exhaled. "His face was ripped in two. The undertaker had to suture it back together."

A chill crept over my body.

"Hundreds of shotgun pellets in his face," Hallelujah continued, anger burning in his eyes, "and the sheriff dismissed them as dental fillings. He didn't say a thing about the bullet holes in his shot-out tires."

As I studied the paper, Hallelujah said, "Dr. T.R.M. Howard in Mound Bayou said some Negroes would sell their grandmas for half a dollar, but Reverend Lee was not one of them."

"Negroes like Ma Pearl," I said, glancing up at him.

"Judas niggers."

"What?"

"Judas niggers," Hallelujah repeated. "Negroes who'd sell their grandmas for half a dollar just to stay in the white man's favor."

I told him what Ma Pearl said about Levi having "a whole lotta stupid" in his head and how she'd kill her own if they registered to vote.

Hallelujah leaped from the stump. "That's bull crap!" he said, banging his fist in his palm. "We have rights too. And that includes the right to vote. A man shouldn't have to die for wanting to vote."

I tugged his shirttail. "Calm down before folks get suspicious."

He slumped down on the stump with a huff.

"Reverend Jenkins know you talk like that?" I asked.

A quick shrug of his right shoulder was Hallelujah's only reply.

"You shouldn't use such strong language. You might start cussing like Queen."

"These white folks around here will make even a preacher cuss," Hallelujah answered.

"Well, don't you start," I said. "Be a shame for a good boy like you to end up in hell."

"I live in Mississippi," he replied tersely. "I'm already in hell."

"Hell is hot, and it's full of demons," I said.

Hallelujah glared at me and said, "And so is Mississippi."

August

Chapter Nine

FRIDAY, AUGUST 19

JULY HAD COMPLETELY MELTED AWAY, AND WE WERE more than halfway into August before we heard from Mama up in Chicago. The cotton-chopping season had ended, and I had nothing to do except work like a donkey around the house while Queen sat around acting like, well, like a queen.

God had sent ol' Gabriel down with more buckets of blazing heat. And being as faithful as the Bible describes him to be, ol' Gabe poured that heat on us good. Everything around us was as parched as a winter peanut. Except the cotton. It was growing strong.

Papa prayed every day that it wouldn't rain. Rain would ruin his crop. Sun would help it prosper. And every day, it seemed, a wide, dark cloud hovered right over the cotton field, then suddenly poofed away without leaving a trace of water. Every night, Papa fell on his knees and thanked God for holding the rain in the clouds for one more day.

It was too hot to do anything besides work in the house anyway. So there I was, down on my knees, scrubbing the kitchen floor, my hands chafing from lye soap, while Queen relaxed on her lazy behind in the parlor, lost in the wonderful world of radio soaps.

School wouldn't start for another two weeks. And I couldn't wait. Folks said the colored school was haunted, said it was built over a cemetery. And since the white folks who built it didn't bother to relocate the sixty-nine Negro corpses that rested beneath it, angry ghosts appeared randomly throughout the day to scare away the intruders. Papa said it just wasn't right to disturb a sacred space that way, said he didn't blame the haints if they showed up. "Wouldn't want folks stepping on my grave either," he said.

Personally, I never saw any haints, unless you count the little round white man with the doughy face who visited on occasion to make sure "you folks have all you need ovah heah."

But I didn't care that the school was haunted. I only cared that it was new, even if everything in it was raggedy junk from the white school. At least we had a school. Most colored children weren't lucky enough to even go to school, especially the ones who lived on somebody else's land. With cotton-picking season right around the corner, they were expected to work. Luckily for me and Queen and Fred Lee, Papa allowed us to attend school even during the harvest season. Ma Pearl, on the other hand, couldn't have cared less.

Grade school was considered a decent education by most

folks in the Delta anyhow. But not for me. I wanted more. I needed more. I couldn't be like Papa and spend the rest of my life working in a cotton field. Nor like Ma Pearl, cleaning up after and serving white women like Mrs. Robinson. I would turn into a madwoman if I had to be surrounded by all the fanciness of a white woman's house all day, then return home and try to find contentment with the drabness of my own.

If only for this reason alone, I wanted—no—I *had* to do like Levi Jackson and some of the others. I had to finish up high school and head off somewhere to a college. Except Levi would never again set foot in a college, thanks to the fool who put a bullet in his head. But at least his younger brothers would have a better chance than he did.

Right after Levi's funeral and before the cotton chopping was all done, Mr. Albert and his wife, Miss Flo-Etta, took their younger sons and joined their older sons in Detroit. He said he was done with Mississippi and would never set foot on that demon soil again. Perhaps Fish, Adam, and Mr. Albert's other young sons would get to go to one of those fancy schools up north, where they claimed white children and colored children sat in the same classrooms—something I figured I would have to see for myself to believe.

My seventh-grade teacher, Miss Johnson, had said that would eventually happen in Mississippi. But she also said it was the actions of people like the NAACP field secretary

Medgar Evers who got us that new colored school built. She said that Mr. Evers had first gone to Alcorn, the colored college where Levi had gone, and studied business. After that, he tried to go study law at that fancy white college they call Ole Miss. Miss Johnson said that as long as colored folks tried to force their way into white schools, white folks would spend money to build colored schools. That way they could claim colored children had the same privileges as white children, and they wouldn't be forced to integrate like they had done in Topeka, Kansas.

But she and Reverend Jenkins both said that they could build all they wanted, but a change was still coming to Mississippi, and soon. Reverend Jenkins himself had attended a funny-sounding colored college named Tougaloo, where he studied literature. So besides preaching, he was also a teacher at the colored high school, and he sold life insurance policies on the side. Hallelujah was planning to study medicine when he went to college. I wanted to learn important things like that too—medicine, or maybe even business or law like Mr. Evers.

I was almost finished with the kitchen floor and was about to get started on sweeping the back porch when Ma Pearl yelled from the parlor. "Rose Lee! Come read this."

I scrambled up from the floor and dried my hands on a dishrag. I welcomed the break from my work, even if it was only to read the mail. Ma Pearl was one of the reasons I knew I had to get as much schooling as possible. She'd been born in 1899, her mama and papa were former slaves, and she couldn't read or write a lick. She couldn't even read the mail when it came in. Papa, however, had taught himself to read when he was a boy. He told me that while his mama cleaned the white woman's house, he read the white children's books, figuring out the words by studying the pictures. He couldn't read all that good, but at least he could read some. Good thing too, since he studied that *Farmer's Almanac* like it was the Bible. His favorite reading, however, was the three-day-old Memphis *Commercial Appeal,* a white-owned newspaper that the Robinsons passed on to Ma Pearl. Papa read the paper in the late evening, after what he called a hard day of cotton-field meditation. He said that after spending a whole day looking inside his own head, it was nice to take a break and look inside someone else's.

I knew before seeing it that the letter in Ma Pearl's hand was from Mama. And I also knew, from the sour look on Ma Pearl's face, that the letter didn't contain that lil' something Mama had promised to send as soon as she got settled.

When Ma Pearl thrust the letter in my face, she cussed under her breath and said, "See what that heffa got to say."

Mama shouldn't have promised money she couldn't

deliver. Now Ma Pearl would be in a dark mood all weekend. And with her not having to go to Mrs. Robinson's again until Monday, I dreaded the three-day wrath we all had coming.

As I studied the letter before I read it out loud, it broke my heart. The penmanship was so poor I couldn't tell whether it had been written by my twenty-eight-year-old mama or my six-year-old stepbrother. Mama had had to quit school at fifteen because she was "in the family way." Despite her age, she had still gotten only as far as sixth grade. Ma Pearl said she was too busy studying Johnny Lee Banks instead of studying her books.

But even with a sixth-grade education, I would think Mama could do better than the mishmash of so-called words I was staring at. Mama's spelling was so bad it read like some kind of secret code.

Dear Mama and Papa,

How ya doin. Fin I hop. We fin to. Pete got lost wen we got her. He went to the rong bildin. A white girl told us we was on the rong side a the free way. She tol us go a cupa mo blocs soth. She was nic. We fond our bildin. It so tall. It bout the talless thing I eva seed. Our partmint aint nar bout big as the hose in Grenwood. But at lees it got a bafrum. We aint got to go otsid. And we got swichs

on the wall for the lites. We aint got to pull no strng to
trun them on. And we got closit to put our cloths in.

Pete lik his job. I aint fond one yet. They say thar
pline hear. But they bout as hard to com by as they is in
Missippi. They say pline white wimens hirin mads. But I
aint come all way to Chicgo to be no mad.

Baby Susta com frum st luis last wek to see us. She
said she goin to Missippi on the 21 to see ya. She gon be
ther for a cupa weks. Pete say it be a whil four we com
back. We got to gil our mony back rit.

Ma Pearl grunted. "You go'n read the dirn letter or burn a
hole in it with yo' eyes?" She stood so close to me that I could
feel her breath on my ear. At that moment, I was glad she
couldn't read.

I swallowed the lump in my throat and tried to figure out a
way to read the letter out loud and not make my mama sound
stupid, especially with Queen sitting right there in the room.
Her mama, Aunt Clara Jean, had finished eighth grade. But I
don't know what Queen was so proud for; her mama dropped
out for the same reason mine did. And at least I knew who
my daddy was. Besides, everybody knew Mama wasn't the
brightest flower in Ma Pearl's bouquet, even if she was the
prettiest.

I quickly finished scanning the letter to get the gist of it so I could say out loud what my mama wasn't competent enough to write in a letter.

"Dear Mama and Papa," I read.

"How y'all doing? Fine I hope. We're fine too. Pete got lost when we got here. He went to the wrong building. A white girl told us we were on the wrong side of the freeway. She told us to go a couple more blocks south. She was nice. We found our building. It's so tall. It's about the tallest thing I've ever seen. Our apartment ain't near as big as the house in Greenwood, but at least it's got a bathroom. And light switches and closets to put our clothes in.

"Pete likes his job. I ain't found one yet. They say there are plenty here. But they're about as hard to come by as they are in Mississippi. They say plenty of white women are hiring maids. But I didn't come all the way to Chicago to be no maid.

"Baby Sister came from Saint Louis last week to see us. She said she's going to Mississippi on the twenty-first to see y'all. She will be there for a couple of weeks. Pete says it'll be a while before we come back. We got to get our money back right."

I stopped reading and folded the letter. The rest was about how she missed me and Fred Lee. I would've felt stupid reading it out loud.

"Folks want you to raise they chi'ren," Ma Pearl said, "but they don't want to send you nothing to help raise 'em with. She better hurr'up and get her money right."

That last sentence seemed to be the only thing Ma Pearl heard in the whole letter. Funny how she never said a word to Aunt Clara Jean when she and Uncle Ollie always seemed to have plenty. Even though they, too, lived on Mr. Robinson's place, their house was bigger than ours, and it even had a bathroom, of sorts. Plus Uncle Ollie owned a car. Not many coloreds living on somebody else's land could make that claim.

Queen took her ear from the radio long enough to ask, "So Baby Susta coming on Sunday?"

"That's what Mama says."

Queen held out her hand. "Lemme see that."

"No," I said sharply, pressing the letter to my chest.

Queen sneered. "Girl, I already know yo' mama can't write no better than Ellie out in the barn." She jumped up, snatched the letter from my grasp, and rolled her eyes. "And I know she don't talk near 'bout as proper as you just made her sound in this letter," she said, scoffing as she glanced at the letter. "I don't even know how you can read this chicken scratch anyway."

She tossed the letter back at me. It hit the floor.

Then she quickly switched from putting down Mama to

criticizing Aunt Belle, who was referred to by everybody, except me, as Baby Susta, or Baby Sister, if you chose to say it right. "Hope she bring me something good," she said as she flopped back down in her chair. "I couldn't even wear half that junk she brought the last time."

I picked up the letter from the floor and placed it in the front pocket of my dress. It wasn't worth the fight to insist that Queen pick it up. "Maybe if you quit eating and sleeping all the time and tried a little work, that behind of yours wouldn't spread so fast," I told her.

With her nose in the air, Queen said to me, "Don't worry 'bout my behind. Worry 'bout them sticks you call legs. Besides, don't nobody wanna be po' as a pole like you."

"I'd rather be po' as a pole than have a behind that sits up like a couple of muskmelons," I said.

Queen sucked her teeth and said, "Git on out there in the field and scare some crows, lil' ugly girl."

"Crows eat corn, not cotton, stupid."

Queen nodded toward my dress pocket, which held Mama's letter. "I wouldn't be so quick to call people stupid if I was you."

Before I could set my mouth to respond, Ma Pearl butted in. "You done cleaning that kitchen, gal?"

"Almost," I muttered.

"Almost ain't never got nothing done. Get on in there and

quit running yo' mouth. Today Friday. Baby Susta be here Sunday. And you know how she like to bring folks down here with her, like Mississippi some kinda zoo that the whole world jest gots to see."

"Yes, ma'am," I mumbled.

Queen, snickering, relaxed in her chair and turned up the volume on the radio.

"Aren't you glad you use Dial?" the radio announcer said. "Don't you wish everybody did?"

As I ambled toward the kitchen, my heart stinging from the letter, my hands stinging from the lye soap, I hated Mama even more for marrying Mr. Pete.

Chapter Ten

FRIDAY, AUGUST 19

THE ONLY BRIGHT SPOT IN MAMA'S LETTER WAS THE announcement that Aunt Belle, the youngest of Ma Pearl's children, was coming from Saint Louis that Sunday, the twenty-first. Only two days away. Of course that meant extra work for me. But I didn't care. Having relatives visit from up north was worth the extra labor of scrubbing down every-thing in the house. Everything had to be bone clean, includ-ing the front yard, which would be swept until it was nearly as clean as the kitchen floor.

Special care had to be taken with Grandma Mandy's old mothball-scented room, between the front room and the kitchen. Ma Pearl kept it as a guest room and worshiped it as a shrine, seeing as it had been the room where Papa's mama slept for the ten years she'd lived with them. From what I'd heard, Grandma Mandy could barely stand the sight of Ma Pearl, yet Ma Pearl did all she could to win her favor. So even with Grandma Mandy seven years dead, her ancient bones cold in the ground, Ma Pearl kept her room unoccupied and as pristine as Mrs. Robinson's parlor, while I had to share a room with wanna-be-swanky Queen.

Unlike Queen, I didn't care nearly as much about the clothes Aunt Belle would bring as I did about seeing how rich colored folks were after they had been living up north for a while. I thought about some of the other things Mama said in that letter, things about light switches and closets. Things Mrs. Robinson had in her house. I thought it was almost magical that whenever I walked into a room in her house, all I had to do was hit a switch on a wall and the light would come on. I couldn't wait to grow up and get me a real house, with a toilet that flushed my doo-doo down to God knows where, instead of an outdoor toilet where everybody's mess sat stagnant and maggot-covered in a hole until a new toilet was built.

And closets? What a dream it would be to put my clothes in their own special little room instead of folded in a cardboard box in a corner. Of course, if I had a closet, I reckon I'd need some decent clothes to hang in it too. But one day —one day it would happen, because I was determined to get myself a good education and make it happen.

When I went out to sweep the back porch, I found Fred Lee sitting on the steps. He was tossing corn at Slick Charlie and his female admirers—the twenty or so hens that supplied us with eggs and the occasional chicken dinner.

"Got a letter from Mama today," I told him.

Fred Lee shrugged, kept tossing corn to the chickens, and didn't utter a word.

I took the letter from my pocket and extended it toward him. "Wanna read it?"

He spat on the ground, then shook his head. Even with his near-charcoal complexion, he still looked like Mama, in my opinion, despite what Ma Pearl said. He had her sleepy eyes and her thin nose and thin lips, unlike me, with my wide nose and full lips.

I placed the letter back in my pocket and began sweeping the porch. But I wasn't nearly as concerned about the dirt as I was about my brother. At only twelve, his thin shoulders were already hunched over, almost as bad as Papa's at fifty-nine.

My aunt Ruthie Mae, the knee baby of the family, was married to a mean man everybody called Slow John. Slow John drank all the time and was always getting into fights. He even stabbed an old man six times in the chest for cheating him at dice. Papa said Slow John was hard like that because he grew up without his mama. Folks said she was shot to death by Slow John's daddy in a juke joint up in Clarksdale.

As I swept the porch and stared at my brother, I wondered if he would become hard like Slow John. When Fred Lee was little, Ma Pearl was always calling him stupid because he wouldn't talk. Until around age four, the most he would do was mumble. Even though I was only five, I tried my hardest to teach him how to talk. By the time he was four and a half, he still knew only a few words. He didn't speak in sentences until he was almost six.

Then Mama left us. Fred Lee shut down again. After that, it took him two years to say more than "umm." Standing there on the back porch that hot August afternoon, nearly a month after Mama had left for Chicago, I couldn't recall two words having come out of Fred Lee's mouth since.

I took a chance on getting caught by Ma Pearl and leaned the broom against the house. I went to the edge of the porch and sat with my brother. Fred Lee had never cared much for touching, so there would be no pat on the knee or arm draped around his shoulders. I folded my hands in my lap instead.

"Wanna talk?" I asked.

Fred Lee shook his head.

"You should," I said.

Fred Lee shrugged.

"Baby Sister's coming Sunday."

Nothing.

"She'll probably bring us something."

Silence.

I should have expected that response from Fred Lee. He didn't give a hoot or holler about stuff like that. Like Papa, he seemed to be content in whatever state he was in, even if that state was the State of Poverty.

Ma Pearl said that Fred Lee was slow in the head like our daddy. She said, "All them Banks is a tad bit touched." Interestingly, according to Ma Pearl, all of mine and Fred Lee's bad traits came from the Banks blood. None of them came from hers.

Seeing that my brother wasn't going to talk, I got up and began sweeping the porch again. Then he decided to talk.

"How come she don't want us?" he asked, his voice coming out choked.

I didn't stop sweeping. But the broom stopped moving, as if it had a mind of its own. I took that as a sign from above and placed the broom against the wall. I sat and had a long-overdue talk with my brother.

At first neither of us said a word. We simply sat there in the sun, listening to the sounds of the chickens clucking in the yard. Occasionally a grunt came from the hog pen as our sow and her three plump pigs cooled themselves in the mud. The pigs would soon become our meat. Then Papa would mate our sow with Uncle Ollie's boar to produce new pigs. They, too, would be fattened up with slop, and the circle of life would continue.

I took a handful of corn and tossed it into the yard. The

chickens left the corn they were already pecking at and raced toward the fresh drop. "Sugar and Li' Man are still babies," I told Fred Lee. "They need Mama more than we do."

I cringed at my own lie.

"Ain't Sugar seven?" Fred Lee asked.

I didn't answer. He already knew Sugar was seven — the age I was when Mama left us, saying we were big enough to take care of ourselves.

"I'm leaving as soon as I can get my hands on some money," Fred Lee said.

I jumped. That was the most I'd ever heard my brother say in his entire life.

"How you suppose you gonna do that?" I asked him. "Every dime we manage to get goes in Ma Pearl's hatbox."

Fred Lee shrugged. "I'll figure out a way. Pick pecans, maybe."

"Gotta have somebody to pick for," I said. "Mr. Robinson already got his pickers. Little children. Nine and under. So he only has to pay them three cents a pound. Then he can go to Greenwood and sell them for twenty cents a pound."

Fred Lee said nothing.

"Picking pecans won't get you enough money to buy a bus ticket nohow," I said.

Fred Lee shrugged, grabbed a handful of corn, and tossed it into the windless space above the yard. He gazed out at the fields, which were bursting forth with bolls, just begging to be picked, weighed, and sold. "We too black for her," he said.

"The blacker the berry, the sweeter the juice," I said, mimicking Hallelujah.

"That's stupid," Fred Lee muttered.

Of course it was. Hallelujah could comfortably make fun like that. His complexion was an acceptable caramel color. He knew he could stand in the sun all day long and never get as black as me and Fred Lee. Besides, only a fool would want to.

The blacker the berry, the quicker it gets thrown out is what he should've said, because that's exactly what I felt like, something thrown out, like the corn Fred Lee and I tossed to those chickens.

Chapter Eleven

SUNDAY, AUGUST 21

AFTER MAMA LEFT US AND MARRIED MR. PETE, Aunt Belle would sit with me nearly every day on the old broken-spring sofa in the front room and fill my heart with dreams. We'd sit there with a Sears and Roebuck catalog spread in our laps and dream over dresses. Pretty, frilly dresses. The prettiest, frilliest dresses a little girl could ever wish for.

I remember pointing at a blue one with a stitched white bodice and a big bow tied in the back. I smiled and asked, "Will you buy me this one?"

"Um-hmm," Aunt Belle said with a nod.

I beamed and pointed at another. "And this one?" It was red with white polka dots. The white collar was round and wide.

"Sho' will," Aunt Belle promised.

I vividly remember a black velvet one with a white lace collar. Aunt Belle promised me that one day it, too, would be mine.

Other than in those catalogs, I never laid eyes on any of those pretty dresses. At only seven years old, I was too young to realize my aunt didn't have the means to purchase them. Less than a year after Mama left, Aunt Belle, at nineteen, left too. She moved to Saint Louis with Papa's youngest sister, Isabelle, after whom she was named. There she attended beauty school. And although she had only finished eighth grade, like Aunt Clara Jean, three years after moving to Saint Louis, she opened her own beauty shop.

Papa said she had grit. As a little child, I thought he meant grits, like what we ate for breakfast. So whenever Ma Pearl cooked them, I ate a big helping because I wanted grit too, like Aunt Belle.

In my eyes, Aunt Belle was rich. Not as rich as Mr. Pete, but richer than most folks I knew. She never bought me those promised dresses, but she brought both Queen and me clothes every August before school started back in September. We weren't allowed to keep these clothes folded in boxes in the corner in our room like the homemade croker-sack dresses. Ma Pearl kept our good clothes in her room, hanging in that old scratched-up chifforobe Mrs. Robinson gave her. And sometimes Queen would be the only one allowed to wear hers. Ma Pearl would find a reason to deny me mine, such as claiming they didn't fit me right. So they remained a collection, untouched, in the chifforobe.

When Sunday finally came, I thought I would burst from excitement. Plus, we didn't have to go to church, as Ma Pearl wanted to have the house ready and the food cooked by the time Aunt Belle arrived.

I sat on the front porch, my legs dangling over the edge. I didn't worry about sweat, splinters, or even snakes as my legs swung anxiously back and forth under the raised porch. I simply enjoyed the scent of collard greens and candied yams floating from the kitchen. I could even smell the buttermilk in the cornbread. Ma Pearl usually cooked on Saturday night, with Papa believing that Sunday was the Sabbath. But this time he made an exception and let her cook on Sunday. So, long before the sun ever left China that morning, she was up fixing chicken and dressing and whipping up cakes—coconut and caramel.

It was straight-up noon, and the sun nearly burned a hole in the top of my head. But as soon as I got up to grab my straw hat to avoid heat stroke, I saw a black car coming down the road with a cloud of dust surrounding it. I knew it was Aunt Belle. It was one of the most beautiful sights I'd ever seen.

I burst through the screen door and yelled, "She's here! Baby Sister's here!"

Queen dropped her magazine and bolted from the chair by the window. If I had been a monkey, she would have crushed my tail, as Papa liked to say. She was out of the screen door before I could even turn around good. She raced across that porch and bounded down the steps faster than

Li' Man and Sugar had that day they told me they were going to Chicago.

It's a good thing she didn't collide with the car, as fast as she was running.

Aunt Belle's car (or rather, Great-Aunt Isabelle's car) pulled slowly into the yard and stopped under the ancient oak tree. Except this time Aunt Belle wasn't driving. A man was. And he was the blackest man I had ever seen in my life. So black that it looked like only a bright yellow shirt and a set of grinning teeth were positioned behind the steering wheel. And just as Ma Pearl predicted, the car held three other northern just-gotta-see-Mississippi spectators as well.

By the time I reached the car, everybody—Ma Pearl, Papa, and Fred Lee—had come out of the house. While Ma Pearl and Queen and I swarmed Aunt Belle's car like bees on a hive, Papa and Fred Lee remained on the porch. I could tell they were studying the stranger in the driver's seat as his wide grin revealed teeth that were whiter than Ma Pearl's bleached bloomers.

Aaron. That was the stranger's name. Aaron. Like Moses's brother in the Bible. Except his name was much longer: Aaron Montgomery Ward Harris. "I was named after the famous Aaron Montgomery Ward who created a mail-order catalog," he said. "Like those you have stacked there in the corner." He smiled proudly as he nodded toward our collection of Sears and Roebuck catalogs. "But feel free to call me Monty."

Like me, Mr. Aaron Montgomery Ward Harris was as dark as midnight without a moon. With his black hand interlocked with Aunt Belle's creamed-coffee one as they sat together on the settee in the parlor, I couldn't help but think of a piano and how the keys worked together to make music. Aunt Belle and Aaron, or Monty, as I had decided to call him, looked happy, like two people making music.

The three northern spectators were a man and a woman —newlyweds, James and Shirley Devine—who looked to be around Aunt Belle's age, and a girl, Ophelia, who looked to be about Queen's age. Ophelia was the sister of the sophisticated Shirley. And she was a Goliath of a girl, big boned and as ugly as an ogre. But sitting crossed-legged on the sofa, wearing a cream-colored pantsuit and as much makeup and the same hairstyle as her full-grown older sister, she made even Queen appear homely.

And she made me feel five years old. Papa allowed me to wear pants only when I went to the field, and even then, they belonged to Fred Lee. And makeup? Never.

The country people—Queen, Fred Lee, and me—sat on raggedy chairs brought to the parlor from the porch. Ma

Pearl and Papa sat in the matching blue chairs, one near the window, the other near the door, while the sophisticated Saint Louis folks sat on the settee and sofa.

"Where y'all staying?" Ma Pearl asked. That was always her first question to Aunt Belle. Never "How was the trip?" Or "How's everybody up there doing?" But always "Where y'all staying?"

"Monty has folks in Greenwood," Aunt Belle answered. "We'll be staying with them."

Aunt Belle had said she could never go back to sleeping under a tin roof or peeing in a pot after having enjoyed the luxuries of living up north. Yet with hope, and without fail, Ma Pearl had me scrub everything from top to bottom and from left to right, anticipating a different answer from her youngest child.

Ma Pearl addressed Monty. "You from here?"

"My mother grew up around Money," he answered. He grinned and added, "Mississippi, that is," then chuckled at his own joke.

"You ain't no kin to Mose Wright 'n'em, is you?" Ma Pearl asked.

Monty thought for a moment before he said, "The name doesn't sound familiar."

"Mose a farmer over there in Money," said Ma Pearl. "A good man. A preacher."

"My mother never mentioned any Wrights," said Monty. "She moved to Saint Louis at age twenty. I was born and raised there, as a matter of fact. But I believe Mother's family might have moved to Greenwood when she was around seven or eight, so she doesn't remember much about Money. Just that it was small. Nothing more than a one-horse town."

"Mose wouldn'ta been livin' in Money then, Pearl," said Papa. "He just moved out there on Mr. Frederick's place 'bout eight, maybe nine years ago."

Ma Pearl squinted at Monty. "You kinda put me in the mind of Preacher Mose. You favor him a lil' bit."

"There's no telling who I'm related to down here," said Monty. "My mother still has family scattered throughout the Delta. Some in Greenwood still. But more in Mound Bayou, the city founded by Negroes. Some of Mother's family moved there in 1898, shortly after the city was founded. But she's never mentioned any Wrights from Money."

Ma Pearl's forehead creased. "How old is you?" she asked Monty.

"Thirty," he answered.

"Belle ain't but twenty-fo'."

"That's only six years' difference, ma'am."

With her expression stoic, Ma Pearl answered, "I can count."

Monty grinned. "I'm sure you can, ma'am."

Ma Pearl, of course, couldn't let him have the last word. She glared at him and said, "Y'all sharing a bed?"

Aunt Belle fidgeted, shifting her weight upon the settee. "We're engaged, Mama," she said. She showed Ma Pearl her ring finger. It held a thin gold band. Atop it sat a dainty diamond.

Ma Pearl snorted. "That ring don't mean y'all can share a bed."

Papa sat straighter in his chair. He removed his pipe from his shirt pocket and placed it between his lips. He didn't bother filling it with Prince Albert.

But before he could say a word, Aunt Belle blurted out, "It's a shame what they did to Mr. Albert's boy, ain't it?"

Ma Pearl's jaw dropped so hard it could've hit the floor. "What you know 'bout that?" she asked.

"Anna Mae and Pete told me."

"How they know and they way up in Chicago?"

"Pete said he read about it in the *Defender*," Aunt Belle answered. "Said it wasn't much, just something about another Negro killing going unpunished in Mississippi. Didn't even have his name. But Pete knew it was one of the Jackson boys. The one that was at Alcorn College."

Papa rubbed his chin. "Hmm, the *Defender*," he said. "That's a colored paper, ain't it?"

Monty nodded and said, "Indeed, it is. The *Defender* is a paper created and run by Negroes, Mr. Carter. It was founded in 1905 by Robert Abbott."

Ma Pearl raised an eyebrow. "Abbott? That don't sound like no colored name to me."

"Neither does Carter," said Monty. "But I assure you, ma'am"— he held up his hand and turned it backwards— "Mr. Abbott was a Negro, with a complexion as dark as mine."

Queen sneered. I could imagine what she was thinking— the same thing she'd said to me too many times: *Wouldn't wanna run into a spook like you after dark.*

"How they know 'bout what's going on in Mississippi?" Ma Pearl asked.

Aunt Belle spoke up. "Just because Mr. Albert wouldn't allow the NAACP to get involved directly doesn't mean they didn't in other ways," she said. "People still talk."

"Um-hmm," Ma Pearl said, pursing her lips. "It's all that talk that caused Albert 'n'em to run off in the night, sked half to death. They know'd them NAACP peoples wadn't go'n keep they mouths shut. And as soon as they'da started lurking round here, white folks get mad and take it out on the rest o' the family."

"Mr. Albert and his family are probably better off in Detroit anyway," said Aunt Belle as she rolled her eyes toward the window, where Mr. Robinson's rows of white cotton stretched till they met the horizon. "At least they don't have to pick that man's cotton."

"Humph!" Ma Pearl said. "He coulda at least stayed one mo' week to help Paul finish choppin' that last stretch o' cotton."

"You're blaming the wrong people," Aunt Belle said. "The NAACP didn't run Albert Jackson from Mississippi. White folks did."

Ma Pearl's forehead creased as she squinted at Aunt Belle. "You ain't messing with them NAACP peoples, is you?"

Without hesitation Aunt Belle snapped open her black patent leather purse and whipped out a small brownish card. She handed it to Ma Pearl.

Ma Pearl grabbed her chest as if her heart had suddenly failed. "Lawd, I knowed we shouldn'ta let you go up there with Isabelle."

Ma Pearl might not have known how to read, but she certainly knew her letters. With a grunt, she read them one by one. "N-A-A-C-P," then the name, "Lucy Isabelle Carter." With a flip of her wrist she flung the card back at Aunt Belle. It landed on the floor. "Didn't know I was raising no dirn fool," she said.

Aunt Belle picked up the card and placed it back in her purse. "I'm not a fool, Mama."

Ma Pearl stared hard at Aunt Belle. "You is a fool. All y'all fools," she said, motioning toward the sofa at the three Saint Louis spectators.

Their eyes bucked.

"Mrs. Carter, I assure—"

With a pudgy pointed finger, Ma Pearl cut off Monty. "You got her into this, didn't you?"

"Monty didn't get me into anything, Mama," said Aunt Belle. "I'm a grown woman. I make my own choices."

"Stupid choices," Ma Pearl said. "Messing with them folks won't do nothing but get a Negro kil't. Where was they when L. B. Turner 'n'em run Albert's boy off the road and shot him?" She paused for an answer, then said, "They sho' wadn't here to stop 'em."

"So they know who did it," said Monty.

Ma Pearl was dumbfounded. She had put her own foot in her mouth, as she liked to claim about other people.

Monty pressed on. "If they know who did it, why won't the sheriff do anything?" He looked from Ma Pearl to Papa and back again. "Why wouldn't his family allow NAACP involvement?"

When nobody answered Monty, my chest tightened. I wanted the sour conversation to stop. Aunt Belle's coming home was the highlight of my summer. Now Ma Pearl was about to ruin it. But before I could open my mouth and risk getting a backhand slap from Ma Pearl, Fred Lee opened his.

"What do them letters stand for?" he asked, his voice timid.

Everybody stared at him as if his skin had suddenly turned white and his hair blond.

After a moment Monty displayed all thirty-two of his gleaming white teeth. "NAACP stands for the National Association for the Advancement of Colored People," he said. "The organization was formed in 1909 to ensure the political, educational, social, and economic equality of rights of all persons and to eliminate racial hatred and racial discrimination."

He sounded like my teacher Miss Johnson reading from the history text. Poor Aunt Belle. She was about to marry a walking, talking *Encyclopedia Britannica*.

"One of our biggest concerns now is to eliminate these Jim Crow laws in states like Mississippi," he continued, "and to prevent decent young colored men like yourself from swinging from a tree with a rope around your neck."

Ophelia the Ogre's eyes popped.

"Or getting shot in the head for wanting to vote, like Levi Jackson," said Aunt Belle, cutting her eyes at Ma Pearl.

Ma Pearl bolted up from her chair and charged at Aunt Belle. "Git outta my house with that crazy nonsense," she said. She towered over Aunt Belle and pointed toward the door. "Go on back to Saint Louis with that crazy aunt of yours."

The Saint Louis spectators looked as if they'd get up and run any minute.

Monty draped his arm around Aunt Belle's shoulders and pulled her closer. With new assurance, Aunt Belle stared hard at Ma Pearl, unmoved by her threat. "I came to visit my family," she said, her voice calm and steady, "and I won't leave until my vacation is over."

Ma Pearl planted thick fists on her thick hips. "You won't be bringing that mess up in my house," she said. "You ain't go'n git me run off this place. Everybody can't run up north."

Papa stood up and put a hand on Ma Pearl's broad shoulder. "Have a seat, Pearl," he said quietly.

Luckily, the tension broke for a moment when Ophelia wiggled in her seat and asked where the toilet was.

Ma Pearl's head jerked toward me. "Show that gal where the toilet at."

The toilet. The toilet! My mind raced. The toilet was outside. I stared at Ophelia in her fancy beige suit and wondered whether she knew that as well.

After a gulp, I waved her toward the door and said, "Follow me."

Though her outfit was dainty, her walk certainly wasn't. Big-boned Ophelia looked like a man in women's clothing. And she had a voice to match.

Still, I was jealous. Especially as the sophisticated scent of her perfume filled the air around us as we strode through the meager surroundings I knew as home. After walking through the front room with the rundown furniture, Grandma Mandy's room with its mothball mustiness, and the kitchen with its antiquated woodstove and icebox, I felt about as proud as a barren hen. By the time we reached the back porch, I was wishing I had simply walked around the outside of our little unpainted house instead.

"Watch your step," I said as we descended the steps from the porch, warning her not so much about the steps, but about the drops of chicken poop scattered throughout the backyard.

Ophelia fanned herself with her hand as we walked the path to the toilet. Her makeup had begun to glisten with sweat. "It's so hot down here," she said. "How do you stand it?"

"It ain't hot in Saint Louis?" I asked.

"Not this hot," she said, wiping sweat off her forehead.

Before we even reached the toilet, its odor attacked the air and wiped out the sweet scent of Ophelia's perfume.

She wrinkled her nose. "Good God, that thing stinks," she said.

"It's a toilet," I said. "It's supposed to stink."

Ophelia laughed a throaty laugh. She pointed at our outdoor toilet and said, "That nasty thing is not a toilet. A toilet is inside a house. A toilet gets flushed after it's used. And it smells like pine after we clean it." She laughed again and said, "That filthy thing is an outhouse."

I balled my right hand into a fist. But I quickly mustered all the strength I could find to relax it before it slammed into Ophelia the Ogre's ugly face.

While she stood there laughing, her face uglier than it was before, I unhooked the latch and yanked open the toilet door. "Go ahead. Use it."

She covered her nose with her hand. "I don't have to use it. I just wanted to see what it looked like."

I planted my hands on my hips and gave her a dirty look. "You had me walk out here in this heat for nothing?"

Still shielding her nose from the stench, Ophelia nodded and said, "I've heard about these things, and I wanted to see one for myself."

After that, I really wanted to punch her in that big ugly nose she was guarding. Instead, I slammed the toilet door, hooked the latch in place, and stormed back toward the house. I couldn't believe I was missing important conversation in the parlor just to show some ungrateful northern spectator what an outside toilet looked like.

While I had been outside giving city Ophelia an education on country living, someone had been out to Aunt Belle's car and returned with two large shopping bags.

"Since your birthday is coming up," Aunt Belle said to Queen, "and you're turning sixteen, I thought pantsuits would be perfect for you. Especially with the way you've filled out."

Pantsuits! Aunt Belle brought us pantsuits! Just like the fancy one Ophelia was wearing.

When Aunt Belle began pulling the bright-colored outfits out of the bag, Queen squealed. "I'll be the only girl in school with pantsuits from the city," she said, beaming.

"Probably the only girl in pantsuits at all," Aunt Belle added.

Papa cleared his throat and shifted in his seat. But Ma Pearl threw up her hands and cried, "Lawd, if that NAACP mess don't git y'all sent straight to hell, wearin' them pantses sho' will."

Aunt Belle handed the two bags to Queen. "Here. I don't need to pull them all out in front of everybody. Take these on to the back and try 'em on."

When she handed the bags to and directed her statement

at Queen, and Queen only, my heart stopped beating for a few seconds, then started back up again. Seeing all the fashionable pantsuits she had brought for Queen, I thought it was only right to ask her if she brought me anything. Maybe someone had neglected to bring them from the car.

"Did you bring *me* anything?" I asked.

Aunt Belle's head jerked up, and she eyed me strangely. Then she looked at Ma Pearl. Then back at me. "Rose Lee, honey, Mama said you wouldn't be needing any school clothes." She looked at Ma Pearl again, her mouth slightly open.

Ma Pearl nodded. "That's right. She ain't going back to school."

My chest tightened as "What?" slipped quietly from my lips.

"You heard me," Ma Pearl said. "You won't be going to no school. You finished seventh grade. That's more'n you need already."

"Ma Pearl—"

"What you need mo' schooling for?" She narrowed her eyes. "You strong. You can work with yo' hands. And Papa go'n need you to pick cotton anyway, with Albert 'n'em gone."

My heart pounding, I turned to Papa. "Can't you get somebody else to help with the cotton? What about Slow John?"

Ma Pearl's eyes bucked. "That fool? He ain't go'n work for nobody."

Monty, with an expression just as perplexed as mine, chimed in. "This child's absence from school is only until the cotton has been picked, correct?"

If looks really had the ability to kill, Monty would have died instantly with the way Ma Pearl stared at him. "This ain't yo' bizness," she said. "This between me and mines. If I say she got all the school'n she need, then she got all the school'n she need. Seventh grade. That's way mor'n I ever got. When she finish the pick'n, she can help me out round the house."

Tears stung my eyes. And a pressure filled my head so quickly that it felt as if it could explode. Plenty of folks who worked in the fields kept their children out of school until the harvest was over, but Ma Pearl was talking foolishness if she expected me to quit school altogether. I had no choice but to speak up. "Miss Johnson said I was one of the smartest students at the school," I said, my voice shaking. "She said I could even go all the way to college if I wanted to. I can't quit school. That would be a waste."

Ma Pearl grunted. "Waste?" she said, her brows raised. "What's a waste is a strong gal like you goin' to school 'stead o' work'n like you should be. You thirteen. Too old for school." She sniffed and added, "Besides, what that lil' foolish teacher know? College ain't free. So how a po' Negro like you s'posed to go?"

My eyes met Papa's. "Can't you find somebody else to help pick the cotton?" I pleaded.

"I said you ain't goin' back. Cotton or no cotton," Ma Pearl interjected. "I need you here at this house takin' some o' the load off me 'stead o' runnin' up there to that school gittin' too smart for yo' own good."

Monty gestured toward Fred Lee and Queen. "What about these two?"

Ma Pearl's nostrils flared. "Don't try to tell me how to raise my grandchi'ren."

"Papa," I pleaded again, my voice cracking.

"We'll talk about this later, Rose Lee," he said quietly.

I was so lost in my misery, I hadn't concerned myself with what Aunt Belle's friends might have been thinking until they began to shift nervously on the sofa. When I saw how they stared at me with pity, my tears crested and flooded down my cheeks. Ma Pearl had not only crushed my spirit. She had also totally humiliated me in the presence of the sophisticated Saint Louis spectators.

Chapter Twelve

WEDNESDAY, AUGUST 24

★   ★

WHILE REVEREND JENKINS READ FROM THE BOOK OF Isaiah, I removed a scrap of paper from my Bible, took a pencil from behind my ear, and scribbled a note to Hallelujah: "Ma Pearl said I can't go back to school."

Shock raced across Hallelujah's face. *What?* he mouthed. He removed a pen from his shirt pocket and scribbled on my note. He handed it back to me.

"Has she lost her mind?" the note read.

I pushed back a chuckle. Laughing was not allowed in church, especially on Wednesday nights, and especially while Reverend Jenkins was reading. We had only begun having Wednesday night services since the beginning of the year. We were Baptist, and Baptist folks usually went to church only on Sunday.

All. Day. Long.

But Reverend Jenkins had made a covenant with the Lord that year and promised to be holier, like the folks at the Church of God in Christ. So he added Wednesday nights to the torture of our church attendance.

Reverend Jenkins's voice boomed from the pulpit: "*'He was oppressed, and he was afflicted, yet he opened not his mouth: he is brought as a lamb to the slaughter, and as a sheep before her shearers is dumb, so he openeth not his mouth.'*"

I snapped to attention. The preacher always seemed to say just the right words at just the right time. That was exactly what I felt like: a lamb to the slaughter, a sheep before my shearer. And I couldn't even open my mouth to defend myself.

I responded to Hallelujah: "She lost her mind a long time ago."

"Queen, too?" Hallelujah wrote back.

When I first read the note, I giggled, imagining he meant Queen had lost her mind like Ma Pearl. Of course, in my opinion, she had. But I scribbled back, "No. Queen gets to go."

Hallelujah mouthed, *What?* He lowered his head and wrote.

I suppressed a smile when I read "The way she hates school!!!"

I wrote back, "Don't be surprised if she drops out at 16."

"What did Mr. Carter say?" Hallelujah wrote.

The scrap of paper was out of space, so I flipped through my Bible — the Bible Reverend Jenkins had given me for my twelfth birthday — for another. I scribbled, "He said we'd talk about it later."

"When?" wrote Hallelujah.

I shrugged and wrote, "Don't know. It's been 3 days already."

I had never known Papa to lie to me. But that's exactly what I had begun to fear he'd done. I couldn't believe he had sided with Ma Pearl to keep me out of school.

Hallelujah wrote, "You think Preacher could talk to Miss Sweet?"

I didn't want to tell Hallelujah what Ma Pearl really thought of his daddy. "That boy ain't nothing but a educated fool," she'd say of Reverend Jenkins. "Can't preach worth a lick. Now, Reverend E. D. Blake over at Little Ebenezer, that's a preacher."

Reverend E. D. Blake wouldn't know a Holy Scripture if it came and sat at the table with him and offered him supper, I wanted to tell her.

I wrote back, "She's made up her mind."

"Can he talk to Mr. Carter?" wrote Hallelujah.

I groaned slightly and scribbled, "He won't even talk to me!"

"Still got 2 weeks. Maybe he's still thinking about it," wrote Hallelujah.

Two weeks. What if Papa said no? What if I really was forced to quit school with only a seventh-grade education?

That was worse than my aunts. At least they all made it through eighth grade. And my poor mama, only sixth. But at least she was pretty enough to have a man like Mr. Pete want to marry her. But I wasn't pretty like Mama, so I wasn't expecting someone like Mr. Pete to whisk me off to the courthouse and marry me—then take me off to Chicago so our children could go to those good schools they bragged about. And I certainly wouldn't have the opportunity to get myself educated like Aunt Belle. Because I didn't have the grit to defy Ma Pearl the way she had.

My chest tightened as I wrote, "How will I ever leave Mississippi if I can't get an education?"

Hallelujah frowned and wrote back, "You will get an education."

"How do you know?" I wrote.

Hallelujah sighed and scribbled. Then he smiled and handed me the note. It read "Just pray. Have faith. God will make a way."

"Stop sounding like a preacher!" I wrote back.

Hallelujah grinned at my note. He loved it when he sounded like a preacher, even though he didn't want to be one. "I wanna be a surgeon like Dr. T.R.M. Howard in Mound Bayou," he often said. "And I'm gonna be the first Negro to attend that new medical school Ole Miss opened in Jackson."

I didn't really care at that point to be the first Negro to do anything. I just wanted to be the first person in my family to graduate from high school.

Hallelujah handed me the note again. "Can Miss Johnson talk to Miss Sweet?"

I wrote back, "She thinks Miss Johnson is stupid."

Hallelujah wrote, "I think she's cute."

I smiled and wrote, "She's a grown woman. You're a boy."

With a sly grin and raised brows, Hallelujah scribbled, "So?"

I wrote, "What do you know? You think catfish-eyed Queen is cute."

Hallelujah blushed, lowered his head, and scribbled on the paper: "Stop passing notes in church."

And I did. I was out of paper.

Chapter Thirteen

THE ONLY GOOD THING ABOUT REVEREND JENKINS forcing us to go to church on Wednesday night was that he fed us afterward. Well, we fed ourselves. Every family brought something to share with everybody else. Like a repast. Except no one had died, unless you count the Holy Ghost, who was killed the minute he set foot in Greater Mount Zion Missionary Baptist Church.

During the night I realized that I had drunk way too much of Miss Doll's sweet tea. This time Queen wouldn't be the only one peeing up the pot through the night.

The pot was kept in a tiny room off the side of Fred Lee's room. For some reason it was called the back room, even though it was actually on the side of the house. The room served as our indoor toilet, without the proper plumbing, of course. Besides keeping the pot in there for nighttime use, the back room was also where we took our daily wash-ups and twice-a-week baths in a number-three tin tub.

I made my way into the dark room and gently waved my

hand before me until I hit the string that hung from the light bulb in the ceiling. Strangely, this pretend-it's-a-bathroom was the only room in the house with electricity. Mr. Robinson, promising Papa that he would convert the room so that it had an actual toilet, with indoor plumbing, had wired the room for lights first but never got around to getting the plumbing put in. But at least we could see without having to light a kerosene lamp when we needed to use the pot at night. Too bad the only privacy was the double sheets hanging in the doorway.

After giving my bladder some relief, I crept back through Fred Lee's room using the moonlight as my guide. I felt my way along the wall until I reached the sheet that hung in the doorway of the room I shared with Queen. When I pulled it back to enter, my heart nearly stopped. I thought I was seeing a ghost. Instead it was Queen, fully dressed and climbing out the window.

My gasp startled her. She stopped, one leg on the floor of our bedroom, the other hanging out the window.

"Queen!" I said, my voice between a shout and a whisper. "What you doing?"

Queen just stood there with her eyes bucked and her mouth gaping. She was wearing one of the new outfits Aunt Belle had brought her—a light pink pantsuit that fit her curvy body like a second skin. Ma Pearl would kill her if she found out she'd sneaked clothes out of the chifforobe. Well, maybe not, since it was Queen.

Letting the sheet drop to shield our room from Fred Lee's, I tiptoed in. "Where you going?" I whispered as I got closer to Queen.

She placed a finger to her mouth and shushed me. She brought her whole body inside the room, then peeped out the window.

"You running away?" I asked, assuming that any bags she had packed must have been tossed outside, seeing that her hands were empty.

With a wave of her hand, Queen shushed me again. "Naw, fool. I ain't running away."

"Then why you sneaking out the window?"

She sucked her teeth and said, "None a yo' ol' ugly business."

The shock of her angry reply made me jump. Then I heard a horn. It sounded as if the tooter just barely touched it, so as to alert only someone who knew to be listening for it.

Queen glanced out the window. "Go back to bed," she hissed at me like an angry snake.

I stalked toward the window. "Who's out there?"

Queen blocked me with her arm. Her nostrils flared. "Like I said, that ain't none a yo' business, ol' ugly spook," she said, her teeth clenched.

When I tried to push past her, she shoved me to the floor. Before I could get back up, she was out the window faster than a gush of wind. I stumbled to the window just in time to see her race to the edge of the field, where a rusted-out white pickup waited.

My stomach twisted. The pickup belonged to Ricky Turner.

Chapter Fourteen

SATURDAY, AUGUST 27

HALLELUJAH STARTED DRIVING WHEN HE WAS ONLY eight years old. After the second Mrs. Clyde B. Jenkins the Second died, Reverend Jenkins was so torn up that he couldn't even remember how to start his own car. So eight-year-old Hallelujah jumped right on into the front seat, started it for him, and drove straight down the road without missing a beat. And at fourteen he was a master behind the wheel.

When he pulled up in front of the house that morning, I beamed. And if I had been the squealing type, I would have done that, too. Hallelujah might have been his daddy's chauffeur at eight years old, but Reverend Jenkins rarely allowed him access to the keys once he was actually almost old enough to drive.

I hopped into the passenger seat of the brown Buick, my grin stretching from my right ear to my left, and commanded, "To Miss Addie's, my good man." I held on tight to my crate of eggs, as I knew what would happen next.

Gravel flew behind the car as Hallelujah sped off. Good

thing Ma Pearl had gone fishing that morning, else she would've barged out of the house like a giant mama bear, yelling, *Gal, git outta that car with that foolish boy!*

Gravel beat on the sides of Reverend Jenkins's Buick like popcorn popping in a skillet of hot grease. Hallelujah and I both hooted, as if we were a couple of city gangsters who had just pulled off the heist of the century. I knew to cherish the moment, as there was no telling when I'd see another one like it.

After catching Queen sneaking off into the night with Ricky Turner, I finally told Ma Pearl and Papa about him chasing me off the road nearly a month before. I told them right in front of Queen, hoping she'd take a hint. She didn't do a thing but roll her eyes at me.

Ma Pearl threw a fiery fit when she realized that Miss Addie never got her eggs and had to make do a whole month without them. "Eggs is needed for everything," Ma Pearl had yelled at me. "You should've told somebody. I oughta slap the black off you right now."

Papa interrupted her rant and said he'd get Preacher to take me the next time. The preacher sent his son instead. So there we were, Hallelujah and I, rumbling down the road to Miss Addie's, when Hallelujah decided to spoil my adventure by telling me that another Negro had been killed in Mississippi for helping colored people register to vote.

"His name is Lamar Smith," Hallelujah said. His voice was quiet, and his eyes were fixed intently on the noisy rock road ahead of us. "He was sixty-three years old. A farmer and a war veteran. He had voted only a few weeks ago. When he was shot down, he was at the courthouse, trying to help other Negroes register to vote."

I, too, stared at the rocky road ahead, saying nothing as Hallelujah gave me the horrible details of this man's murder. By the time we pulled into Miss Addie's yard, which was only big enough to accommodate the Buick, I was trembling and had broken into a cold sweat.

"You better stop all that shaking before you break them eggs," Hallelujah said, nodding toward the crate in my lap.

I tried to smile at his attempt to calm my nerves. But how could I smile when a sixty-three-year-old man had been gunned down in broad daylight just for voting and taking other Negroes to the courthouse to vote?

Ten o'clock in the morning?

Right on the front lawn of the courthouse?

The sheriff saw the killer leaving the scene covered in blood, and he did nothing?

Mississippi had to be the most evil place in the world.

I thought about the ages of the people who had been killed in just a few short months. Reverend George Lee was fifty-one. This man, Lamar Smith, was sixty-three. And Levi

Jackson had just turned twenty-one. They all risked their lives to try to make a change.

Reverend George Lee, from what I was told, was a man of means, like Mr. Pete. But rather than running up north, he chose to stay down south and fight for his rights. I didn't know much about Lamar Smith, except his age and that he had fought in the war, but he was older than Papa. Yet he decided to go to the courthouse and help other colored people register to vote. Then there was Levi, who was almost finished with college. He could have waited one more year, then left Mississippi and started a new—better—life somewhere else. Instead, he risked his life, even though he knew that Reverend George Lee had been killed only a few months before.

I could now understand why people like Mr. Pete chose to leave. He had his own land, on which he grew plenty of cotton. He had a nice house in Greenwood. He was better off than a lot of white folks in Leflore County, or even in Mississippi. Yet if he did something as simple as register to vote, like one of them, he could be killed.

At first, after seeing Mama and everyone else leaving Mississippi for a better life up north, I wanted to go only because I wanted that kind of life too. But after hearing that white folks in Mississippi would kill anybody, regardless of age, for simply wanting to exercise their right to vote, I wanted to leave before I was old enough to face the life-and-death decision of whether to stand up for my rights or just sit back and leave things the way they were.

Hallelujah turned off the motor, got out, and then ran around to the passenger side and opened the door for me. Either Reverend Jenkins had taught him well, or he didn't want to take a chance on my dropping Miss Addie's eggs.

Miss Addie's yard was so small that we were practically at the rickety front steps when we got out of the car. I was almost afraid to climb the steps and walk across the tattered porch, even though I had done it too many times to count. Each time, I wondered whether it would be the last.

At nearly 102, Miss Addie had been born a slave. And since she lived on Mr. Robinson's place and her last name happened to be Robinson as well, we all assumed that her family had been owned by Mr. Robinson's family. And from the looks of her house, it appeared she was still living in a slave shack.

But slave or not, Miss Addie, like the abolitionist Frederick Douglass—whom my old teacher Miss Johnson frequently quoted—could read and write. And from what I had heard, she was a person with rather strange insight, and she had delivered not only nearly every colored baby in Stillwater but a few white ones as well.

Before I could tap on the door, she called out in her crackly voice, "Y'all come on in."

Miss Addie's house had three rooms—a front room, a middle room, and a back room, which held a table, no chairs, a woodstove, and a tiny icebox. The house was what folks called a shotgun house. If you shot a gun at the front door, the bullet would zoom straight through the house and go right out the back door, assuming nobody (or nothing) was in its path.

Miss Addie's front room served as her bedroom as well as her living room. In it she had no other furniture besides her bed, a rocking chair, a spit cup for her snuff, and a large tree stump that sat right in the middle of the floor, as if someone had chopped down a giant tree and built the shack right around it, which I think they did.

The middle room was where Miss Addie's granddaughter, Jinx, slept. Jinx, who was also Miss Addie's caregiver, was a forty-something-year-old spinster who sat around giggling all the time when there was nothing actually funny. I'm not sure whether Jinx was her real name or not, but I imagine that when it came time for choosing which relative would live with and care for Miss Addie, someone probably pointed at her and said, *Jinx! You're it!*

I was hoping that Jinx wouldn't be there when we arrived. But as soon as Hallelujah and I stepped through the door, she emerged from the middle room, giggling for no apparent reason and asking for the eggs. "How come you didn't bring 'em last time?" she asked me.

Miss Addie, rocking back and forth in her rocker, said with some exasperation, "I told you dat boy run her off da road, Jinx."

Jinx giggled, hugging the egg crate to her chest, as if I might take it back. "How you know a boy run her off the road, Mama?" she said. "You ain't left this house in ten years."

Miss Addie picked up her spit cup—a tin can that once held store-bought peaches. She spat in the can, then wiped dripping snuff from her chin with a dingy handkerchief. "These old eyes sees what others cain't," she said.

With eyes nearly as silver as dimes, Miss Addie, some folks claimed, was born with a caul, or sixth sense, and therefore could "sense" things that other people couldn't. But most folks, like Jinx and Ma Pearl, just thought she was plain ol' senile.

"Set a spell, chi'ren," she said, motioning toward the stump.

Jinx giggled and said, "I'll put the eggs in the icebox."

Before she left the room, Miss Addie said, "Brang these chi'ren some dem teacakes you made the other day."

"No, thank you," I said quickly. "We ate before we left." Besides being a giggler, Jinx was also a nose picker. And from what I had heard, she couldn't cook worth a lick anyway.

"They taste funny, Mama," Jinx said, giggling. "I didn't have no eggs, remember?" For some reason, she found that extremely funny and broke into a giggling fit as she headed to the back of the house.

"How's yo' papa 'n'em?" Miss Addie asked me, although she stared straight at Hallelujah.

"Everybody's fine," I answered. She was still staring hard at Hallelujah.

Hallelujah fidgeted.

Miss Addie pointed a bony black finger at him and narrowed her silvery eyes. "You ain't the boy, is you?"

"Me?" Hallelujah asked, pointing his thumb at his chest. He chuckled. "No, ma'am. Rosa and I are friends. I would never run her off the road. I gave her a ride here."

Miss Addie moaned as if she were in pain. "Um-umph, not that," she said, shaking her head. "It's somp'n else. But I cain't quite git a holt of it."

Hallelujah glanced at me and grimaced. We had both heard stories of Miss Addie's so-called visions, which even Reverend Jenkins said were no more than her recounting stories from her hundred-year-old past.

Jinx reappeared in the doorway. With her head tilted to one side and her hand over her heart, she was serious for once and not giggling. "Mama, what you talking 'bout?" she asked.

Miss Addie kept her eyes fixed on Hallelujah. "Dat boy," she said, pointing. "Somp'n 'bout dat boy."

Jinx shook her head and said, "Mama, don't start that crazy hoodoo talk with these chi'rens here."

"Dis ain't no hoodoo!" Miss Addie snapped. "Dis da truth.

Somp'n 'bout to happen. Somp'n 'bout to shake up Miss'sippi jest like dat flood of twenty-seven shaked us up. It came heah to wash 'way da sins o' dis place."

Jinx stormed into the room. "Stop it, Mama," she said. "Stop scaring these chi'ren. Every day, you sit round here ack'n like some kinda witch cooking up spells. You too old and too close to death for this kinda stuff. You go'n end up going straight to hell."

But Miss Addie didn't stop. She wrapped her thin arms around her frail body and rocked vigorously in her chair. "Yes, Lawdy, baby, somp'n 'bout to happen. Somp'n 'bout to happen. Somp'n 'bout to shake dis place."

Jinx giggled nervously and said, "Don't y'all pay Mama no mind. Ain't nothin' 'bout to happen, 'cause she don't see nothin' 'cept the angel Gabra, who 'bout to come take her home soon."

Miss Addie stopped rocking and stared at Jinx. "Ain't no anja 'bout ta come git me. My time ain't close as you thank it is. But dis place," she said, motioning around the room. "Dis place. Her time done come. Somp'n 'bout to happen. Lawdy, somp'n 'bout to happen."

Even though there wasn't a whiff of cool air in that tiny room, chills covered my arms. I was ready to leave.

"Well, we have to go now," I told Miss Addie. I nudged Hallelujah.

Rather than hearing me, it seemed that Miss Addie had fallen into a trance. She pointed toward the ceiling and said, "Look! Do you see it?"

Hallelujah and I looked up at the same time. I don't know what he saw, but all I saw was sunlight streaming in through the cracks in the ceiling.

"Yes, Lawdy, baby," Miss Addie said as she threw her head back. "The time is com'n dat all mens should repent!" She dropped her head to her chest, then began to sway and moan. The sunlight that was streaming in through the cracks in the ceiling suddenly disappeared. The sky had clouded. The room grew darker, as if a giant hand had covered the whole house and was blocking out any sunshine that had previously managed to seep in.

Miss Addie's moaning grew louder as the room grew darker. It seemed as if she would moan forever. When she finally stopped, the room was as quiet as a graveyard.

"Jinx!" she yelled.

We all jumped.

Jinx stepped forward. "I'm right here, Mama," she said quietly, like a child chastised and found guilty.

Miss Addie grinned, as if nothing unusual had happened, and said, "Git these chi'ren some dem teacakes 'fo they leave."

Chapter Fifteen

SATURDAY, AUGUST 27

I HADN'T BEEN ABLE TO GET A FULL NIGHT'S SLEEP since the night I got up to use the pot and caught Queen sneaking out the window. And that Saturday night was no different. She lay over on her bed, breathing softly, but I couldn't tell whether she was really asleep or just faking. I decided she was faking. So I did the same, with my face turned toward her bed in case she tried to sneak out.

Sure enough, after what felt like an hour of lying there playing possum, I heard a truck in the distance. It cut off suddenly, but I could still hear some clanking, as if the truck were coasting along without its engine running.

Queen's bed creaked.

When she eased off the bed, I saw that she was fully dressed. Again, in one of her new outfits. A powder blue pantsuit.

I sprang up to a sitting position.

Queen nearly jumped to the ceiling. "You scared me!" she said, half yelling, but mostly whispering.

I crossed my arms over my chest and asked, "You going somewhere?"

Her face, illuminated by moonlight, quickly went from surprised to hateful. "Mind your own business, spook!" she hissed at me as she headed toward the window.

I got up from my bed and followed her. "You're gonna get in trouble."

"Not if you keep yo' dumb mouth shut."

"I don't mean that kind of trouble."

Queen waved me off. "You don't know nothing, ol' ugly girl. You just a baby."

"I know sneaking out at night with a boy can *get* you a baby."

Queen's face hardened. She grabbed my wrist and twisted my arm so hard it popped.

I winced and tried to wriggle free. But for someone who never did any work, Queen was surprisingly strong.

Twisting my arm harder, she leaned her face nearly nose to nose with mine and snarled, "If you say one word about this, I will break this arm *and* twist that ugly head right off yo' skinny . . . black . . . neck."

She breathed heavily in my face. Her breath smelled like mints. Those, too, she obviously stole from Ma Pearl's chifforobe when she'd swiped the powder blue outfit she was wearing.

Before I could wrestle free from her grip, the faint tap of a horn had Queen dropping my arm and dashing out the window faster than Flash Gordon.

"I hope you get eaten up by mosquitoes!" I yelled after her.

I fell onto my bed feeling just what she'd called me: stupid. Why should I care what happened to her? She was meaner than a bear caught in a beehive, as Ma Pearl would say. So she deserved whatever she had coming. I couldn't believe Ma Pearl was making *me* leave school and letting *her* stay in. She wasn't doing anything with her life but throwing it away. I, at least, had dreams.

I lay flat on my back and rubbed my wrist. My skin burned where Queen had dug her long fingernails into it. I didn't know what time it was, but I knew it was late and I should've been sleeping. Before I knew it, Slick Charlie would be crowing, the scent of coffee, biscuits, and salt pork would be stuck in the stuffy air, and Ma Pearl would be storming through the house with her war cry: "Rise 'n shine, Saints! It's time for church!"

Of course, that wouldn't include Queen, who would be curled up in a ball, moaning, "Oh, Ma Pearl, I can't go to church this morning. I got the cramps."

I flipped my pillow to the cooler side, rolled over to face the wall, and tried to sleep. But it was no use. Everything and everybody raced through my mind, especially poor Hallelujah, who was in love with Queen, and probably with Miss Johnson, too, only because of their light complexions. Why was everybody so afraid of blackness?

Well, everybody except Aunt Belle, whom I hadn't seen all week because of Ma Pearl and her big mouth. To be fair, I couldn't blame Aunt Belle's absence entirely on Ma Pearl. It was Aunt Belle herself who was too busy working on behalf of the NAACP and didn't have time for her family.

She and Monty, along with their northern comrades, were driving all over Leflore, Sunflower, and Bolivar Counties rounding up backwoods Negroes, trying to convince them to register to vote. Didn't she realize that Reverend George Lee and Mr. Lamar Smith, a proud colored man who fought in a war, were lying stone cold in their graves for doing the same thing? I never thought I'd agree with Ma Pearl, but now this NAACP thing was affecting my own kin, and I was afraid. I didn't want my aunt gunned down in the prime of her life. Nor did I want her body mutilated and hanging from a tree. I wanted her at the house with us, sitting around eating good food, telling funny stories, and laughing—filling my head with dreams of what life was like up north.

My chest ached, and I wanted to go find her, snatch that little NAACP card from her black patent leather purse, and burn it before her very eyes. Like any other Negro, I wanted change too, but not at the expense of my own family.

When sleep finally came, I found myself in a dream where I was trapped inside Miss Addie's tiny house. Her silver eyes aglow, she stood over me, swaying, and chanting, "Somp'n 'bout to happen. Somp'n 'bout to happen."

I called for Jinx to make her stop. But Jinx was nowhere in the house. I was all alone with Miss Addie, and I had no way to escape. The walls closed in, and the little house came crumbling down upon me.

Chapter Sixteen

SUNDAY, AUGUST 28

I SAT UP STRAIGHT IN MY BED, GASPING FOR AIR. My heart raced so fast I felt it would rush right out of my chest.

Sunlight filtered into the room through the thin beige curtain.

Queen was back in her bed, curled into her covers like a baby who just got over the colic and could finally sleep. Since I hadn't heard her sneak in and hadn't heard Slick Charlie when he crowed, the dream, which felt so short, was obviously much longer.

Exhausted from the lack of sleep and the weariness of my worries, I forced my body off the bed and to the back room to use the pot. As I sat there, I realized that the aroma of coffee seeped through the walls, but its accompaniments—the biscuits and the Sunday-morning salt pork—were missing. Nor had Ma Pearl yelled for us to rise and shine.

I felt an ache in the pit of my stomach as I crept back to my room to dress. Fred Lee was still in bed. This was unusual for a Sunday morning. I threw a housecoat on over my nightgown and headed to the kitchen. My heart leaped when

I saw Aunt Belle sitting at the table. Her hands were wrapped around a cup of coffee as she stared at Ma Pearl, who sat across from her. They were both silent.

As hot as it was in our house, I suddenly felt chilled. The looks on Aunt Belle's and Ma Pearl's faces immediately signaled something was wrong. I wrapped my housecoat tighter around my body and hesitantly crossed the threshold into the kitchen.

Aunt Belle's head jerked in my direction even though I hadn't made a sound.

I'm not sure why, but the first words out of my mouth were, "Where's Papa?"

"Papa's with Preacher," Ma Pearl answered briskly.

"And Monty," Aunt Belle added. Both of their expressions were tense.

I looked from face to face, confused. My thoughts raced. *It's Sunday morning. Ma Pearl didn't wake her troops for church. Aunt Belle is here in the kitchen, her hands wrapped around a chipped white mug filled with black coffee. Yet they both say to me, "Papa's with Preacher. And Monty."*

Something wasn't right. "How come Papa's with Reverend Jenkins?" I asked, my voice quivering. "Something happened at church?"

Aunt Belle removed her right hand from the coffee cup and extended it toward me. "Come sit down," she said quietly.

As I entered the kitchen, a jolt of nervousness attacked my stomach. I stumbled to the chair next to Aunt Belle and sat.

She took my hand and held it in hers. Her hand was warm from the coffee. "A Negro boy is missing," she said.

My heart beat faster. "Hallelujah?"

Aunt Belle squeezed my hand. "No, sweetie," she said, shaking her head, looking apologetic.

"It's one of Mose Wright's grandboys," Ma Pearl interjected, her tone indifferent. "Down here from Chicago."

"Nephew, Mama," said Aunt Belle. "It's his nephew that's missing."

"Missing?" I asked. "What you mean by missing?"

"We're not sure," answered Aunt Belle. "Monty's cousin in Greenwood got a call early this morning from another cousin who lives near Money. Said he heard that two white men burst into Mose Wright's house before day this morning and took the boy. Monty insisted on going there, so I called Reverend Jenkins to go with him. When Reverend Jenkins stopped by here to let Papa know there'd be no church today, Papa offered to ride with them and insisted I stay here with Mama." She glanced at Ma Pearl, as if the idea repulsed her.

"My Papa?" I asked.

Ma Pearl glared at Aunt Belle. "To keep this gal from runnin' over there."

Mose Wright? The name sounded familiar. "Ain't that the man you asked Monty if he was kin to?" I asked Ma Pearl.

Ma Pearl pushed her chair from the table and heaved herself to a standing position. "Um-hmm," she said. "That's him. And I bet you any 'mount of money, that boy of his was down here stirring up trouble, jest like this gal and her boyfriend is doing," she said, glaring at Aunt Belle. "That NAACP nonsense go'n git us all kil't."

Aunt Belle's forehead wrinkled. "This has nothing to do with the NAACP, Mama. I doubt that boy was old enough to know anything about the NAACP. But I can assure you, the NAACP will not let this thing go unnoticed. It's time somebody put a stop to all this white terror."

Leaning forward and placing her huge hands on the edge of the table, Ma Pearl braced herself for one of her rants. She stood there, silently glaring at Aunt Belle as if she were the devil himself sitting at her kitchen table. "White terror, huh?" she said, smirking. "Chile, you ain't see'd no white terror yet. These NAACP peoples keep coming down here interrupting these people's way of life, these white folks liable to burn down every shack on every plantation in order to keep things the way they is round here."

Aunt Belle stared at Ma Pearl and shook her head with pity. "Mama, haven't you ever dreamed of something better for yourself than cleaning up after Mrs. Robinson and her children?" With one hand, she gestured around the room. "Wouldn't you like to own a house one day? Have a kitchen with some running water and a real gas stove? And what about your grandchildren? Don't you want something better for them?"

"That what Isabelle got up there in Saint Louis?" Ma Pearl asked. "A fancy house to call her own?" Ma Pearl snatched up her empty cup, turned on her heel, and stalked over to the stove. As she picked up the coffeepot, she chuckled. "You been in Saint Louis, what? Five years? Now, you know something?" She refilled her cup as she chuckled again. "Isabelle tell you how she got that house?"

Aunt Belle didn't answer. She simply stared into her coffee cup, her expression somber.

"You don't know nothing, do you, gal? That fancy house yo' aunt got up there in Saint Louis?" Ma Pearl paused and stared at me. "I ain't go'n say how she got that fancy house in front this chile here," she said. "But I know one thang: all that living up north go'n do is teach you how to be a dirn fool."

Tears bulged in Aunt Belle's eyes. She wiped them with the back of her hand. I couldn't tell whether she was sad or angry, but what came out of her mouth next told me she felt sorry for Ma Pearl. "Slave mentality, Mama," she said. "These whites down here have you thinking you're somehow less than they are because of the color of your skin." She shook her head. "You're not. I'm not," she said, pointing to her chest. She glanced around the room, gesturing with her hand. "None of us are."

Ma Pearl's nostrils flared. "And you got a fool mentality, gal. White mens wouldn'ta took that boy for no reason. He did something." She paused and took a sip of her coffee. "He did something a'right. And it's go'n cause trouble for all the other Negroes round here. You wait and see. If I told you once, I told you a thousand times: one Negro do something, and white folks get mad at all us. Like we all is one."

"Coloreds outnumber whites in this county, Mama," Aunt Belle said. "We shouldn't let them run over us like this."

Ma Pearl strolled over to the table and set her cup down. "Us?" she asked with raised brows. "You don't live her no mo'." She waved her hand in the air. "You a city gal now. Coming down here in yo' fancy car with yo' fancy friends. Wearing fancy clothes, bringing these gals fancy clothes, trying to make them like you. White folks don't take too lightly to niggas trying to act like them. And that's exactly what you city niggas do—try to act like you white. Like you as good as them."

"We are," Aunt Belle answered tersely, her voice quaking.

Ma Pearl snorted a laugh. "You think if I dress up that sow out there in the hog pen I'm go'n let her come in here and sleep in my bed? Nah," she said, shaking her head. "'Cause she still a hog, no matter how clean and dressed up she is. And niggas is still niggas, no matter how dressed up they is."

Aunt Belle sighed. "Mama," she said, pausing, shaking her head. "You should want something better for yourself than this." She motioned her hand to signify not just the house, but all of Mississippi, it seemed.

Ma Pearl lumbered over to the back door and stared out through the screen. She stood there, not saying a word, only contemplating as she observed her backyard full of chickens, a few hogs, and a cow mooing in a small patch of a pasture. "Things is better than they used to be," she said, still not turning to face Aunt Belle. "And they wouldn't be so bad as they is if the gov'ment wadn't trying to force the whites down here to act like the whites up north."

"Mama, why are you so afraid of white people?"

"You ain't see'd what I done see'd," Ma Pearl said. She turned abruptly, nearly spilling her coffee. She stared icily at Aunt Belle. "That boy ain't missing," she said. "He dead. Just like every other nigga that got outta place with the white man. And ain't nobody go'n do a dirn thing about it."

"The NAA—"

Before Aunt Belle could finish spelling out the letters, Ma Pearl cut her off. "The NAACP can go to hell for all I care. More Negroes been kil't since they came down here than ever before. Whites, too, if they find theyselves on the wrong side of the line. The NAACP can't stop a Negro from being lynched, and they can't make the sheriff put a peckerwood in jail for doing the lynching. This Miss'sippi. Ain't nothing go'n never change."

Chapter Seventeen

SUNDAY, AUGUST 28

WITH MA PEARL'S WORDS RINGING IN MY EARS, I left the kitchen and went back to my room. I had to lie down and ease the pain throbbing in my head.

When I sighed and collapsed on my bed, Queen stirred in hers. She sat up, stretched, and asked me what time it was.

I shrugged and mumbled that it was a little after ten.

Yawning, she asked, "What's going on? How come Ma Pearl didn't wake us up?"

"A colored boy from Chicago is missing. White men took him from his uncle's house in Money."

Queen shrugged and asked, "We ain't going to church?"

I shook my head. "Reverend Jenkins is over in Money. Papa, too."

She sniffed the air and said, "Ma Pearl didn't cook?"

"Queen," I said, scowling, "a colored boy is missing. Two white men came to his uncle's house in the middle of the night and took him."

"That don't mean Ma Pearl can't cook," she said, jumping up off the bed. "Can't believe I got to git my own food."

"Don't you ever care about anybody other than yourself?"

"Niggas oughta quit acting a fool round here," she said, yanking back the sheet in the doorframe. "Nothing I can do 'bout him missing. He probably somewhere hanging from a tree by now anyways."

I lay on my bed, shaking. A colored boy from Chicago was missing in Mississippi, and my own cousin was too callous to care.

No. He wasn't missing.

He had been taken.

By two white men.

And they knew exactly where he was.

Fear gripped me and wouldn't let go. What if Queen was right? What if he was hanging somewhere from a tree? It wasn't as if we hadn't heard plenty of stories like that before. What kind of place was I living in, where white men could just walk into the house of a colored person and take away his kin? What if it had been Fred Lee? Would Papa have just let him go? Or would he have put up a fight?

At the thought, a sick feeling invaded my stomach. Papa might not have fought.

When the sheet hanging in the doorframe of the bedroom moved and I saw that the hand moving it wore a diamond engagement ring, I shut my eyes and pretended to sleep.

"You didn't go to sleep that fast," said Aunt Belle.

I didn't answer.

"I see your eyes moving under your lids. And your breathing is all wrong. You ain't asleep, Rose Lee."

I opened my eyes and stared at Aunt Belle standing in the doorway.

"You okay?" she asked.

Though she smiled, worry crisscrossed her face. I wanted to smile back at her and tell her I was okay, but my emotions wouldn't allow me. It wasn't until that moment that I realized how angry I was at her. She had been in Mississippi for a whole week, and I had seen her only once—on the day she arrived. The day when all she could talk about was the NAACP and what needed to change in Mississippi, and not a word about what life was like for her up north. The day she brought fancy pantsuits for Queen and none for me. The day she allowed Ma Pearl to humiliate me in front of all her sophisticated Saint Louis friends and didn't utter a word in my defense.

I turned my eyes from her and stared at the ceiling. Even now, she wasn't really in that room to see me. She only wanted to know how I was feeling about what was going on around me. It took a missing Chicago boy just to get her to the house. And that's only because Papa took her place and forced her to stay with Ma Pearl.

Without an invitation, she entered the room and sat on

Queen's bed. "Sorry I haven't been around much," she said, sighing.

Much? You haven't been around at all, I wanted to tell her. But I didn't say anything. I was no longer a brokenhearted seven-year-old whose head she could fill with dreams from a Sears and Roebuck catalog. I was a thirteen-year-old who finally realized that when black birds flew north, they outgrew the ones they left in the South. Unless the ones they left were old enough to vote. Then they came back and asked them to risk their lives by registering. And for what? To be gunned down before they could even set foot in the courthouse?

Ma Pearl was probably right. The boy from Chicago was probably stirring up trouble just like Aunt Belle and Monty were doing. Without my permission, words suddenly flew out of my mouth. "Don't you care if you die or not?"

"What?" Aunt Belle asked, as if my words had startled her.

I sat up on the bed and faced her. "Don't you care about dying?" I asked, my voice shaking.

"Of course I care about dying. We all care," she said. "But that doesn't mean we should shrink back and not fight for our rights."

"You have your rights. Nobody is gonna kill you for voting in Saint Louis like they did Levi Jackson or that old man Lamar Smith."

"But that's why we're here."

I turned my face from her and said, "I thought you were here to visit your family. That's what you told Ma Pearl. And that's what you've been doing for the past few years, visiting family, not rounding up people to register to vote."

Aunt Belle came and sat beside me on my bed. "Things have changed, Rose. Do you know what Brown versus Board of Education means?"

I nodded. "The Supreme Court outlawed school segregation in the state of Kansas."

"That's right," Aunt Belle said. "And soon it will happen all over the country." She shifted her weight on the bed and asked, "Do you know what the White Citizens' Council is?"

Again I nodded. "Hallelujah told me about them."

"That group formed right here in the Delta, in Indianola, not too far from Stillwater. They formed shortly after the Supreme Court passed down their ruling. Their membership spread like fire throughout the South. They want to make sure the government doesn't force integration on the South the way it had to do in Kansas."

"They're in more than one state?"

Aunt Belle nodded. "Alabama, Arkansas, Louisiana. They're all over the South."

I told her about what I heard at the Robinsons' a few days after Levi's death, how I heard Mr. Robinson himself say they had to put a stop to the NAACP, calling them the National Association for the Agitation of Colored People. "Mr. Robinson even threatened Papa and Ma Pearl that he'd throw them off his place if they got involved with the NAACP."

"Then you know why we're here," Aunt Belle said. "The White Citizens' Council uses those scare tactics to keep Negroes from registering to vote. They know that if colored people voted, the South would lose its fight to keep Jim Crow laws intact."

"They ain't just scaring people, Aunt Belle. They're killing them," I said. "Levi is dead. Lamar Smith is dead. Reverend Lee is dead. And for all we know, that boy from Chicago — Mr. Mose Wright's nephew — could be dead. And like Ma Pearl said, we don't know what he did to make those white men angry enough to take him from his uncle's house."

Aunt Belle's expression grew dark. "Well, I assure you it wasn't registering to vote. The boy is fourteen and from Chicago. And for all we know, he didn't *do* anything. It wouldn't be the first time these crackers lynched a colored man just because they felt like it."

I grabbed my chest. "You think he was lynched?"

Aunt Belle shook her head. "No, no, no. I'm sorry. I didn't mean to say that." She looked away, but not before I saw the tears in her eyes.

"Aunt Belle," I said quietly, "do you think he's dead?"

She grabbed my hand and squeezed it. "Let's not think that way, okay?"

I nodded, but the thought lingered in my mind like a bad dream. I didn't know the boy from Chicago, but I knew my own little brother. And I would want to die myself if something happened to him, especially if he was taken in the middle of the night by white men.

Aunt Belle turned back to me and said, "Come here." She embraced me and held me tight. "I know you're scared. This is a hard place to live in, and it's a hard time to live here as well. But you've got to be brave. We're in a war. And there has never been a war fought where everyone lived. Some folks will have to die."

My body shook. "But I don't want that somebody to be you," I said. "Can't you just stop? Can't you just go back to Saint Louis? Why do you have to risk your life just so colored people in the South will vote?"

Aunt Belle pulled away and held me by my shoulders. "When I first left for Saint Louis, I swore I would never set foot in Mississippi again," she said. "Then I came back to visit, and I saw the plight of my people. It broke my heart. Once I met Monty and learned so much about our history from him, I wanted to do something about it. I wanted to come back and help my people."

I shook my head and muttered, "I don't wanna be here. I

wanna leave. Go to Chicago. Saint Louis. Anywhere. As long as it ain't the South."

"And you will," Aunt Belle said. "When you're old enough."

"What about now? Why can't you take me back with you when you leave next week?"

Aunt Belle shook her head. "I can't."

"Why not?"

Her forehead creased. "Besides the fact that Mama won't let you leave?"

I didn't answer.

Aunt Belle sighed and said, "I can't. I just can't right now, because I didn't come down here to take you back to Saint Louis, so I'm not prepared to take care of you."

"I don't need you to take care of me," I said, my voice pleading. "I know how to take care of myself. I can cook and clean and do anything a grown person can do."

With solemn eyes, Aunt Belle simply shook her head and said, "I'm so sorry, Rose. But I just can't right now. That's not why I came."

Aunt Belle's words closed in and crushed me, just the way Miss Addie's shack had crushed me in my nightmare. And at that moment I wished the nightmare had been true. I would have preferred being buried under the rubble of Miss Addie's fallen shack than sitting there holding the ruins of my crushed dreams.

Chapter Eighteen

SUNDAY, AUGUST 28

After Aunt Belle left my room, I slept for hours. And I didn't care if Ma Pearl got mad at me. She could have come in and beat me with that black strap of hers, and I wouldn't have cared. Aunt Belle had disappointed me so badly that I didn't really care if I just suffocated in my hot room. The air was thick and muggy from what I assumed was middle-of-the-afternoon heat. I had no idea what time it was, but Queen's bed was made. Not neatly, but made, nonetheless. Since we didn't have church, she was probably already gone to visit her mama and her six siblings, which she occasionally did on Saturday and Sunday afternoons, although it was more like babysitting while Aunt Clara Jean went from house to house gossiping.

My body was stiff, and my head ached. Too much sleep. My body wasn't used to sleeping past sunrise. I got up and stumbled through Fred Lee's room, hoping someone was kind enough to have left me a basin of water so I could wash my face. There was none. I'd have to go outside to the pump and get my own. But at least someone, obviously Fred Lee, not Queen, had emptied the pot of the previous night's contents. One less chore for the day.

On my way to the kitchen, I couldn't help noticing the voices coming from the parlor, which was to the right of the front room. The voices belonged to Papa, Ma Pearl, Aunt Belle, and Monty. They were talking about the missing boy.

In the front room was a large rectangular mirror that Ma Pearl had gotten from Mrs. Robinson. Though the mirror was cracked straight down the middle, it still served its purpose of showing reflections — twice. It hung on the wall next to a large picture of a longhaired, smiling Jesus — also courtesy of Mrs. Robinson. Through the mirror I could see Papa perched in his chair, directing his attention toward the settee, where I assumed Aunt Belle and Monty sat.

"I knowed he did something," I heard Ma Pearl say.

Standing on tiptoe, I could see that she was sitting in the chair next to the window, her arms folded defiantly across her bosom.

"Since when did speaking to a woman become a crime?" asked Aunt Belle, her tone icy.

"Any fool know it's a crime when you is colored and the woman is white," retorted Ma Pearl. "That boy oughta knowed better." She paused, then said, "His mama oughta taught him better."

"The boy is fourteen, Mrs. Carter," said Monty. "He was

born and raised up north. Things are different there. Negro youths and white youths attend the same schools even, so it's only natural the boy would assume a few words to the woman wouldn't harm anything. He was probably only being polite."

"Things ain't no different up north," Ma Pearl said. "Y'all jest fool yo'selves into thinking they is. Colored is colored, and white is white. I don't care where you run to. Chicago. Saint Louis. Detroit. It's all the same. You a fool if you think they ain't. They jest ain't got the signs posted, is all."

"Mose's boys said his nephew didn't say a word to the woman, as far as they know," Papa said. "It's her white word against his colored one."

"But he did whistle when she came out of the store, according to one of the boys," said Monty.

In the mirror, I saw Papa shaking his head. "Po' Mose," he said. "If them boys would've told him 'bout the boy doing the whistling, he could've been ready. He could've sent him on back to Chicago, or at least he would've had his shotgun ready. He wouldn't've let them come in his house like that and walk 'way with his kin. He wouldn't've," he said, shaking his head. "I know Mose. He wouldn't've just let 'em take that boy like that."

Papa himself had two shotguns. I wondered if he had them loaded and ready. Many Negroes, according to Papa, had armed themselves with shotguns and pistols. But I'd never heard of one using them to defend himself against a white man. It seemed the only folks Negroes shot were one another. Sometimes in self-defense, and sometimes just out of plain anger.

"And that boy's poor mama," Aunt Belle said quietly. "Lord, she must be some kind of sick with worry."

"Imagine how Mose felt when he had to call her," said Papa.

Ma Pearl threw in her nickel's worth. "If the boy's mama was so worried, she woulda kept him up there in Chicago. Any fool know Mississippi ain't no place for quick-tongued niggas."

"Woman, you're just plain evil!" Monty cried. "How can you say something so cruel? That poor woman's son is missing. In Mississippi at that. White men with pistols came in the middle of the night and took him from his bed. Didn't even want him to take the time to put on a pair of socks, for God's sake. And you have the nerve to blame his mama for letting him come down here?"

Unfazed, Ma Pearl answered curtly, "And you jest plain stupid. And disrespectful. And you can git the devil on outta my house." She glowered at Monty and swung her thick arm toward the direction of the door.

I heard the settee creak as Monty stood.

"Sit down, son," Papa said. "I wear the pants in this house." To Ma Pearl he said, "Pearl, I've had enough of yo' nonsense. Mr. Bryant and his brother had no right to come in Mose's house like that in the middle of the night and take what didn't belong to them. No right at all," he said, shaking his head. "Mose is tore to pieces over this, and his wife done up and left too. Said she wasn't coming back. Never setting a foot in that house again."

How I secretly wished Ma Pearl would do the same!

"This ain't the time to blame nobody 'bout how they raised they chi'ren," said Papa. "This is the time to pull together. To help. To pray that the boy is returned safe."

Ma Pearl grunted but otherwise remained silent. Papa might not have been a man with an imposing stature, but when he spoke sternly, even Ma Pearl listened.

"Maybe he's lost somewhere," said Aunt Belle. "Maybe they just scared him and let him go, so maybe he wandered off in the woods somewhere and can't find his way back to Preacher Wright's house."

I thought about nine-year-old Obadiah Malone running through the woods to get away from Ricky Turner. When his daddy found him, he had passed out. What if this boy was lying somewhere in the woods, passed out from the loss of blood or dehydrated from the heat? Being from Chicago, surely he wouldn't know how to find his way through the woods.

"You believe that lie, baby?" asked Monty. "You believe

two white men would force a Negro from his bed at gunpoint in the middle of the night, have a little chat with him, and then let him go?"

The room grew quiet.

"We can hope," Papa finally said.

Ma Pearl shifted in her chair. "You say Mr. Bryant was one of the mens that took the boy?"

"That's what Mose say," Papa answered. "Said he wanted to talk to the boy from Chicago. The one that did all that talk up at his sto'."

"And a big bald-head one was the other man?" asked Ma Pearl.

"Um-hmm," said Papa. "Mose say he was the one with the pistol. Said he walked through the house like he owned it. Yelled at anybody that woke up to go back to sleep. Threatened Mose. Told him if he wanted to live to see sixty-five, he best forget his face." With a sigh, Papa dropped his head. "Mose say he'll never forget that face."

"I heard of Bryant. And the bald-head one sound like his brother. Milam," Ma Pearl said brusquely. "Lawd, I hope it ain't J. W. I believe he the man Doll say her nephew work for in Glendora. She say he one o' the meanest white mens in Mississippi. Meaner than a bear caught in a beehive. Fought in the war. Learnt how to beat mens to death with his pistol."

The room was quiet again. My legs grew weak from

standing on my toes to peer into the parlor through the cracked mirror. I needed to go get water so I could wash up. But I couldn't move. My curiosity kept my ears glued to the parlor and my eyes on that mirror.

Finally Ma Pearl spoke. "Y'all know that boy dead."

"Mama!" Aunt Belle snapped.

"They might as well be looking for a body 'stead o' waiting for the boy to show up at the front do'," Ma Pearl said. "If Big Milam is the one that got a holt of him, he dead."

What if Ma Pearl was right? What if the boy was dead while everybody was waiting for him to show up at the house? What if Miss Addie was right about something bad about to happen in Mississippi? What if colored folks were about to start getting killed for any old reason and regardless of their age?

Reverend George Lee in May.

Levi Jackson in July.

That old man Lamar Smith in the middle of August.

And now a fourteen-year-old boy from Chicago might be dead too? And August hadn't even ended.

My head spun, and I no longer felt like going to the kitchen to warm up water for washing. I no longer felt like doing anything but crawling back into bed and hiding my head under the pillow. I had to do something to block out the horrible thoughts swirling through my head.

September

Chapter Nineteen

THURSDAY, SEPTEMBER 1

WHEN I WAS ALMOST TEN AND REALIZED THAT GOD wasn't going to lighten my skin any more than he was going to let the moon rule the day, I began to wonder what it was like to be white. More specifically, I used to wonder what I would be like if I were white. Would I be nice like old Mrs. Jamison, whose husband owned a clothing store uptown? It was rumored that she allowed her colored maid to enter her house through the front door as well as eat with her at the dining room table. The only time Ma Pearl got to see Mrs. Robinson's front door was when she had to answer it. Or would I be spiteful like Ricky Turner and chase Negroes off the road with my pickup just for the fun of it? I always figured I would be a nice white person, that I wouldn't hate Negroes or mistreat them. But maybe that was because I was a Negro and knew what it felt like to be mistreated simply because my skin was brown. And among my own people, I also knew what it felt like to be shunned simply because my skin was *too* brown.

Hallelujah once showed me a copy of *Jet* magazine that

had an article called "The Most Beautiful Women in Negro Society." On the cover was a woman labeled "Pretty Detroit Socialite." She looked as white as Mrs. Robinson.

Hallelujah, twelve years old at the time, cooed and clucked over her, claiming that he'd marry a pretty woman just like that one day. I didn't see one picture of a woman with dark skin among those listed as "the most beautiful women in Negro society."

Also in *Jet* I saw an advertisement for a product that could make my skin light. After that, I started bleaching my skin with the stuff Aunt Clara Jean used to keep her complexion "even." Every time I went to her house, I'd sneak into her bedroom, grab the jar of Nadinola Bleaching Cream from her dresser, then smear the cream all over my face. The label read "Lightens skin fast!" and "Results guaranteed!" I'd return home thinking that in no time at all, my skin would be pretty and caramel like the rest of the women in my family, with the exception of Aunt Ruthie. Of course, just like the prayer, the cream didn't work, as it had to be used daily in order to see results.

A lot of good the cream would have done anyway, seeing how much time I spent in the sun, chopping and picking cotton. That's where I was supposed to be that morning. Instead, I was somewhere I wasn't even allowed: Ma Pearl and Papa's bedroom. I should have been in the field picking cotton, but I just couldn't go. I couldn't take it a third day in a row, especially knowing I wouldn't get to go to school the next week when everyone else went.

Heavy-hearted doesn't begin to describe what I was feeling that morning. Since the Chicago boy was still missing, so was Aunt Belle. She and Monty were riding all over the Delta in search of any signs of the boy and in search of answers as to how something like that could have happened. I couldn't believe she cared more about someone she had never met than she did about her own family. She had only a few days left before she returned to Saint Louis, and she couldn't bother spending them with us.

That morning, I was sick and tired of being *sick and tired*. So, like my wanna-be-a-movie-star cousin Queen, I faked an illness. Not cramps, but a summer cold. The dry, hacking cough and sneezing were easy to conjure with a little help from a black-pepper-filled handkerchief, but the fever was a bit harder to fake. Sitting close to the woodstove helped, though.

As I stood before Ma Pearl's dresser and studied my reflection in the clouded mirror, I felt as black as a crow and uglier than a mule. The room was dark because of the thick curtains Ma Pearl had made to block out the sunlight, but that didn't prevent me from seeing the frightening figure before me. My bony shoulders jutted out from the sleeveless croker-sack dress. And my shapeless arms were so skinny it's a wonder I was able to even work the pump long enough to fill a bucket with water.

I stared at my reflection and felt guilty for wishing I were more like Queen. Despite her ugly catfish eyes, her light complexion and long hair still made her attractive. And she was shaped just right, like the women in *Jet,* who showed no shame when displaying their perfect bodies in what looked like nothing more than bras and bloomers.

With Ma Pearl at Mrs. Robinson's and Queen still sound asleep, I knew it would be safe to slip my dress off for a second and see what I looked like in my bra and bloomers. I knew I'd look nothing like the models in the magazine, but something in the back of my mind made me wonder. Why I turned the radio on for this occasion, I will never know. But I did. I turned the dial several times to quiet down the static; then the music came through.

Nat King Cole. "Unforgettable." While listening to the crooning, I slipped my dress over my head and let it drop to the floor. But after I wiggled out of my dingy white slip, I cringed at the sight in the mirror.

A skinny, furless bear. That's what I looked like. Tall. Brown. Skinny. Like a bear who forgot to wake from hibernation and starved through three winters. A vision that was certainly not *unforgettable.*

When the song ended, I placed one hand on my hip and the other behind my head. Tilting my hip to the side, I pretended I was posing for *Jet* magazine. I whispered at my reflection, "Rose Lee Carter, pretty Chicago socialite." Yes. Chicago. That's where I would go. Forget Saint Louis. I would have to find a way to make my mama love me enough to return for me and Fred Lee so she could raise us right along with Li' Man and Sugar.

I switched to the other hip. "She left Mississippi at age thirteen. Attended the best schools in Chicago. Graduated at the top of her class. She is now a college student studying to be a teacher. Or a lawyer. Or a doctor. Or maybe even a movie star."

I quickly recognized the next song. A thousand times I had watched Queen dance around the parlor, snapping her fingers and shaking her hips as she listened to it. With the beat so catchy, I couldn't help swinging my hips from side to side too, wondering what it would be like to be one of those northern socialites.

The song was something about a sandman bringing dreams. Snapping my fingers, I danced until I worked up a sweat. I knew I probably looked like a fool standing before the mirror, dancing in my undergarments, but at the moment, I didn't feel like one. I felt free. Happy. Rejuvenated. Ready to move up north and conquer the world.

"Mr. Sandman," the song said, "bring me a dream."

Hallelujah. He was kind of cute. Probably the cutest boy I'd ever seen. But he liked Queen, not me. Everybody liked Queen. Everybody liked beautiful, light-skinned Queen.

But at that moment, I didn't care. I hugged my body and pretended I was dancing in one of those juke joints where Ma Pearl claimed that Slow John caroused on Saturday nights. I hummed to myself.

"Mr. Sandman, hmm, hmm, h—"

"Gal, what is you doing?" Ma Pearl cried from the doorway.

Shock flashed through my body like lightning. "Ma Pearl!" I gasped as I scrambled to get my dress off the floor and over my head.

Ma Pearl, her arms folded, her eyes cold, stared at me from the doorway. "What the devil is you doing in my room, Rose Lee?"

I feared my heart would beat out of my chest. "I—I—" I didn't know what to say. There I was, undressed, dancing in front of a mirror, in a room where I wasn't even allowed, on a day I'd pretended to be sick so I wouldn't have to work in the field, and I couldn't think of a lie that was less humiliating than the truth.

"I ast you a question, Rose Lee," Ma Pearl said.

My mind scrambled for an answer. When it didn't find

one quickly enough, Ma Pearl stormed toward the wall where the black strap of terror proudly hung. She yanked it from the nail and said, "Guess I have to speak to the backside, since the mouth on vacation."

Recognizing the familiar threat as an invitation for a beating, my brain quickly conjured up an answer. "It was too hot in my room," I said, my words rushing together. "My fever felt like it was getting worse. That's why I came in here. Your room ain't as hot." I pointed toward the blackout curtains, my hand shaking.

Ma Pearl narrowed her eyes. "And why was you half nekked?"

"I took off my dress to cool off faster."

"Um-hmm," Ma Pearl said, staring at me from head to toe.

She made me feel ashamed even with my dress on.

"You better be glad that boy in the front room waitin' for you," she said, frowning. "Otherwise I'd beat the devil outta you for lying to me. Talkin' 'bout a fever. You got a fever all right."

"Ma Pearl, it wasn't like that," I said, wishing I could melt into the floor and disappear.

She jerked her head toward the door. "Git on in there and see what that boy want. He running round here frantic. Like he go'n die if he don't talk to you."

Butterflies fluttered in my stomach. "What boy?" I asked.

"Preacher's boy." Ma Pearl frowned. "Who else be looking for yo' lil' black self?"

"Hallelujah," I whispered. Guilt overcame me. Just knowing I had been standing before the mirror, undressed, swaying to music and thinking about Hallelujah, made me feel dirty and ashamed. I wanted to cry, but I knew I couldn't. Ma Pearl didn't tolerate tears unless she had administered a beating strong enough to warrant them.

Seeing that she had deflated me, she sniffed haughtily and said, "Git on outta my room and quit ack'n like a dirn fool. You see that boy all the time."

Slapping me hard on my backside as I passed her, she added, "That's for running down my dirn radio batt'ries."

I felt as low as a smashed spider as I stumbled into the front room, where Hallelujah, fedora in hand, sat on the three-legged sofa near the front door. "Rosa Lee," he said, his voice sounding relieved. "I thought something had happened to you."

Swallowing the tears before they formed, I motioned him to follow me outside to the front porch.

"I went to the field looking for you, and Mr. Carter said you were sick in bed," Hallelujah said, his voice rushing out. He slumped into one of the close-to-broken chairs on the porch. I leaned against a post instead.

"I'm okay," I mumbled, staring at the floorboards.

Hallelujah placed his fedora back on his head and leaned forward in the chair. "I knocked and knocked and nobody answered. I was worried."

When I didn't say anything, Hallelujah began to nervously tap his foot. "Mr. Carter told me to go get Miss Sweet. I ran to the Robinsons' and found Miss Sweet starching shirts in the backyard." Still nervously tapping his foot, he wrapped his arms around his stomach, as if to calm himself. "I didn't know what to think when you didn't answer the door," he said, his tone somber.

"I'm okay" was all I could muster. Tears threatened to gush. I felt like a fool letting Ma Pearl catch me like that. I felt even more like a fool standing outside on the porch with Hallelujah after I'd just been inside dancing undressed in front of the mirror. I didn't think the day could get any worse until Hallelujah uttered his next words.

"They found him, Rosa Lee," he said quietly.

I shook my head. "What?"

Hallelujah's voice choked when he spoke. "They found the boy from Chicago."

Found. I grabbed my chest. From the look on Hallelujah's face, I knew it was worse than when Obadiah Malone was found, passed out, near Stillwater Lake.

"They found him yesterday," Hallelujah said. "Preacher just got word this morning."

My throat went dry. "Wh-wh-where?" I managed to ask. "Where did they find him?"

"The Tallahatchie River."

The landscape swirled. I grabbed the porch post to keep from falling.

Hallelujah took a handkerchief from his shirt pocket and wiped sweat from his forehead. "A fisherman found him caught up in a bunch of tree roots. They tied a cotton-gin fan around his neck with barbed wire," he said, his voice strained. "Tried to keep him down with the weight."

Hallelujah stared toward the ancient oak in the front yard. His eyes seemed to be fixed on that tree for an eternity before he finally said, "He floated to the surface anyway. No matter how hard they tried," he said, swallowing, fighting back tears, "they couldn't hide it. They couldn't hide their crime."

Chapter Twenty

SATURDAY, SEPTEMBER 3

When I was little, Aunt Belle read me a book she had found in the trash at the Robinsons'. I remember the book's cover. It was red, yellow, black, and tattered. And I remember the title: *Remarkable Story of Chicken Little*. I asked Aunt Belle what "remarkable" meant. She said it meant that the story was unbelievable. After she read it, I understood why. Chicken Little thought the sky was falling—that the world, as she knew it, was coming to an end.

She was wrong. And because of her foolish mistake, she and all her neighbors were coaxed straight into a fox's den and eaten by the fox. And like Chicken Little, because of one foolish mistake, a boy was dead.

That Saturday morning, as I sat on the front porch with Papa and waited for Uncle Ollie to arrive, I, too, felt as if the sky were falling. The blanketlike cloud draped over us with such blackness it seemed as if God had asked his faithful angel Gabriel to paint it that way. It seemed that any minute the sky would open up and wash us all away.

Maybe Hallelujah was right. Maybe Mississippi itself

was hell. No. Mississippi was worse than hell. At least in hell you know who the enemy is. And at least, if you believe the Bible, you know how to keep yourself from going there. But in Mississippi you never knew what little thing could spark a flame and get you killed. Registering to vote. Voting. Or even something as little as whistling at a white woman.

But it wasn't just the storm clouds that darkened my morning. It was Aunt Belle; she had left without bothering to say goodbye. The minute she found out about the Chicago boy's funeral, she sent word by Reverend Jenkins that she and her northern comrades were leaving—heading to Chicago. I figured that's probably where she was at that very moment—in Chicago—preparing to attend a funeral for someone she'd never met while the folks who loved her sat under the heavy weight of a thunderous Mississippi sky.

As Papa and I waited for Uncle Ollie, we didn't dare sit in the house. Ma Pearl was in a huff—slinging pots and pans around as if they had scorned her. She had planned to go fishing that morning, but both the thunder and the news that a dead body had been floating in the river for three days kept her at home.

Papa and I sat in silence as we watched the black clouds roll across the sky, looking as if there was no end to them. Thunder rumbled in the distance, yet it was still so hot that it felt as if the heat could burn a person's skin off. No one thought the weather would turn so suddenly, as the day before had been sunny. Now it felt as if those thick clouds had trapped the heat over Stillwater the way heat got trapped inside the belly of our black woodstove.

At a quarter of ten, Uncle Ollie's old Ford came rumbling up the road. The car was black with lots of dents, but it got Uncle Ollie, along with all the family members he often chauffeured, where they needed to go. And that Saturday, Papa and I were going to visit his little black bird in the woods — my aunt Ruthie.

Aunt Ruthie and her husband, Slow John, didn't live on anybody's place. They simply lived in a shack hidden so deep in the woods that even a bear couldn't find it. And since they didn't live on anybody's place, Slow John, an uneducated, rowdy drunk, had no one to work for — no sharecropping or tenant farming. And because of his bad spirits (and the many other spirits he consumed on a daily basis), he rarely held a job more than a week at a time.

Slow John and Aunt Ruthie were so poor they didn't even have a problem with rats. Those rats took one look at that empty kitchen, shook their heads, and walked away.

Uncle Ollie's car shook and rattled as he drove over tree roots that snaked throughout Aunt Ruthie's grassless front yard. As soon as the car stopped, just short of the splintered front steps, three of Aunt Ruthie's children — Li' John, Virgil, and Mary Lee—rushed off the sagging porch and raced to the car.

"Papa!" they cried. They had just seen him the month before, but they acted as if they hadn't seen him in a year.

The screen door creaked open, and Aunt Ruthie stepped out on the porch. She might have had a complexion like cocoa, but she was one of the most beautiful women I knew. She kept her long hair pressed and curled. And when she smiled, her face lit up so bright it could soften even the hardest heart, except that evil Slow John's.

Her slender body was draped in the same dress she seemed to wear every time I saw her, a lime green one with faded red flowers. With one hand on her hip and the other over her heart, she called out to the car, "Y'all come on in, Papa."

Aunt Ruthie's house always smelled like lemons. Every door and window in the house was kept open during the summer. And with so many trees surrounding it, it was always cool, even if the air everywhere else in Stillwater sat stiff at a hundred degrees. But wintertime was a different story. Aunt Ruthie's house had so many cracks in the walls and floors that it was as cold as the outdoors.

Visiting Aunt Ruthie made me appreciate why Ma Pearl didn't want to get thrown off Mr. Robinson's place. There was a time when Aunt Ruthie and Slow John, like the rest of the family, had resided there as well. From what I heard, Slow John stole money from Mr. Robinson and blamed another worker. But the truth came out when Slow John was foolish enough to go in to town the next week and buy a bunch of new clothes from Mr. Jamison's store. Mr. Jamison immediately notified Mr. Robinson that one of his "nigras" had come into the store flashing a heap of money. After that, Slow John was never again able to secure a spot on a white man's place, except for that shack, which was owned by an out-of-town landlord who couldn't care less about his property.

"Papa, you didn't have to do that," Aunt Ruthie said when she saw us hauling sacks of food from the car. She said that every time. And every time, Papa replied, "Ah, this ain't nothing, Ruthie. We got plenty at the house. No sense in us having all this extra."

"Li' John, y'all take them sacks to the kitchen," Aunt Ruthie said.

Uncle Ollie handed his sack to Li' John, but Papa and I held on to ours like we always did. "Me and Rose got this, Ruthie," he said.

We followed Li' John through the bedroom to the right of the front room, then on to the kitchen from there. Aunt Ruthie had only one bedroom in her house: it was for her and Slow John. The children slept on pallets in the front room and the kitchen. Girls in the front room, boys in the kitchen.

Every time I entered Aunt Ruthie's kitchen, I thought about the nursery rhyme "Old Mother Hubbard," whose cupboard, too, was bare.

As we helped seven-year-old Li' John and six-year-old Virgil place food in the safe, Papa clucked his tongue. "Bible say a man who won't take care o' his own is worse than a infidel. Lord Jesus, help that man do better by his family."

I also thought of how the Bible says that if a man didn't work, he ought not to eat. Yet there was Papa, once again supplying that lazy man's kitchen with food. But I quickly dismissed the thought when I looked into the eyes of Aunt Ruthie's daughters, four-year-old Mary Lee and two-year-old Alice, staring hungrily at the bags of beans, as if they couldn't wait to smell them simmering in a pot.

"Y'all set a spell," Aunt Ruthie said when we went back to the front room. She shooed all the children, even the baby, who had just begun to crawl, outside to play on the front porch. I prayed that they didn't get struck by lightning, seeing how the house was surrounded by all those trees.

While Ma Pearl's house was furnished with Mrs. Robinson's halfway decent castoffs, Aunt Ruthie's house was furnished with whatever anybody else in the family could've easily burned as rubbish in their backyards. That day, I made a promise to myself that when I found my way out of Mississippi and got an education and a job, I would buy Aunt

Ruthie a house, just like I planned to buy one for Papa. I would fill her house with beautiful brand-new furniture and fill her kitchen with so much food that she would feel like she lived in a store.

Aunt Ruthie settled her skinny self down on a brown chair that had been thrown out by Aunt Clara Jean and turned to me, saying, "I bet you miss your mama."

I swallowed the truth. "Yes, ma'am," I said.

"Anna Mae sho' is lucky," Aunt Ruthie said. "Always has been," she added, sighing.

"How the chi'ren?" Papa asked.

"They fine, Papa," said Aunt Ruthie. "You hear how they out there runnin' round that porch makin' all that racket."

"Um-hmm," Papa said, nodding, staring toward the wide window that overlooked the porch.

Even with hungry bellies, Aunt Ruthie's children could smile. Their daddy might have been a trifling drunk, but their mama was always there. Always caring. Always loving them with everything she had.

"Ready for school?" Aunt Ruthie asked me.

I looked at Papa, then I replied tersely, "I won't be going to school next week."

"You won't?" Aunt Ruthie asked, her brow furrowed.

Just thinking about school made a lump rise in my throat. I shook my head because I couldn't answer.

"How come?" she asked.

This time Papa spoke for me. "Rose is needed at the house. I'm shawt on help for the pickin', and Pearl gittin' to the point where she need mo' help too."

"This jest till the harvest in, like we used to do, right?" Aunt Ruthie asked. "She goin' back in November, ain't she?"

When Papa shook his head and said no, I felt like fainting.

Aunt Ruthie grimaced and said, "You go'n take Rose outta school, as smart as she is?"

Papa sighed, but he didn't answer Aunt Ruthie, just like he wouldn't answer me. Instead, just like he had done when he questioned Mr. Pete on the day they left for Chicago, he crossed his right leg over his left knee, removed his pipe and Prince Albert tobacco from his shirt pocket, filled the pipe, and placed it between his lips. He puffed, even though there was no smoke, while Aunt Ruthie and I regarded him with the same curiosity with which he had regarded Mr. Pete when Mr. Pete had made a decision others could not seem to comprehend.

Chapter Twenty-One

SUNDAY, SEPTEMBER 4

I DOUBTED THERE WAS A NEGRO IN STILLWATER, other than Slow John, who wasn't in church that morning. Even Uncle Ollie came. And Aunt Ruthie, which was rare. She and her children huddled in the last row of the church, near the window. Aunt Ruthie once told me that she didn't like church, because when they came, folks stared at them as if they didn't belong. I stopped staring when I realized I was acting like one of those folks.

I snapped to attention and stopped glancing around being nosy when Miss Doll belted out, *"Je-e-e-sus, keep—me neccar thy cross. There a pre—cious foun-n-n-tain. Free to all a he-e-ealin' stream—flows from Cav—re-e-e's moun-n-n-tain.'"*

The congregation joined in. *"In the cross . . . in the cross . . . be my glo-o-o-ree-e-e evu-u-uh. Till my rap-tured soul shall find . . . rest . . . beyond . . . the ri-i-i-ver.'"*

It didn't take long for me to tune them out, and my eyes—and mind—began to wander again. River. The Tallahatchie. A body weighted down with a seventy-pound cotton-gin fan.

I had never been inside a cotton gin, but they always looked scary to me. A huge barnlike building where cotton was processed. Very spooky.

Seventy pounds is a lot of weight. I had picked that much cotton before, and I could never lift the sack. I shivered as I imagined someone binding an object that heavy around my neck, then throwing my body into the river. What if that had been Hallelujah? Or Fred Lee? It didn't matter who he was, really, because he still belonged to somebody. Somebody who loved him.

By the time my mind drifted from the Tallahatchie River and found its way back to Greater Mount Zion Missionary Baptist Church, the congregation had completed their moaning of "Jesus Keep Me Near the Cross," and the seven-member choir had begun to sing another song about Calvary.

> *"Calvary,*
> *Calvary, Calvary, Lord!*
> *Surely He died on Calvary.*
> *Don't you hear Him callin' His Father?"*

About midway through the song, Miss Doll changed the lyrics. *"Can't you hear him callin' his mother? Can't you hear him callin' his mother?"* she sang again and again.

Several women removed handkerchiefs from their purses and began dabbing their eyes. Ma Pearl's eyes bulged as though she might cry as well.

"Scorned and beaten, despised of men," Deacon Edwards, the thinnest man I had ever seen in my thirteen years, cried over the singing. His words blended into the singing as though they were part of the lyrics. "A dog got a better chance at living than a Negro in Mississippi," he said.

The choir continued to moan "Calvary," as several "amens" were murmured among the members.

Miss Doll's voice got louder. *"Can't you hear him callin' his mother? Can't you hear him callin' his mother? Surely, oh surely, he died in Mississippi."*

Miss Doll could no longer contain her tears, and they came spilling from her eyes. Women began to shout and holler, and the ushers sprang into action. The air around me was thick, and I thought I would suffocate. I had been going to church all my life, and I had never felt "the Spirit" until that moment. I don't know what came over me, but my body began to tremble and tears gushed from my eyes as well.

Ma Pearl gave me a handkerchief, and I buried my face in it. Even though many others were crying, I somehow felt embarrassed to allow them to see my emotions so openly displayed.

"Jesus, forgive me of my sins, seen and unseen," came a shout from the back. The voice belonged to Aunt Ruthie.

I peered back, but Ma Pearl's head turned so fast, I was sure she would snap her neck. Aunt Ruthie, according to her, was what the Apostle Paul called himself: the chief of sinners. The only sin I knew Aunt Ruthie committed was marrying that old slue-footed Slow John, which was both a sin and a shame.

Aunt Ruthie stood, her arms splayed as though hanging on a cross. Her face turned heavenward, tears flowing, she cried out for mercy. Her children, all holding on to her, cried too.

By the time the choir and Deacon Edwards finished, the only dry eyes in the little church belonged to Ma Pearl. And even hers were a little moist.

My body rocked with emotion. Emotion I had never felt before. I remembered how I felt at my first funeral. How I cried because children—grown children—cried for their mother. And I remembered how I felt at Levi's funeral. But something was different this time. This wasn't a funeral, yet I felt as though it were. Somehow I felt that something worse had happened than what happened to Levi. This boy, Emmett, they say his name was, had only been visiting. He wasn't like the rest of us—born in Mississippi, stuck in Mississippi, just waiting for our chance to get out of Mississippi. He'd come here to visit, to spend time with relatives, enjoying good food and laughter, the way I had wanted Aunt Belle to. Instead he made one mistake, and he was sent back home in a pine box.

Sometimes I wished God would give Gabriel a big eraser and say, *Gabe, I made a mistake. I should have made everybody one color. So take this eraser, go down to earth, and erase the color. Make everybody colorless so they can all feel special.*

As tears streamed down my face and as Deacon Edwards moaned and sang, "'I love the Lawd. He heard my cry. I-I-I-I l-o-o-o-ve d-e-e-e Law-awd. He-e-e-e hear-r-r-r-d my-y-y-y cry. And pitied every groan,'" I realized I was crying not for Levi Jackson nor for Emmett Till, but for myself, Rose Lee Carter. Because I was a Negro. A person of color. A person who could be killed simply because my skin had a color. And that color happened to be a dark shade of brown.

But really the shade of brown didn't matter one bit. A Negro didn't have be brown to be hated. He needed only to be labeled "Negro" by the blood running through his veins. The skin on the upper side of his hand could have been as light as the skin on his palms, like Queen's, but because he was a Negro, he was despised and hated.

By the time the last shout had died to a whimper, Reverend Jenkins stood in the pulpit, armed with his Bible and, strangely, a newspaper. "For those of you blessed enough to own a Bible," he said, "turn, if you will, to the book of Saint Matthew, the chapter being twenty-eight, and we shall commence reading at verse twelve."

A few pages ruffled, as only a handful of people owned Bibles or, at best, could read them.

Reverend Jenkins read aloud while those of us who could, read silently:

> "*AND WHEN THEY WERE ASSEMBLED WITH THE ELDERS, AND HAD TAKEN COUNSEL, THEY GAVE LARGE MONEY UNTO THE SOLDIERS,*
>
> *SAYING, 'SAY YE, HIS DISCIPLES CAME BY NIGHT, AND STOLE HIM AWAY WHILE WE SLEPT.'*"

"Now, we know from the Bible," Reverend Jenkins said as he stepped from behind the podium and began pacing, "Jesus was *raaaaised* from the dead."

A few "amens" came from the deacons.

"But look at this, folks," said Reverend Jenkins. "When word of the Resurrection reached the ears of the chief priests, what did they do?"

"Preach, Preacher!" yelled Deacon Edwards, who obviously didn't know the answer.

Reverend Jenkins strode back to the podium. "They *as-seeembled* with the elders and took *counselllllll.*" He looked over at the deacons sitting crisply in the front row, smiled, and said, "In other words, they met with the deacons and came up with a plan."

Reverend Jenkins paced again. "Can you imagine them," he asked, "huddled around a table, whispering, 'Where is he? What happened to him? How could he get out? His disciples must have taken him.' Another shook his head and said, 'We had soldiers guarding that tomb. That's impossible.' They straightened their robes and said, 'But we can't let this get back to Pilate. We'll look like fools. He'll know we killed an innocent man.'"

"So what did they do?" Reverend Jenkins asked, heading back to the podium.

There was a moment of silence. No "amens." No "Preach, Preacher!" Just . . . silence.

Reverend Jenkins slammed his Bible so hard on the podium that dust fell from the ceiling. "They lied!" he said. "They paid off the soldiers to say the disciples came and stole the body while they slept. Now what kind of cockamamie story is that? Roman soldiers guarding the tomb? And all asleep at the same time? Pilate would have had them all killed for sleeping on the job."

A few chuckles arose from the congregation; otherwise, the whole room was stiffly still and silent. The only noises were Reverend Jenkins and the whirring hum of box fans. It was the first time I had ever seen everybody awake during a sermon.

Reverend Jenkins removed his glasses, wiped them with a handkerchief, and placed them back on his face. He stared at the congregation for a moment, then placed the newspaper on the podium and spread it open. Whispers vibrated throughout the congregation.

"Suffer me a moment, if you will, as I read portions of this article from this morning's edition of the Memphis *Commercial Appeal*," Reverend Jenkins said.

Ma Pearl grunted.

Reverend Jenkins held the paper up to display the headline. "Charleston Sheriff Says Body in River Wasn't Young Till," he read. He placed the paper back on the podium. "I had written and rehearsed an entirely different sermon for today. But when I got this paper this morning, special delivery from a close friend, I knew I had to address this issue."

An even quieter hush fell over the congregation as Reverend Jenkins read from the paper:

> *"Sheriff H. C. Strider said yesterday he doesn't*
> *believe the body pulled from the Tallahatchie River*

*in Mississippi was that of a Negro Boy who was
whisked from his uncle's home accused of whistling
at a white woman.*

*"'The body we took from the river looked more
like that of a grown man instead of a young boy,'
the Tallahatchie County Sheriff said in Charleston,
Miss."*

Reverend Jenkins stopped reading and stared at the congregation. "Y'all know of any Negro men missing in Mississippi?"

Heads shook, and voices murmured, "No, sir."

Reverend Jenkins grimaced and continued reading.

*"Sheriff Strider said the victim looked at least
eighteen years old and probably had been in the
water four or five days."*

Reverend Jenkins chuckled and said, "Four or five days, huh? I ask you again, y'all heard of any Negroes gone missing in the last few days other than the Chicago boy, Emmett Till?"

Murmurs filled the church.

Reverend Jenkins quieted the crowd with the wave of his hand, then continued reading.

"He said there was a large silver ring on the boy's middle finger of his right hand.

"'Mose said he couldn't identify the ring and would have to talk to his boys to see if they could identify it,' Sheriff Strider said. He was speaking of Mose Wright, Till's uncle with whom he had been staying.

"Sheriff Strider said he believes Till is still alive."

"Till is still alive. Now, what kind of nonsense is that?" Reverend Jenkins asked. "Sheriff Strider is a big fat liar. And I do mean FAT!" He threw the paper toward a fan in the pulpit. Pages flew in all directions.

He pushed back his suit coat and stuffed his hands into his pants pockets. He paced back and forth in front of the pulpit.

After a moment he stopped pacing. As his right hand came out of his pocket, he held it palm up and stared at it. "On the one hand," he said, "we have a man everybody knows to be dead, and the powers that be concoct a story to say that his disciples stole him."

Then the left hand. "And on the other hand, we have a body that's been packed in a pine box, placed on a train, and shipped back to Chicago, and the powers that be say it's the wrong body. If it was the wrong body, then why did they try to make Preacher Wright bury it the same day they found it floating in the river?"

As his hands swiftly went back into his pockets, Reverend Jenkins paced the floor. "You know what identified him?"

After no response from the congregation, Reverend Jenkins held up his hand. "His ring. His father's ring. A signet ring. They stripped him of his clothes," he said, pacing and waving his hands. "They took off his shoes." He pointed at his feet. "But they didn't think to take the ring off his finger. Had it not been for the ring," he said, smiling, holding up his hand again, "Sheriff Strider might've been able to convince the people of a lie."

Chapter Twenty-Two

SUNDAY, SEPTEMBER 4

MA PEARL WAVED A DRUMSTICK AT ME. "YOU KNOW revival next week, don'cha?"

I broke off a piece of cornbread, pinched up a few fingers of collard greens, and mashed them together. I stuffed them into my mouth. "Didn't we have revival already? In June?" I muttered, my mouth full.

"Having it again. A special one. Too many y'all young folks ain't saved."

Plenty of grown folks ain't saved either. "Oh," I answered, lowering my eyes, diverting my attention to a crack in the floor. I was trapped. Nobody was in the house except the two of us. And I had no excuse to get away from sitting in the kitchen eating Sunday dinner with Ma Pearl.

Uncle Ollie had come by the house shortly after church was out. His voice was panicked as he told Papa that his boar had somehow escaped the hog pen and was on the loose. That hog was as huge as a whale, meaner than Ma Pearl, and considered dangerous outside the pen. So Uncle Ollie, Papa, and Fred Lee had gone out to search for it, leaving the dinner company to consist of Ma Pearl and me. And the last thing I wanted to talk about was revival and the mourners' bench.

"It's time," Ma Pearl said. "Past time. You thirteen. Should've been down in the water befo' you was twelve. Ain't nothing certain. You see that boy dead at fo'teen. That could be you."

My skin prickled. Every summer, including this one, I'd ignored Ma Pearl when she spoke of revival and going to the mourners' bench. She had begun hounding me to "get religion" shortly after Mama left us and married Mr. Pete. I was only seven at the time, but Hallelujah, who was only eight, had gotten religion two years prior, when he was six. So on the day I turned twelve, even Reverend Jenkins had begun warning me about my "soul's salvation" as he handed me that glossy black Bible with the words "King James" engraved in gold.

Revival was a weeklong ordeal, where "sinners" were assigned a special pew up front. Monday night through Friday night, they sat on that bench, gloom covering their faces as they waited for "a sign from de Lawd." Saved church members took turns praying for them at the altar. And during each prayer, the "mourners" (biblically known as sinners) were required to kneel before the mourners' bench and pray along. Once a mourner received a sign from the Lord, he or she "crossed over" and became a candidate for baptism.

I didn't want to go through all that trouble, sitting on a special pew at the front of the church while folks prayed over me like maniacs, spraying their spit all over the place. Nor did I want to spend the whole week, while home, praying "without ceasing," stopping only to eat. The "mourners" even had to keep a pious face while working in the field (which wasn't hard to do, considering the circumstances). They weren't even allowed to talk to anyone until after they received their sign and crossed over. All their time was spent "mourning" for their sins.

But Ma Pearl was right about one thing. I had felt as if I had all the time in the world—until the Chicago boy was killed. With the way colored folks were being murdered in Mississippi, I knew I needed to give a little thought to my soul.

"What about Fred Lee?" I asked. "And Queen?"

Ma Pearl took a bite out of a chicken thigh, as she had already stripped the drumstick down to the marrow. Breaking her own rule, she spoke with her mouth full. "They goin' too," she said. "All o' you shoulda been to the moanin' bench long time ago," she said. "Don't know why I let y'all lay up in my house loaded down with sin nohow. I shoulda sent all o' you to the bench back in June."

She paused, wiping grease from her mouth with a dishrag. "Twelve, thirteen, and fifteen," she said. "All y'all too dirn old to be running round here without religion."

I scooped candied yams onto my fork, but didn't eat them. I thought about how Queen had been to the mourners' bench three times already and had never crossed over, regardless of how many times Ma Pearl knelt right down beside her at that bench and prayed over her until her voice gave out. What if I, like Queen, never received my sign? What if I humiliated Ma Pearl year after year by going to the bench until I was nearly grown, and I never got religion? I was about to make a case for myself, but Ma Pearl started up again.

"Shoulda never let that boy start preaching," she said, referring to Reverend Jenkins. "He ruin'n y'all with all this nonsense 'bout being saved by grace. No wonder y'all cain't git a sign. The preacher ain't taught you how to ast for one."

Reverend Jenkins used to preach at an African Methodist Episcopal, or AME, church before he started preaching at Greater Mount Zion. He didn't believe in the mourners' bench, but he suffered through it for the old folks' sake. Reverend E. D. Blake used to be our preacher. Every Sunday it was fire and brimstone, until Papa and some of the other deacons found out about Reverend Blake's questionable behavior outside of church. He left Greater Mount Zion and began preaching at Little Ebenezer soon after. Reverend Jenkins started filling in after that. He was well received by Papa and the other deacons, and he stayed permanently. But Ma Pearl favored Reverend Blake and his preaching, regardless of how folks claimed he behaved when he wasn't wearing his preacher's robe.

From the kitchen we heard the front door open. "Yoo-hoo! Housekeeping!"

I wanted to get up, leave my tasty food, and run. Aunt Clara Jean was here. And from the rumble of feet, it was obvious she'd brought those rowdy chaps of hers, too.

"Back here!" Ma Pearl called from the kitchen.

"Lawd, Jesus, something smell good back here," Aunt Clara Jean said as she lumbered toward the kitchen. Like Ma Pearl, she was big, boisterous, and brusque. A perfect mismatch for tiny, sweet Uncle Ollie.

"Mama, what you cook?" she asked as she pulled out a chair without an invitation. "Junior, y'all go on outside 'n play hide-the-switch or something," she said, shooing her little ones away. "Queen, you go on in there and lay down."

"What's wrong with Queen?" Ma Pearl asked.

"Sick," Aunt Clara Jean answered. "Done thowed up everything she ett today."

"She ain't got the summer flu, is she?" Ma Pearl asked.

Aunt Clara Jean reached across me and grabbed a chicken wing from the pan in the middle of the table. "She ain't got no fever or nothing like that. Jest said she wadn't feeling good, then started running to the bathroom to thow up."

Queen entered the kitchen. She looked whiter than any one of the Robinsons. Pale skin. Droopy eyes. And dry lips.

Ma Pearl beckoned to her. She placed the back of her hand on Queen's forehead. "She ain't warm," she said to Aunt Clara Jean. "What else ailing you?" she asked Queen.

"Just a little headache," Queen said, placing her hand on her forehead.

"Git you a glass o' that tea and go back there and git'n the bed," Ma Pearl said.

Queen nodded, got a glass from the safe, and poured herself some tea.

After she left the kitchen, Aunt Clara Jean leaned toward Ma Pearl and, with her forehead creased, whispered, "You reckon Queen might be 'specting?"

Ma Pearl's nostrils flared. "Heck, nah. I don't let these gals leave this house 'cept to go to church. The only place Queen been is yo' house. If she in trouble, it didn't happen under my roof."

Aunt Clara Jean smirked as she snatched a wedge of cornbread from the skillet. "You didn't let me and Anna Mae leave the house either," she said, chortling.

Ma Pearl shot Aunt Clara Jean an icy look. "Queen ain't in trouble."

When Aunt Clara Jean didn't respond, Ma Pearl turned

her attention toward me. "Wouldn't surprise me none if this lil' heffa here get herself in trouble soon."

"Me?" I said, leaning back, my thumb pointed at my chest.

"Her?" Aunt Clara Jean said, her head cocked toward me. She laughed and said, "Don't nobody want that ol' black thang."

"Humph," said Ma Pearl. "You shoulda see'd what I caught her doing in my bedroom last week."

Aunt Clara Jean's head snapped toward me. "What?" she asked, wide-eyed, eager for gossip.

My blood felt like it drained as Ma Pearl proceeded not only to give a play-by-play of the fiasco of my dancing scene in her bedroom, but also to embellish the story with details that were way beyond my thirteen-year-old imagination. "All moanin' and groanin'," she said, frowning with disgust.

Aunt Clara Jean looked down her nose at me and said, "Umph, umph, umph. She fast, jest like her mama."

I felt tears begin to bulge. "Ma Pearl, you know that ain't true," I said, my lips trembling.

Ma Pearl narrowed her eyes at me. "You wadn't in front of my mirror dancing like a tramp off the street?"

Before I could stop them, tears fell in clumps into my food. I took my chance on a skillet flying to the back of my head and got up from the table and ran out the back door.

My whole body shook as I raced down the steps, across the backyard, and straight to the cotton field, the sound of Ma Pearl's and Aunt Clara Jean's cackling following me all the way.

I ran all the way to the far end of the field before I stopped and collapsed in the dust. The tall green leaves and white cotton bolls hid me as I lay there and sobbed—promising myself that I would one day kill Ma Pearl and Aunt Clara Jean.

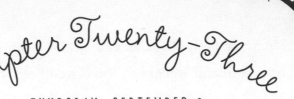

Chapter Twenty-Three

PAPA WAS WRONG WHEN HE SAID I NEVER FORGET. No matter how hard I tried, I couldn't remember what my daddy's face looked like. I had seen him only once, from a distance, when he came to see Fred Lee shortly after he was born. Every year when the cotton was full and ready for harvesting, I thought about that day.

Fred Lee and I were both nursing at Mama's breast, but she still had to go to the field to pick cotton just the same. She would come back to the house every few hours to nurse Fred Lee, then allow me — at nearly two years old — to have the rest of whatever was left of her milk when he was done.

On one of those days, there was a knock at the door. It was our daddy, Johnny Lee Banks. Mama stood at the slightly open door, her back to me, and told him, "I can't see you no mo'."

"I didn't come to see you," he replied. "I jest wanna see the baby."

I thought he was talking about me until Mama said, "You can't see him neither."

"They say he don't look nothing like me," my daddy replied. "I wanna see for myself."

"You need to leave 'fo my mama catch you here," Mama said, pushing on the door.

Instead, the door opened wider, and Johnny Lee tried to push past Mama. She pushed him back out the door, but not before I saw his face. I guess I didn't see it long enough to hold it in my memory. But his voice is still there. It dragged, just like Fred Lee's.

I couldn't remember my daddy's face, but poor Queen had never even seen her daddy's face. Nor did she know his name. Fred Lee had seen our daddy once, when he had gone to town with Uncle Ollie. Neither said anything to the other, but Uncle Ollie had pointed him out from a distance and said, "There go yo' pappy, boy."

Queen was following in the same footsteps as our mamas. Maybe she'd get lucky like Aunt Clara Jean and find a kind man like Uncle Ollie who would marry her and start a new family. Or perhaps she'd end up like Mama and find a rich man who desired a pretty woman to raise his children.

Well, I didn't want to end up like any of them, not Mama, not Aunt Clara Jean, and certainly not Aunt Ruthie, who, to escape Ma Pearl's house, married Slow John. From what I'd heard, she had been offered the same opportunity as Aunt

Belle. Papa's sister Isabelle had come from Saint Louis and offered to take her back when she was sixteen, said she could attend a cooking school and become a chef. But Ma Pearl refused to let her go. Two years later Aunt Ruthie slipped off in the night and married Slow John.

Angry with her or not, I knew I'd pattern my life after Aunt Belle. Like Aunt Belle, I knew I'd have to escape through someone taking me up north. And I knew I had to learn a trade. I would've preferred finishing high school and going to college, but at the time, anything would have been better than chopping and picking cotton. Or squeezing milk from an ornery heifer before the sun came up in the morning.

That Thursday afternoon, after having baked in the sun for four days straight, I'd made up my mind not to kill Ma Pearl and Aunt Clara Jean after all. They weren't worth me frying in the electric chair. Besides, I had devised a plan.

After Emmett Till's funeral, Aunt Belle and Monty had decided to return to Mississippi to see what assistance they could offer the NAACP. They would arrive on Sunday and stay for two weeks. By the end of those two weeks I hoped to convince Aunt Belle to take me back with her. In my heart I knew Chicago was not an option. If Mama didn't want me and Fred Lee when we were Li' Man and Sugar's age, then she certainly didn't want us when we were just about grown. She renounced us as her children the day she began referring to us as Sister and Brother and had Li' Man and Sugar call us Aunt Rose and Uncle Fred.

In the meantime, while I waited for my chance to be a part of the great colored migration, I had to drag that sack through the field and collect Mr. Robinson's cotton while Queen and Fred Lee went to school. Queen had thrown up every morning. And every evening after school she fell asleep before her head hit the pillow. Ma Pearl was still asking her if she had the summer flu. She refused to believe her precious Queen was capable of doing any wrong.

That Thursday was also the fourth night of revival. Ma Pearl made us all go to the mourners' bench. But I wasn't trying to get religion. Why would I want to go to heaven if she and Aunt Clara Jean would be there? I'd take my chances in hell before spending an eternity with them.

So every night, Monday through Wednesday, I had sat on that front pew—the mourners' bench. I sang when everyone else sang, shouted when everyone else shouted, and got down on my knees and bowed when everyone else prayed. But I didn't pray for religion. I asked God to put a curse on Ma Pearl and Aunt Clara Jean instead. I knew it was selfish and evil, but after exhausting myself with tears in that cotton field, evil was all I could feel toward them.

I knew I needed religion or, more specifically, a faith, something to believe in. But I didn't have to kneel and pray before a bench in the front row of the church, with a bunch of people moaning and praying over me, to get it.

Reverend Jenkins said that all we had to do was confess that we were sinners and ask for forgiveness. But the old folks said that was nonsense. You couldn't get religion without a sign.

"You gotta be still and ask the Lawd for a sign," Deacon Edwards had cried out every night of revival. "Pray, 'Lawd Jesus, I is a wretch undone. Please, Suh, look and have mercy. If I got religion, please show me some sign.'"

And I did. I prayed that Deacon Edwards would lose his voice so he would stop screaming all over the place. I also prayed that Aunt Belle would change her mind and take me to Saint Louis.

I would find my faith eventually, when I was ready. And not when Ma Pearl said I should.

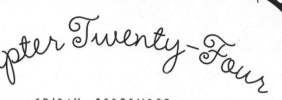

Chapter Twenty-Four

FRIDAY, SEPTEMBER 9

I LOVE THE LAWD; HE HEARD MY CRY,'" DEACON Edwards sang out. The rest of the church joined in as he dragged out the words:

"'I-I-I l-o-o-o-ve d-e-e-e Law-awd. He-e-e-e hear-r-r-r-d my-y-y-y cry.'"

Deacon Edwards: "'And pitied every groan.'"

The church: "'A-a-and pi-i-i-tie-e-ed e-e-e-ver-e-e-ey gro-o-oan.'"

Friday had finally come, and the mourners' bench wasn't as packed as it had been on Monday. There were only a few of us, six to be exact, still waiting for a sign. On Monday the front pews had been so packed, there was barely room for our arms, which were smashed to our sides as our hands lay folded in our laps. But on Friday the choir stand was packed and the mourners' bench sparse, as the newly saved saints glared piously down at those of us still waiting to receive a message from heaven.

Queen had crossed over on Tuesday night. Finally. I guess the death of Emmett Till was enough to scare even the worst of sinners toward salvation. When I asked her what sign she had asked God for, she told me it was none of my business and to worry about getting my own sign. So much for being saved. She perched on the front row of the choir stand, her legs crossed, her lips pursed, her nose pointing, fanning her proud face with a paper funeral-home fan that displayed a picture of Jesus knocking at a door.

Well, I had asked for only one sign, and I knew I wasn't about to get it. Deacon Edwards was in full swing, leading the opening prayer, praying for the last of the mourners on the bench. If all of us didn't cross over that night, revival would not be considered a complete success. So he prayed fervently, sweating and spitting while folks moaned and shouted as if a funeral were in progress.

The prayer portion of the night seemed to drag on forever. After Deacon Edwards, Miss Doll prayed. Ma Pearl, of course, couldn't let either of them outshine her. She prayed, it seemed, for nearly a half-hour. While she prayed, I—rather than asking for my soul's salvation—asked that she'd choke on her spit, which was flying all over the front of the church.

After all prayers had been delivered on behalf of us sinners, Reverend Mims, a small man from a nearby farming community, approached the podium to deliver the message. We always had a guest preacher for revival, as it was a well-known fact that an educated preacher like Reverend Jenkins couldn't save souls with his rhetoric. It took fire and brim-stone for that. Reverend Mims, though small, was an impos-ing figure. His voice was loud and intimidating, making me feel as though it were the devil knocking at my heart, wishing to come in instead of Jesus. And he was as black as a witch's hat, as Ma Pearl liked to say, with almond-shaped eyes as yellow as gold.

Since he never used a Bible, Reverend Mims simply began speaking. "Jesus said, 'Behold, I stand at the do' and knock. If any man open it, I'll come in and have supper with him.' How many y'all want the Lawd to come to yo' table this evening and have supper with ya?" he asked, pointing at the six of us left on the mourners' bench. He waved his hand toward the choir stand. "Look at all these folks who said yes when the Lawd knocked. Don't you want to join them at the table?"

The room erupted in "amens."

Now that he'd gotten the crowd stirred, Reverend Mims leaned back, cupped his right hand to the side of his mouth as if to shout his message to heaven, and said, "Praise ya, Lawd, for these souls that's go'n one day join you at yo' grand table in heaven. We all go'n feast on milk and honey. Come on taste and see that the Lawd is good." He dropped his hand and danced a little jig around the pulpit as if he had said something remarkable.

The congregation, it appeared, agreed. Folks started dancing and shouting about milk and honey, wearing a long white robe, and sitting at the Lawd's table, as if it would happen that night. When Fred Lee and I made eye contact, it took every ounce of resolve to keep myself from laughing. I knew I shouldn't have been playing around during such a serious and sacred time, but I wanted to come to religion on my own terms, not Ma Pearl's.

"Y'all young folks better be ready to meet the Lawd at any time," Reverend Mims shouted over the shouting. "When death come to look for souls, he ain't looking at nobody's age. He'll take ya at eighty-four, sixty-four, forty-four, twenty-four, fourteen, or even four. Yes, he take babies, too. He'll take you whether you a man or a woman, boy or girl, white or black. He'll take you whether you live in Mississippi or just visiting."

Folks started shouting and falling all over the floor.

"Is you ready?" Reverend Mims shouted over the chaos. "Is you ready?" He stared straight at Fred Lee when he said those words. Throughout the week Fred Lee had only been playing around, like me. He said he wasn't "stud'n no mourners' bench." Now he sat as still as stone as Reverend Mims pierced his soul with his words and his ugly yellow eyes.

"A fo'teen-year-old boy. Just a boy," he said, his voice rising. "Visiting. Taking a vacation 'fore going back to school. Wanted to see Miss'sippi. Wanted to see how things is down here, like so many others who been up there in the North all they life." He paused, closed his eyes, and moaned.

A few shouts of "amen" rose from the church.

Reverend Mims opened his eyes and set them on the mourners on the bench. *"'Time is filled with swift transition,'* the old song says. *'Naught of earth unmoved can stand, Build yo' hopes on things eternal. Hold to God's unchanging hand.'"*

It didn't take long before the pianist struck up a note, and the church joined in with, *"'Everybody ought hold to his hand, to God's unchanging hand. Hold to his hand, to God's unchanging hand. Build yo' hopes on things eter-r-r-nal. Hold to God's unchanging hand.'"*

"Behold, I stand at the do' and knock," Reverend Mims said over the singing, his hand cupped around his mouth, his golden eyes shining toward heaven. "If any man will just open up, I'll come in."

After a moment he directed his gaze back at Fred Lee and pointed. "Boy, is you ready?" he asked. "Is you ready to die?" He feigned a puzzled look. "No?" he said, as if Fred Lee had answered him. His next question seemed to be aimed at all of us left on the mourners' bench. "Y'all think that boy from Chicago was ready to die? Y'all think he would've followed them white mens outta his uncle's house if he knowed they was go'n kill him? That boy didn't come to Miss'sippi to die. That boy come to Miss'sippi to live. To eat some good ol'-fashion' home cooking. To smell the scent of fresh air. To see green fields and white cotton bolls. Instead he saw the bottom of the Tallahatchie River. Death don't 'scriminate, and it don't give you no warning. Be ready!"

I gasped when Fred Lee stood. All week long, like me, he had not taken the mourners' bench seriously. As he took the seat of the right hand of fellowship, I couldn't believe that with one sermon, a little country preacher had convinced him otherwise.

Shouts erupted from the crowd, with Ma Pearl shouting the loudest.

I didn't shout, but I smiled. I was happy that my little brother got religion, even if I wasn't ready to make that commitment myself. It took the church several minutes to finish shouting and dancing over Fred Lee's conversion.

But even after another ten minutes of spewing fire and brimstone, Reverend Mims couldn't move the last five of us mourners from that bench.

Chapter Twenty-Five

TUESDAY, SEPTEMBER 13

I DIDN'T BOTHER WIPING THE SWEAT THAT POOLED beneath my eyes. I simply trudged toward the edge of the field, homebound, lugging the stuffed-to-the-brim cotton sack behind me. That evening, it seemed my sack was heavier than I ever remembered. I hadn't worked any harder than usual, but the sack seemed a bigger burden regardless. Perhaps it was because for the past week and a half I had watched Queen and Fred Lee hop into Uncle Ollie's car and head into town for school while I headed out to the field with Papa.

It made no sense. I was the smartest of the three, but I was the one stuck in the field. I could understand that Fred Lee was only in seventh grade, and perhaps Ma Pearl and Papa wanted him to at least finish that much. But Queen was headed off to the tenth grade. She was the one who had more schooling than she needed, not me. And she was pretty enough that any man would want to marry her, like Mr. Pete married Mama. But that ungrateful girl was wasting her time with the likes of Ricky Turner and wouldn't even give a smart colored boy like Hallelujah the time of day. I'd be happy if someone as smart as Hallelujah was bent on marrying me. Not that I was looking at marriage as my way out. But like almost any other girl, I looked forward to a family of my own someday too.

My clothes clung to my sweaty body, and all I wanted was a cool bath in the tin tub. But since it was only Tuesday, I knew I wouldn't get one. I'd have to wait for Wednesday, then again on Saturday. In the meantime, I had to make do with a wash-up, a bird bath, as Ma Pearl called it. Besides, there on the front steps sat Hallelujah, waiting for me.

Friend or not, I resented him sitting there in his freshly pressed clothes, that fedora atop his head, his penny loafers shining—not even a drop of sweat on his nose. But then I remembered that he had promised to bring me something to read, and my heart skipped a few beats. He had promised to bring me a book Reverend Jenkins had ordered for him from a teachers' catalog. The book was called *Native Son,* and it was written by a colored man named Richard Wright, who was supposedly born and raised right here in Mississippi. Like that phenomenon of colored and white children sitting side by side in classrooms up north, a colored man from Mississippi with his name on the outside of a book is something I'd have to see to believe.

By the time I reached the edge of the porch, Hallelujah was grinning.

I dropped my sack on the ground and asked, "What you so cheerful for?"

"Look what I got," he said, waving a magazine toward me.

"Contraband?" I said, staring at and, for the first time, resenting the copy of *Jet*. The cover was powder blue and white, and it, of course, had a picture of a beautiful Negro woman on the cover. "Where's the book you said you'd bring me?"

Hallelujah scowled. "Preacher said *Native Son* wasn't a proper book to be sharing with a lady."

I winced and said, "I ain't no lady. If I was a lady, I wouldn't be wearing myself out in that cotton field. I'd be sitting under a shade tree like Mrs. Robinson and sipping on some ice-cold lemonade."

Hallelujah laughed and placed the magazine in my hand. "This is better than the book right now," he said. "It's last week's edition. There's an article about Emmett Till. Page three."

"Oh," I said, my perspective changing as I took the magazine from his hand.

"How Dark Negroes 'Pass' Down South," the cover read. That, at least, sounded like information I could use. But when I opened the magazine to the article on Emmett Till, my jaw dropped. "Oh my God, Hallelujah. He looks so much like you."

"Looked," Hallelujah corrected me. Then he said, "I know.

Gave me chills when I saw it. Preacher even said we have the same birthday. July twenty-fifth."

I stared at the picture, a professional shot of a smiling, handsome boy wearing a fedora, a starched shirt, and a tie—what Hallelujah wore every Sunday. I couldn't believe the resemblance, as if they could have been brothers.

"Glad he didn't wear glasses," Hallelujah said, his voice low. "That would've been too close."

"Uncanny," I whispered. "That's the word Miss Johnson would use."

When I glanced at Hallelujah, I noticed that goose bumps were creeping up his neck. I wondered whether he was thinking about our visit to Miss Addie's and her strange reaction when she saw him. I sure was. I rubbed away goose bumps from my own arms as I pondered on how she "sensed" that something bad might happen by just looking at Hallelujah.

I started reading the article out loud: "'A fourteen-year-old Chicago junior high school student, Emmett (Bobo) Till, who was kidnapped by a trio of gun-toting whites early Sunday morning while visiting relatives in Money, Miss., was feared a lynch victim because he "whistled at a white girl."'"

I looked up at Hallelujah. "I thought folks have been saying that the third man might be colored."

Hallelujah shrugged. "What difference does it make? If he was colored, he's still as guilty as the whites."

I read on silently.

"What you think of Preacher Mose sticking around for the trial?" Hallelujah asked.

"What trial?"

"The trial for Roy Bryant and J. W. Milam next week."

"A trial?" I asked, glancing up from the magazine. "Next week?"

Hallelujah nodded.

"In Mississippi? For a white man killing a Negro?"

Hallelujah grinned. "Two white men. And they could go to prison for life if found guilty."

"Praise the Lord," I said.

"Sinners can't praise the Lord."

I narrowed my eyes at him. "They do every Sunday at Greater Mount Zion."

Exasperated by my remark, Hallelujah ripped the magazine from my hands and turned to the article on Emmett Till. He read, "'. . . the sheriff ordered the family of sixty-four-year-old Rev. Moses Wright, a retired Church of God in Christ minister and the boy's uncle, to "take his family from the town for their own safety." The minister, however, refused to leave his home after making arrangements to hide his wife, three sons, and two visiting Chicago grandsons, Curtis Jones and Wheeler Parker.'" He peered at me and asked, "You think you could be that brave?"

"He's braver than most Negroes," I said. "I don't know if I'd be bold enough to hang around. Not after what they did to his nephew."

"I would," said Hallelujah. "I wouldn't let those crackers run me from my home either. I'd stay and testify too."

"You wouldn't," I challenged him.

He nodded. "Would so. My daddy would too. He said Preacher Wright is one of the bravest men he knows."

"If he's so is brave, how come he let them take his nephew in the first place?"

Hallelujah stared at me as though I had turned as orange as the sun. After a moment his forehead wrinkled. "He didn't know they'd kill him, Rosa. They said they wanted to talk to him. He trusted them. Wouldn't any colored man do the same if two white men came to his house in the middle of the night asking to speak to one of his kin?"

"Scoot over," I said, plopping down on the step next to him. "I guess if there was a colored man with him, like Reverend Mose believed, then he wouldn't think they'd do something so violent." I took off my hat and fanned myself. "I bet even Papa would've let Fred Lee go if two white men came saying he'd done something wrong and they wanted to talk to him."

As I fanned myself with my straw hat, I realized how badly I needed that bath. "Sorry if I stink," I said.

Hallelujah pinched his nose. "Pee-eww. Yes, you do."

Playfully, I slapped the fedora off his head. "So how was school today?" I asked.

Hallelujah narrowed his eyes at me as he retrieved his hat from the yard.

He sat back down on the step and fanned himself with the hat. "Folks keep whispering about the Chicago boy and the NAACP, and Miss Wilson's about to have a fit worrying about white folks getting word of it."

Miss Wilson was a new teacher at the colored school. She had been out of college for only a year, with plans to move up north. But her mama, although she was only in her fifties, got sick with what Ma Pearl called "old-timer's disease." And since her mama refused to leave her home, Miss Wilson remained in Stillwater to care for her.

"Miss Wilson can't afford to lose her job," I said.

With a roll of his eyes, Hallelujah said, "She ain't nothing like Miss Johnson."

"I bet she ain't," I said, rolling my eyes back at him.

Hallelujah scowled and placed his hat on his head. "I ain't talking about the way she looks."

After silence sat between us for a minute, Hallelujah finally spoke. "You know how Miss Johnson is. She's brave like Preacher Mose. She'd encourage us to talk about what happened."

"What's Miss Wilson like?"

"As scared as a chicken in a fox den."

I chuckled, but Hallelujah didn't even bother with a smile. "She wants us to put on a patriotic play for the fall and sing that stupid song about *'This land is your land. This land is my land.'*"

"So?"

Hallelujah's brows shot up. "So?" He motioned toward the cotton field. "Is that your land you just picked cotton from?"

"You already know it's Mr. Robinson's land," I said, annoyed at him.

He nodded toward the cotton sack. "How much you gonna get for spending the day in the blazing hot sun filling that thing with cotton?"

"Nothing," I muttered.

"Because this land ain't your land," he said, smiling, satisfied.

I recalled what Mr. Pete had said to Papa before they left for Chicago: *A Negro can own all the land in Mississippi and still be treated worse than a hog.* "You know that's why Mr. Pete left, don't you?"

Hallelujah scoffed. "What good is it for a Negro to own acres of cotton if the white man owns the scales?"

I laughed and told him how I always thought Mr. Pete was rich.

"No such thing as a rich Negro in the Mississippi Delta," he replied. "Unless you count Dr. Howard in Mound Bayou. But that's because Mound Bayou was built by Negroes and is run by Negroes."

"Papa said that all Mr. Pete got for his land was enough to buy a fancy car and drive it to Chicago. He thinks it's a shame he's working for Armour and Company, making soap."

Hallelujah winced. "He'll make more in a factory in Chicago than he would've made growing cotton in Mississippi. But if he was white . . ."

He didn't finish the statement. He simply stared out at the rows and rows of cotton and glowered.

"You gonna do the play?" I asked.

"No."

"What'd Reverend Jenkins say?"

Hallelujah shrugged. "Haven't told him. But he'll probably agree with me."

"Just do it," I said. "Don't cause any trouble for Miss Wilson."

Hallelujah gave me a sideways glance. "Did you read the last few lines in that article?"

"I read the whole thing."

"'If this slaughtering of Negroes is allowed to continue,'" he read from the magazine, "'Mississippi will have a civil war. Negroes are going to take only so much.'" He slapped the magazine shut. "Those were the words of Dr. T.R.M. Howard of Mound Bayou. And I agree with him. Jim Crow has muted colored folks in Mississippi for too long. It's time for us to speak up and be heard."

"And get shot."

"They're gonna kill us anyway. Might as well die a hero."

"Or a fool."

Hallelujah dismissed my comment with a wave of his hand. "If there's gonna be a civil war in Mississippi between colored and white, I'll be the first to sign up."

"And maybe the first to die."

"They can't kill all of us."

"Says who?"

"Eisenhower would send troops down here before he let that happen."

I laughed. "You think the president of the United States cares about Negroes in Mississippi?"

"Abraham Lincoln did."

I stood and stretched. "Well, I, for one, ain't ready to die," I said, yawning. "I want to live. And not in Mississippi."

"Well, I'm not running. I'm staying. And I'm fighting."

"Thought you were going to Ohio."

"I am. But not anytime soon. Like I said, if there's gonna be a civil war between coloreds and whites, I'm up for the task. If old man Preacher Wright won't run, then neither will I."

Maybe Hallelujah was right. Maybe it was time to fight. If Mississippi was willing to have a trial for two white men who killed a Negro, maybe the battle was already halfway won. But of course, there were always people who did what they could to dodge a war—like Ma Pearl's brother Elmer, who Papa said refused to fight in the First World War. Uncle Elmer said the fight wasn't his business, much like Ma Pearl was always claiming the fight between coloreds and whites wasn't hers.

Was it mine? I wasn't so sure. I didn't know if I could be as brave as Hallelujah or Preacher Mose or even Levi Jackson, who risked his life to fight for change.

"I'm proud of you. You know that?" I said, smiling at Hallelujah.

He tipped his hat. "You should be. I'm a man who's going places. And right now I'm about to go in there and feast on whatever Miss Sweet cooked up for supper."

I turned up my nose. "Cornbread. Warmed-up speckled butter beans we had at dinnertime today. Fried corn. Okra and stewed tomatoes."

"Beats the air soup Preacher's serving up at our place," Hallelujah said, patting his stomach.

I tilted my head to one side and squinted to keep the evening sun from my eyes. "You been there before, haven't you?"

"Where?"

"Money."

Hallelujah shrugged. "A few times."

"You ever been to that store? The one where they say Emmett Till talked to the woman?"

He nodded.

"You see her?"

Hallelujah turned his gaze from me and stared at the ground. "Twice."

"She pretty?"

Hallelujah nodded.

"Would you have done it?"

"Whistled at her?"

"Yeah."

Hallelujah stared at me for what felt like an entire five minutes before he finally said, "Heck, no. I'll fight, but I ain't crazy enough to start one."

Chapter Twenty-Six

WEDNESDAY, SEPTEMBER 14

It was late, and we had just settled in for the night after attending church. We were all kind of piddling around before we went to bed. I sat in the front room with Fred Lee, who was reading his history text while I looked at the funny pages from a week-old copy of the Jackson *Clarion-Ledger*. After reading through several chapters of the book of Jeremiah — the "weeping prophet" — during church service, I needed something to give me happy thoughts before going to sleep.

Across from us in the parlor sat Ma Pearl, Papa, and Queen. Ma Pearl and Queen listened to a show on the radio while Papa browsed the pages of a Sears and Roebuck catalog.

When the knock came, it surprised us. No one ever visited that late at night.

We all froze. Except Papa. Springs creaked when he rose from his chair.

He touched his finger to his lips, requesting our silence.

As quietly as he could, except for the squeaking floorboards, he crept to his bedroom to retrieve his shotgun.

Boom. Boom. Boom. Boom. The knock came again. My heart pounded so fast I thought it would beat out of my chest.

With his shotgun at his side, Papa called through the door, "Who there?"

"It's me, Papa," a weak voice came from the other side. "Open the door."

"Ruthie?" Papa called.

When he opened the door, Aunt Ruthie and her children flooded inside. The children clung to her like cuckle bugs.

Ma Pearl, with Queen at her heels, stormed from the parlor. "Gal, what the devil is you doin' with these chi'rens out this time a night?"

Aunt Ruthie stood in the middle of the floor, her face illuminated by the glow of the kerosene lamp. The two younger children, their faces buried in the fabric of her faded plaid dress, hugged her knees; the older ones circled her waist. The baby was cradled in her arms.

"Ruthie," Papa said, his face puzzled, "what is you doin' here?" He placed the shotgun against the wall and peered out the door. "How y'all get here?"

"Walked," Aunt Ruthie muttered, her head hanging, a wide-brimmed straw hat covering her face.

"Walked?" asked Papa. "Seven miles?

Aunt Ruthie nodded.

"In the dark?"

Without raising her head, Aunt Ruthie lifted her arm and mumbled hoarsely, "I had a flashlight."

Her voice rattled, like she'd been crying.

"What you doin' walking seven miles in the dark with these babies?" Papa asked.

Before Aunt Ruthie could answer, Ma Pearl yanked the hat off her head. One of the baby's diapers was wrapped around her head. Blood had soaked through.

"Lawd, Ruthie," Ma Pearl snapped. "You done let that ol' drunk fool beat you again?"

"What happened, Ruthie?" Papa asked gently.

Aunt Ruthie choked back a sob. "He hit me in the head with his steel-toe boot."

"Lawd-a-mercy," Papa whispered.

Queen went over to Aunt Ruthie and took the baby from her arms. When Aunt Ruthie's tears crested, so did mine. I wiped them quickly with the back of my hand.

"Rose, you and Fret'Lee make a pallet on the floor in Grandma Mandy's room for them chi'ren," Papa said. "Ruthie and the baby can have the bed." He turned to Aunt Ruthie and said, "Come on back here. Let me clean you up."

But Ma Pearl wouldn't let her go without a fight. She planted herself right in front of Aunt Ruthie's face. "Don't make no sense how you let that man beat on you, gal," she said. "And he'n even feed'n you and them chi'ren?" She shook her head. "You shoulda left that fool long time ago."

Aunt Ruthie, rubbing her arm and still staring at the floor, choked back sobs. "I'm leaving," she said. "For good. This the last time he go'n hit me."

As if hearing her voice triggered their memories, the children began to cry. Papa, in a sterner voice this time, said, "Take them chi'ren on to the back, Rose and Fred."

Fred Lee had already set his book aside, but I was still sitting on the sofa with the funny pages spread in my lap. I felt immobilized. Everybody talked about Slow John beating Aunt Ruthie, but I always hoped it was an exaggeration. Now I was seeing it for myself. Her children huddled around her, crying—clinging to her, as if at any minute she could be taken away from them—was a testimony of how frightening it must have been. Aunt Ruthie herself stood there looking equally frightened, as if the boogeyman himself had chased her and the children through the dark night, along those wooded predator-filled roads, to the safety of her parents' house. And all she received from her own mama was chastisement, blaming it all on her.

Then, as if Ma Pearl's words finally registered, Papa asked Aunt Ruthie, "These chi'ren ett?"

Aunt Ruthie glanced at Ma Pearl, then at Papa. "They ett," she said softly. "They ain't hongry."

Ma Pearl snorted. "I bet they ain't." She stepped aside as Fred Lee and I pried the children from the folds of Aunt Ruthie's dress.

"Lord, my chile ain't got a bit o' sense," Ma Pearl said, throwing her hands into the air. "Let'n that man beat the devil outta her."

"That's enough from you, Pearl," Papa said. "This gal can't help that man so hard. She here now. That's all that matter."

"Humph," Ma Pearl said. "She been here befo'. She'll go back soon that jackass show up saying he sorry."

"I ain't goin' back" was the last thing I heard Aunt Ruthie say before Fred Lee and I ushered the children to the back. I prayed she was speaking the truth.

While Fred Lee and I got old quilts from the chest in Grandma Mandy's room, surprisingly, Queen came in and calmed the children. All four of them huddled around her as she sat on the side of Grandma Mandy's bed and held the baby. At that moment, as she rubbed their backs and whispered, "Hush now. It's go'n be all right," I almost liked her. I almost forgot how mean and ugly she could be most of the time.

By the time we got everyone settled—the children resting

on a pallet, Aunt Ruthie cleaned up and in the kitchen sharing a cup of coffee with Papa, Ma Pearl and Queen back to their radio show — I headed to bed, as it seemed cruel to continue reading the funny pages when there was so much sadness in the house. As I passed through Fred Lee's room and said good night to him, there was another knock at the door. My heart knew it was Slow John, and again it threatened to pound out of my chest.

As much as I wanted to run to my bed and hide my head under a pillow (actually I wanted to hide my whole body under the bed), my feet wouldn't allow me. As if drawn by a force unknown, they turned and headed toward the front of the house.

Boom. Boom. Boom. Boom.

"Who there?" Papa asked. I'm sure he knew as well as we all did that it was Slow John.

"I came to git my wife," Slow John bellowed from the other side of the door.

Papa didn't open the door. He picked up his shotgun instead. "Go home and git some rest, John," he called through the door. "Sleep off them spirits."

"I ain't drunk, old man," Slow John answered. "I ain't goin' nowhere b'dout my wife."

"Ruthie and the chi'ren stayin' here tonight," said Papa.

Boom. Boom. Boom. Boom. "Open this do', old man."

"Git off my porch, John," Papa said. "'Fore I blast you off."

From the other side of the door, Slow John let out a drunken laugh. "You won't shoot me, you old fool."

Papa cocked his shotgun. "I'll shoot you and take your body to the sheriff myself. Even dig your grave if they ast me."

For a moment, there was silence on the other side of the door, then the shuffling of feet. By the heaviness of his steps, I could tell that Slow John was wearing the steel-toe boots he'd used to whack Aunt Ruthie in the head.

Wump! Slow John kicked the door. "Come outta there, Ruthie, 'fo I come in there and git you," he yelled.

Aunt Ruthie jumped. She had been leaning against the doorframe to Grandma Mandy's bedroom, but now she stood, stiff-backed and trembling.

"My daughter ain't leaving this house, so you might as well go home," Papa said.

"She ain't yo' daughter no mo', old man," said Slow John. "She my wife."

"Ruthie!" he called loudly. "I sorry. I sorry for what I done to you. I swear I ain't go'n do it no mo'." He paused for a moment, then said, "Got a new job, too, baby. Mr. Callahan said he give me work d'morrow. I told him, 'Suh, I be there first thang in the moan'n. I couldn't wait to git home and tell you 'bout it." Another pause, then: "It broke my heart to find you gone."

After a long silence, there was loud weeping on the other side of the door, then, "Ruthie, baby. Please. I loves you. I go'n kill myself if you don't come back."

The look on Aunt Ruthie's face was hard to read. Her empty stare. Was it fear? Or pity?

"Ruthie," Papa said, "you a grown woman. You make your own choices. You chose to marry that man. It's your choice to go or stay. I can't decide for you."

Aunt Ruthie took a step toward the door.

"Dirn fool," Ma Pearl hissed.

With a tremble in her voice, Aunt Ruthie called through the door. "I can't wake up the chi'ren right now, John. I'll be home in the morning."

"I needs you home d'night."

"In the morning," Aunt Ruthie repeated. Her voice shook so badly that she could hardly speak. "You go on to the house and git some sleep," she said to Slow John, staring sheepishly at Papa.

After a long silence, Slow John answered, "I gots to go d'work in the moan'n. I need to take y'all home d'night."

Aunt Ruthie wrapped her arms around her waist, dropped her head, and muttered, "A'right."

"Lawd, have mercy!" Ma Pearl cried. She threw her giant hands in the air and stormed toward her bedroom.

Papa gave out one more warning. "Ruthie," he said, almost as a sigh.

"Let'r go, Paul," Ma Pearl called over her shoulder. "She'll learn 'ventually. That school o' hard knocks is a dirn good teacher."

With tears rolling down my cheeks, I, too, turned and went to my room, knowing my heart couldn't take the sight of Aunt Ruthie walking through that door, especially with fresh blood seeping through the clean rag Papa had just wrapped around her busted head.

Beer!" Monty yelled. "Beer. In a courthouse. During a murder trial. Stupid and senseless," he hissed.

I sat on the floor in Grandma Mandy's old mothball-scented room next to the kitchen, my ear pressed against the wall, straining to pick up every word of the conversation from the adults huddled around the kitchen table. There was so much excitement over the third day of the trial of Roy Bryant and J. W. Milam that I was sure the week of September 19, 1955, would go down as one of the best weeks in Negro history in Mississippi. Our little unpainted house on Mr. Robinson's place buzzed with commotion that Wednesday night, and with so much hope. After Reverend Mose Wright had stood before a courtroom full of white people and pointed out J. W. Milam for the jury, Reverend Jenkins and Monty couldn't stop bragging of his bravery.

But obviously Monty was livid over someone drinking beer during the trial. Having never been in a courtroom myself, I had no idea whether this was normal behavior.

"Mississippi is making a mockery of the justice system,"

he said. "No one should be allowed to drink beer during a trial. It's just plain stupid."

"When you have the judge setting the example," Reverend Jenkins chimed in, "what can you expect? He sat there and sipped on a Coca-Cola."

"This kind of tomfoolery would never be tolerated in a northern courtroom," said Monty.

"Baby, calm down," Aunt Belle said with a slight laugh. "We can't worry about what these people do or do not allow to go on in their courtroom, as long as they let the Negro press in to report the story. God knows we can't depend on the white press to tell the truth."

"Amen to that, Baby Sister," said Reverend Jenkins. "Thank God for the Negro press—"

"But did you see that press table?" interjected Monty. "All our people cramped around a card table against the wall? And they made Congressman Diggs sit there too? And what's with that fat sheriff strolling in there, greeting them with 'Hello, niggers' every morning?"

"Baby, we're not gonna let the negatives overshadow the positives, okay?" said Aunt Belle. "Reverend Mose did a fine job. Stood right there in the midst of all that white, pointed, and said, 'There he is.'"

I was exhausted from a long day of picking cotton, frustrated at all the learning I was missing at school, but somehow

I stayed there on the floor, my legs stretched before me, my head resting against the wall, the nutty scent of Maxwell House coffee lingering in the air. The conversation of colored people discussing the trial of two white men accused of lynching a Negro made me feel good. But then there was Ma Pearl, and she simply had to toss in her two coins.

"I don't like all this crazy talk up in my house," she said. "Coloreds and whites was gittin' 'long jest fine 'fo all these NAACP peoples showed up."

"God, Mama," Aunt Belle said. "How can you call this master-slave existence getting along?"

"I ain't nobody's slave," Ma Pearl said. "I gits paid for my work."

Even from the other side of the wall, it seemed I could hear Aunt Belle's eyebrows shoot up when she asked, "What? Three dollars a week?" She sighed and said, "It's a shame how that woman got you thinking she loves you."

"Y'all young folks thank you know everything," Ma Pearl said. "Don't know nothing. Thank them northern Negroes go'n be round when the Klan show up at ol' Mose's do'step tonight? Nah, they ain't. They go'n be somewhere hidin' behind they own locked do's."

The kitchen was silent for so long it was as if they all had suddenly fallen asleep.

Finally Ma Pearl spoke again. "Not all white peoples is bad," she said.

"Yes, Mama, we understand," said Aunt Belle. "Negroes have their good white people just like white folks have their good nigras. And it was them good nigras that helped Roy Bryant and J. W. Milam kidnap Emmett Till. Any word yet from Miss Doll about where her nephew and Milam's other good nigras have run off to since this trial started?"

"I don't know noth'n 'bout that," Ma Pearl answered brusquely. "If them NAACP peoples wanna know where Doll's nephew at, they can ast *her*, 'cause it ain't my bizness."

"Well, we know that he and the others know something," offered Monty. "The word among our people is that the sheriff is holding Milam's workers in a jail somewhere in a town called Charleston until this trial is over. Now, just why do you suppose the sheriff would go through so much trouble?"

"Like I said, ain't none o' my bizness what Milam's niggers do," Ma Pearl answered.

Monty puffed out his chest. "Well, *our people* will find them. And when we do, we *will* get some answers."

"And jest who is *yo' peoples?*" Ma Pearl inquired.

"The NAACP, of course," answered Monty.

"I wish I could get my hands on Milam's *Judas* niggers," Aunt Belle hissed. "I'd beat 'em worse than Bryant and Milam beat poor Emmett. And if I had a pistol, I'd use *it* on Bryant and Milam!"

"Gal, Saint Louis done really ruint you!" Ma Pearl snapped. "I didn't raise you like this. That boy dead 'cause his mama didn't teach him to respect white folks. Now you talkin' foolish jest like I bet he was. Talkin' 'bout shootin' white mens. Gal, I taught you better'n that."

"Miss Sweet!" Reverend Jenkins yelled. His voice was so loud I jumped.

When he spoke again, his voice had calmed to his preaching level. "I understand there's a certain bond between the older Negroes and the whites, but we're living in a new time, and Mississippi needs to change with the times. Respect is something I agree with, but the constant bowing down to whites because of Jim Crow scare tactics has got to stop. True, the young man had no business whistling at Mrs. Bryant, but not because she's white and he was a Negro, but because he was a fourteen-year-old boy and she is a grown, married woman. That's the kind of respect we need to teach our children. Respect for their elders, respect for authority, respect for their fellow human beings. Not respect based on some antiquated Southern way of life."

When the silence came again, I should have known that Ma Pearl was getting her ammunition together to fight back.

"Preeeeacher," she addressed Reverend Jenkins sarcastically, "you sit here in my kitchen telling me how things got to change. But the man who own this house says I best leave things the way they is. Tells me I gots to leave if I let these northern Negroes tell me how I oughta live in Mississippi. Now you tell me this: Where we go'n go if we git thowed off this place? You got a house for me? You go'n let me and Paul and all these chi'ren of mines live in town with you and yo' boy? I 'spect y'all got 'nuff room for all us with all that money you makin' taintin' the chi'ren through the week and fleecin' the flock on Sunday."

Reverend Jenkins chuckled. "First of all, Miss Sweet, I teach our children, not taint them. And second, last I checked, my flock didn't have enough wool for me to fleece."

"Humph" was all Ma Pearl could counter with.

"You could always come to Saint Louis, Mama," Aunt Belle said softly.

Saint Louis? My heart felt like it momentarily stopped.

I would gladly go to Saint Louis with you! I wanted to cry out to Aunt Belle. *If only you'd ask!* Saint Louis — Chicago — even Detroit. It didn't matter, as long as it wasn't Mississippi. Why was she extending an invitation to Ma Pearl and not me? I know she said she wasn't prepared to take me with her. But how much preparation could she possibly need? Her two weeks were almost over, and I still hadn't had an opportunity to speak to her in private. If only I had the chance, I could perhaps convince her that I, too, was worthy of the North.

Ma Pearl snubbed her offer anyway, saying, "And live with you and that tramp Isabelle?"

"Pearl!" said Papa. "That kinda talk ain't called for."

"Y'all NAACP lovers tell me this," Ma Pearl said. "Where Mose at now? Jest answer me that. Y'all sittin' up in here braggin' 'bout what he did in that courtroom, now tell me: Where he at?"

No answer. So Ma Pearl answered herself. "He holed up somewhere, hidin'. Sked outta his mind. That's where he at. 'Cause there ain't nothin' none y'all can do to protect him."

I heard a sigh, as if someone was about to answer, but Ma Pearl spoke again. "If I said it once, I said it a thousand times. Them NAACP peoples ain't go'n do nothin' but git more folks round here kil't."

In my heart, I wanted to be brave like Preacher Mose and stand up to white people—stand in a crowded courtroom and point a finger at someone like Ricky Turner and say, *There he is! He's the one that tried to run me off the road, then spat tobacco juice at me! He's the one that chased nine-year-old Obadiah Malone into the woods and all the way to Stillwater Lake! He's the kind of evil person who would kill a Negro for no reason!*

But as Papa always said, the spirit might be willing, but the flesh is sometimes weak.

After hearing what Ma Pearl said about Preacher Mose, I suspected that in the courtroom his spirit was willing, but in the dark of the night, his flesh became weak. And when it came to standing up to white folks in Mississippi, my flesh, like Preacher Mose's, weakened when I thought of the horrors they could do to me.

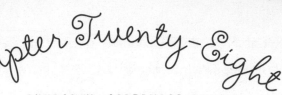

Chapter Twenty-Eight

THURSDAY, SEPTEMBER 22

During church on the previous two Wednesday nights, I had been so tired after picking cotton all day that I barely kept my eyes open while Reverend Jenkins droned on with his lesson. As a matter of fact, I welcomed any prayers the congregation decided to offer, because it gave me a chance to rest my eyes. And I especially welcomed Deacon Edwards. That man could call upon the Lord for a good fifteen minutes without even stopping to catch his breath. But that Thursday night, when Reverend Jenkins decided to hold a prayer meeting before the last day of the trial, sleep was the furthest thing from my mind.

Church was packed. It was more of a victory celebration than a prayer meeting. Even Aunt Belle and Monty were there, as well as a few other folks from around Leflore County who didn't regularly attend Greater Mount Zion Church.

"Today was a great day for the Negro in Mississippi," Reverend Jenkins had said at the beginning of the service. "A historic victory."

Not only had Preacher Mose stood before a courtroom

packed with white people and pointed out a white murderer the day before, but on that Thursday, Mamie Till, the Chicago boy's mother, had bravely testified before the court that she was one hundred percent sure the body found in the river was that of her son, Emmett Louis Till.

Sheriff Strider and the lawyers defending the "accused" murderers were adamant in trying to convince the jury that the body pulled from the river had been there too long to be that of Emmett Till, even making a mockery of the colored undertaker during the trial. They were still holding on to the claim that the NAACP had gone through all that trouble to secure a dead Negro's body, tie a seventy-pound gin fan around his neck with barbed wire, and throw it into the Tallahatchie River just so they could pick a fight with whites in Mississippi. Aunt Belle said she had even overheard one white person laugh and say, "Ain't that just like a nigger to try to swim across the Tallahatchie with a gin fan tied around his neck."

Whether they tried to make a mockery of the trial or not, Aunt Belle and Monty were convinced that with the testimony of two surprise witnesses, Roy Bryant and J. W. Milam had to be found guilty. An eighteen-year-old colored man named Willie Reed had been brave enough to testify before that menacing crowd that he had seen the two accused men take a Negro boy into a barn, and after that he heard screams and beatings. Willie Reed's aunt, Amanda Bradley, had also been brave enough to go to a Mississippi courthouse and point Milam out among his own folks. She, too, had heard the screams coming from the barn that morning and had seen Milam leaving it.

With all that was going on in our little part of Mississippi, I felt invigorated. I felt hopeful. Colored folks were being brave and openly pointing a finger at whites who had committed crimes, and it was all because of a city boy who forgot he was supposed to act a certain way around whites in Mississippi.

After enough folks in the church exhausted themselves with shouting, Deacon Edwards dropped to his knees before the prayer bench at the altar and let out a moan. "Ummm, I just wanna say thank ya!" he shouted. "Thank ya for giving courage to the Negro t'day, Lawd. Thank ya that yo' angels of mercy surrounded Miz Till as she entered that hostile coatroom. Thank ya for watchin' over Brother Willie Reed as he told 'em what he see'd that moan'n when the mens beat that po' boy. Look and have mercy, Lawd. Keep yo' eye on the young lady that told the coat what she heard that moan'n. Let them be safe, Lawd. Don't let there be no 'taliation 'gainst them." When he paused and began to moan, the women of the church began to shout, as they always did. It was then that I felt a tap on my shoulder. When I turned, the girl behind me, Lula Brown, motioned toward the back of the church, where Hallelujah stood near the door. He motioned for me to join him. The moment I had the opportunity, I sneaked out under the pretense of going to the toilet, which wasn't a lie, entirely. After sitting through all that singing and shouting, my bladder was stretched to its limit.

After leaving the toilet, I met Hallelujah at Reverend Jenkins's car, where he sat on the hood. I climbed up on the hood of the Buick and stretched out my legs. The shouting inside the church had quieted, and Reverend Jenkins stood in the pulpit. Outside, several other teenagers loitered around the church, sitting on cars, chatting, smoking, or doing whatever else they felt like doing while the old people inside praised the Lord.

"I don't have a good feeling about this," Hallelujah said.

"So you have a bad feeling?"

I leaned back and rested on the windshield, my arms folded behind my head. The night was clear, and stars blanketed the sky. The air was muggy and smelled of cotton, and I actually felt like taking a nap right there on the hood of Reverend Jenkins's car. Unfortunately, my friend wanted to talk.

Hallelujah leaned back and rested against the windshield as well. He sighed. "At first I was all excited about what's been happening this week. Preacher Mose being brave enough to point out the killers in court. Mrs. Till coming down here and all. And man, Willie Reed having the nerve to actually sit in a Mississippi courtroom and say he saw white men take a Negro into a barn and then heard a beating . . . that was something."

I raised up and rested on my right elbow. I stared at him. "So what's your problem?"

Hallelujah sighed again. "What's gonna happen if these two white men are found guilty?"

"They'll rot in jail," I said as I again rested my head against the windshield. A smile stretched across my face. Two white men could go to prison for killing a Negro. In Mississippi. If that could happen, anything was possible.

"And what if they don't?" Hallelujah asked. "What if the jury says they're not guilty?"

I shot up on my elbow again. "How can a jury find them not guilty? Two people testified they heard the beating. Willie Reed saw J. W. Milam with the boy. Ain't that what everybody's been saying? That he witnessed it?"

Hallelujah stared at the sky, but he didn't answer me.

After what seemed like forever, he finally said, "Imagine this, Rosa." He turned to me and said, "Lean back, close your eyes, and imagine this."

I did as I was told.

"Now, I know you can't stand Queen," he said. "But imagine if Queen did something really horrible, and you knew she needed to be punished. But imagine the punishment coming from Miss Sweet, someone you can't stand even more."

"Hey," I said, my eyes popping open. "Stop judging my feelings about my kinfolk."

Hallelujah shrugged. "Not judging. Just telling the truth. I know you don't like Queen, but I know Miss Sweet plagues you even more. Am I right?" he asked, his brows raised.

I laughed. "I don't know where you're going with all this, but if Ma Pearl beat Queen for *any* reason, folks would hear me laughing all the way to Chicago."

"Okay, maybe that wasn't the best example. Let's see," he said, tapping his finger to his lips.

I exhaled loudly to let him know I was annoyed.

He sprang up on his elbows and asked, "You know what Preacher said Sheriff Strider told the press?"

"I have no idea," I answered, a bit exasperated with him speaking in riddles.

"He said we don't have any trouble down here until some Southern niggers go up north and the NAACP talks to 'em and they come back home. He said if they'd keep their noses and mouths outta our business, folks in Mississippi would be able to do more in enforcing the laws."

I narrowed my eyes at him and said, "Stop speaking in parables and just tell me what you're trying to say."

"What I'm saying is white folks aren't gonna convict their own because of outsiders interfering. You do know that every lawyer in Sumner is defending those two murderers, don't you?"

"Nope. Didn't know that."

"They're teaming up against us, Rosa."

"Of course they are. Haven't they always?"

"My aunt Bertha went to Sumner the week before the trial. You know what she saw when she went inside a few stores?"

I didn't answer.

"Money jars on the counters. She said from what she heard, every store in town was collecting money to help defend those killers."

My heart took a dive. "Our people are teaming up too," I said, trying to remain hopeful. "Look at all the folks down here watching the trial. Aunt Belle closed her shop to come down here. She's losing money. Everybody's doing what they can to help push them to a guilty verdict."

"It won't be enough," Hallelujah said dryly.

"Since when did you become Mr. Gloom and Doom?"

"When I realized we're up against a powerful system."

"Meaning?"

"Meaning," he said, holding a finger up for each point he made, "we have five lawyers defending those murderers. We have every white person in Leflore and Tallahatchie Counties with their threatening eyes glued to the jury, daring them to side with those rabble-rousers called the NAACP and convict two of their own. And we have an all-white male jury. Of course we both know that neither women nor coloreds could be on the jury anyway. But that's beside the point."

"But what about Willie Reed's testimony? He saw them. *And* he heard them."

Hallelujah shook his head. "Won't matter."

I pointed toward the church. Even while Reverend Jenkins was preaching, folks were still waving and shouting. "Your daddy is a smart man," I said. "If he didn't think we were gonna win, he wouldn't be in there stirring up the crowd."

Hallelujah stared at the illuminated windows of Greater Mount Zion for so long it was as if he were in a trance. We could hear Reverend Jenkins, but we couldn't decipher his words. Whatever they were, they were words of hope. Yet what Hallelujah was saying made sense, as if this whole trial were just for show. Emmett Till had been dead for less than a month, but the trial for his killers was almost over. One more day, Friday, September 23. From what Aunt Belle had told me, there would be something called closing arguments; then the jury would make a decision. I suddenly felt sick to my stomach as I watched all those people celebrate something that might not happen.

"Preacher knows," Hallelujah finally said, his voice low.

"Knows what?"

"That those killers won't go to prison."

"Then why is he in there making people shout?"

"He's not stirring them up over what he thinks might happen tomorrow. He's trying to get them ready for the future."

"Riddles," I said, exhaling. "Talk to me straight. I'm not a philosopher like you. I don't even go to school anymore."

"Things are gonna change, Rosa. If Mose Wright and Willie Reed can stand in a courtroom and tell on white people, maybe people will be braver."

"These people," I said, gesturing toward the church. I fell back on the windshield and took a breath. "I doubt it."

"Only time will tell," Hallelujah said quietly.

"Did he ever want to be anything else other than a preacher and a teacher?"

"Preacher?" Hallelujah asked, his brows raised. He thought for a moment, then sighed. "He had dreams of going up north, he told me once. But that was when he had a wife. I don't know if he's ever wanted to be anything more than a preacher and a teacher, though. He sells the insurance policies for the extra, but he says colored folks don't realize they need life insurance just like white folks do."

"You think he ever wanted to be a lawyer?"

Hallelujah glanced toward the church. "Nah. He doesn't care too much for arguing. Just teaching and preaching."

"You think Mr. Evers might get to be one?"

"A lawyer?" said Hallelujah. "Sure, if he can ever get into a law school."

"I wonder why people like Mr. Evers don't just leave Mississippi," I said as I thought about how much I wished I could leave. "Folks like him and that doctor in Mound Bayou could just pack up like Mr. Pete did and go. They could go anywhere they want. Instead, they're here. Fighting for rights."

Hallelujah sighed. "Preacher said it wouldn't be good if everybody left. Imagine what this place would be like if everybody who could just up and went?"

I leaned back and stared at the sky. "Stars can't shine without darkness," I said.

"What?"

"Stars can't shine without darkness."

"What's that supposed to mean?"

"I have no idea. I don't even know where the words came from. But seeing those bright stars reflecting against that black sky, I thought about how my great-aunt Isabelle once brought this little boy from Saint Louis to Mississippi for the first time. He was surprised to see stars. He'd never seen a star in his life. He said Saint Louis didn't have stars. Aunt Isabelle corrected him and said the stars couldn't be seen in the city at night because of all the lights. The stars shine perfectly in Stillwater, especially out in the country, because there's no light dimming their brightness."

"And you accuse me of talking in riddles," Hallelujah said, raising up on his elbow.

"I still don't know what it means," I said. "It just popped into my head as I was looking at the sky."

"Let me know when you figure it out."

"Well, it won't be tonight," I said, leaping off the hood of the car. "I've gotta get back inside before Ma Pearl realizes how long I've been gone."

"Wait," Hallelujah said. "I think I know what it means."

"What?" I asked, eager to know what he thought my strange utterance meant.

"Stars can't shine without darkness," Hallelujah repeated. "You've got to have some darkness to know what light is. If every Negro who *could* leave packed up and left, the struggle wouldn't be the same."

I frowned, indicating that I still didn't understand.

Hallelujah pointed at the church. "Your aunt in there . . . she owns a beauty shop, right?"

I nodded.

"What if she had stayed here, in Mississippi, and opened a shop?"

"White folks would find a way to sabotage it, like they do your aunt Bertha's store, perhaps?"

Hallelujah nodded. "Perhaps. But I'm willing to bet," he said, staring intently toward the illuminated windows of the church, "if she had been able to open a shop here, in a place where our people are shunned and oppressed, it would have made her feel even more accomplished than she already does."

"Stars shine brighter in the darkness," I said quietly.

Hallelujah crossed his arms over his chest and nodded. "Dreams have more meaning when you have to fight for them," he said. "That's why folks like my father choose to stay. They know they have a right to be here, and they're willing to do whatever it takes to make those rights equal."

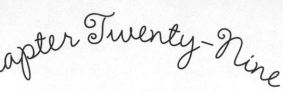

Chapter Twenty-Nine

FRIDAY, SEPTEMBER 23

WHEN I WAS LITTLE, WATCHING A TEENAGE AUNT Belle grow into womanhood, I thought she was the toughest, bravest person I knew. Papa was certainly right about her having grit. Unlike Mama and the rest of my aunts, Aunt Belle was never afraid of Ma Pearl. Aunt Ruthie told me once that she had the same opportunity as Aunt Belle — to go to Saint Louis and become a beautician. She said every time Great-Aunt Isabelle came to Mississippi, Aunt Ruthie would do her hair. And every time, Great-Aunt Isabelle would say to Ma Pearl, "Sweet, you need to let me take this girl back to Saint Louis. I'll send her to beauty school so she can get licensed to do hair and make a decent living for herself. She won't need much training with all the talent she already got." And every time, Ma Pearl refused, even when Great-Aunt Isabelle suggested allowing Aunt Ruthie to be trained as a chef rather than a beautician. But the vocation didn't really matter. Aunt Ruthie said that Ma Pearl was too suspicious of Great-Aunt Isabelle, convincing herself that her spinster sister-in-law made her money running a brothel rather than a boarding house.

"She ain't go'n take my daughter to the city and ruin her," Ma Pearl had said.

So Aunt Ruthie ended up marrying Slow John instead and became a punching bag rather than a beautician, a chef, or "ruined."

When Great-Aunt Isabelle saw the same talent in Aunt Belle, she asked Ma Pearl again to let her take the child back to Saint Louis with her. Again, Ma Pearl said no. At age nineteen, Aunt Belle—who had hidden away half the money she earned caring for various white women's children and ironing the shirts of various white women's husbands—packed her bags and caught a train to Saint Louis without Ma Pearl's blessings. Yes, Aunt Belle had grit. Which is why I was so surprised to see her sitting, doubled over on the sofa in the parlor, her head in Monty's lap, sobbing so hard that her body quaked.

Monty, rubbing her back, looked as if he, too, might cry any minute.

The trial for the two white men who had killed Emmett Till was over. And just as Hallelujah had predicted, the jury had set them free.

For as long as I live, I don't think I'll ever forget the looks on Aunt Belle's and Monty's faces when they walked through the front door. It was as if they had returned from a funeral. In a sense, I guess it could've been considered a funeral, seeing how hope had died that day.

"It was all a farce," Aunt Belle said, her voice choked and garbled with tears. "The whole trial was just for show. They never planned to convict those men."

Monty said nothing. With his eyes cast downward, he only nodded and rubbed her back.

Aunt Belle raised her head and wiped her face with the back of her hand. "Did you see them kissing? Did you see that evil devil and his wife stand right there in front of a camera and lock their faces together for all the world to see? Like they were having a private moment in their own bedroom?"

Monty sniffed back a sob and answered hoarsely, "Yeah, baby. I saw."

"If anybody did any flirting in that store," Aunt Belle said, her teeth clenched, "it was probably that little tramp herself."

"Calm down, baby," Monty told her. "Don't make yourself sick over this."

"I'm not making myself sick. That mockery of a trial just made me sick." She sniffed and said, "And those two murderers smoking cigars like they just had babies? Disgusting."

"Cheering and clapping like they had won an election," Monty said icily.

"Well, they won all right. They certainly left me feeling defeated."

Defeated. That's what we were. Every last Negro, not just in Mississippi, but in the nation. Even the northern Negroes, with their entourage of cameras and notebooks, NAACP leaders and prominent members, congressmen and dignitaries, couldn't defeat the Jim Crow ways of Mississippi.

It made my heart sick to see Aunt Belle so broken and to see so many people's hopes crushed. Aunt Belle had lost money while she was down here that additional two weeks. Monty, who had already used up all his vacation when he came with Aunt Belle in August, took time off without pay. He even said he risked losing his job. How many others, I wondered, had lost time and money for this trial, only to hear a Mississippi jury say, "Not guilty."

"Less than an hour," Aunt Belle whispered. "It took them less than an hour to come back out and tell that lie."

"One hour and eight minutes, to be exact," Monty said. He then added, in a southern drawl, "'And that's 'cause we stopped to drink sody pop. If we hadna been thusty, we coulda been done in a few minutes.'"

At Monty's joke, Aunt Belle chuckled like a sad clown. "Did those fools really believe the NAACP would dig up a corpse and put it in the river?"

"Of course they didn't," Monty said. "You heard the

attorney: 'Every last Anglo-Saxon one of you has the courage to set these men free in the face of this preshuh. Yoah ancestahs would absolutely turn over in their graves if you don't set these boys loose. We have got to use our legal system to protect our God-given freedoms.'"

Monty's rendition of the trial in a southern accent obviously calmed Aunt Belle's nerves a bit. She sat up and wiped her face with a handkerchief instead of her hand. "Well, their Anglo-Saxon ancestors are about to do a lot of turning now, because Negroes are not about to let this thing rest. Those two might have gotten away with murder, but things are about to change in Mississippi."

"Not just Mississippi," said Monty, "but the South."

"Something's about to happen," I whispered.

"What?" Aunt Belle asked.

"Something's about to happen," I said, louder. "That's what Miss Addie kept saying."

"Miss Addie, the old midwife?" asked Aunt Belle.

I nodded. "She said something was about to shake up Mississippi."

"Humph," Aunt Belle said, her expression questioning. "Maybe that old woman really does have a sixth sense after all."

"Well, whether the old lady is a soothsayer or not," said Monty, "something's gotta change."

"You ain't even from here," Ma Pearl blurted out as she stormed into the parlor, wiping her hands on a dishrag. "Why you care so much about what Mississippi do?"

Monty nodded at Ma Pearl. "And a good afternoon to you too, Mrs. Carter."

Ma Pearl snorted. "Northern and uppity is what you is, boy. Folks like you is the reason them peckerwoods is walking free rat now."

Monty pointed at his chest and said, "It's because of folks like me that there was ever a trial in the first place."

"You dirn right," Ma Pearl said, undaunted. "If that lil' uppity Chicago boy hadn't been up in that sto' running his mouth, he would be with his mama 'stead of in a grave."

"Lord Jesus, have mercy!" Aunt Belle said. She threw up her hands. "Let me get out of this crazy woman's house before I start to hate her."

Ma Pearl, her face like flint, her hands in fists, leaned toward Aunt Belle. "If you cain't take the truth, go on back up there where you run off to in the first place. I ain't never ast you to come back to my house. You the one keep running back this way."

Both Monty and Aunt Belle seemed to spring from the sofa at the same time. But Aunt Belle faced down Ma Pearl. "We'll be more than happy to get out of this hellhole," she said. "I don't know why I've wasted so much time here in the first place. Mississippi will never change because of Negroes like you, Mama. You're the same kind of Negro that helped those two men kidnap and kill Emmett Till. Won't even register and exercise your right to vote. So in love with that white woman that she ain't even got to wipe her own behind. Before her stuff even hits the toilet, you there waiting with a wad of tissue in your hand to take care of it for her."

WHAP! With every ounce of strength in her huge body, Ma Pearl swung her fist into Aunt Belle's jaw and knocked her across the room. Aunt Belle crashed in the corner, scattering dust and Sears and Roebuck catalogs across the floor.

"Belle!" Monty screamed.

Sprawled on the floor, Aunt Belle moaned and rubbed her jaw. Monty rushed to her and lifted her upper body off the floor. He smoothed Aunt Belle's hair from her face. "Baby, you all right?"

Still rubbing her jaw, Aunt Belle, with closed eyes, could only moan.

Monty stared up at Ma Pearl. "Woman, have you lost your mind?"

"Talk to yo' girlfriend. She done lost her mind talking to me like that in my own house."

Monty cradled Aunt Belle's head. "I can't believe you hit your own daughter," he said, staring at Ma Pearl as if he wanted to do the same to her.

"Hit you, too, if you talk to me like that in my own house."

I rushed over to Monty when I saw him struggling to get Aunt Belle to the sofa. We lifted Aunt Belle, who was still moaning, onto the sofa. "I'll put some cold water on a towel for her face," I said.

Ma Pearl pointed at me. "Don't you take not one chip of ice from my icebox either. You better make do with pump water."

At that moment Papa entered the parlor. He had washed up and changed his clothes as he prepared to eat supper. "Pearl," he said, his brows raised, "what's going on in here?"

"Paul, you wouldn't believe what that gal just said to me." Ma Pearl pointed at Aunt Belle and said, "She done called me everything but a child of God."

"Mr Carter," Monty said, "I assure you that Belle was only responding to Mrs. Carter's antagonistic ways. Under normal circumstances, there is no way she would use such fresh language in the presence of her elders."

"Hold on a minute, son," Papa said, his palms raised. "I'm a country boy. Speak to me with plain words."

"Ma Pearl started it," I said. My hands shot up to my mouth, knowing they were already too late to stop the words.

Ma Pearl stormed toward me.

But rather than Papa, Monty stopped her. "If you even

think about putting your hands on this child, woman, I will deal with you myself."

A lump rose in my throat.

Papa grabbed Ma Pearl by the shoulders. "Pearl, it's time for you to head back to the kitchen. Rose, go get that wet towel for Baby Susta's jaw," he said to me.

After having subverted Ma Pearl, I knew to use the front door and walk all the way around the house to the pump rather than get water from the bucket in the kitchen. By the time I returned with the towel, Papa was sitting in his chair with his unlit tobacco-filled pipe in his mouth.

Aunt Belle was stretched out on the sofa, her head resting in Monty's lap as he and Papa chatted. The Sears and Roebuck catalogs were, again, neatly stacked in the corner.

I handed Monty the towel, and he placed it on Aunt Belle's jaw.

"You all right?" I asked her.

"Um-hmm," she replied, half moaning, her words garbled. "I bith my tongue. But I'm okay. She's beath me worth with that blat strapth of hers."

The black strap of terror, its sting worse than that of a thousand hornets. I shivered as I recalled the many lashes I had received from it myself.

"She had no right to hit you with her fist like a man," Monty said.

"I shouldnth sassth my mama," Aunt Belle replied. "I was raisth bettha."

Monty smoothed a curl from her face. "Stop trying to talk and rest that swollen jaw. Can't have you looking like Frankenstein."

"Donth makth me laugth," Aunt Belle said, chuckling. "It hurths."

"So they ain't going to prison," Papa said softly.

His words snapped Monty and Aunt Belle out of their banter and back to reality.

"No, sir, Mr. Carter, they're not," Monty said, the grimness returning to his face. "A jury of their peers found them not guilty. They get to go home, back to their families, back to being the good citizens of Mississippi that they always have been."

Monty's sarcasm hung in the air like thick perfume. Good citizens of Mississippi. Good citizens who had put a northern Negro in his place and sent a message to the rest of the country: Mississippi makes its own rules, and nobody can make us do otherwise, not the NAACP, not the Negro press, not even the president of the United States. We can kill all the Negroes we want. You can make us have a trial, but you can't make us find our white citizens guilty.

"Mr. Carter, you registered to vote?" Monty asked, his eyes squinting, challenging Papa.

Papa removed his pipe and shook his head no, even though he knew Monty already knew the answer to that question. "What good would it do, son?"

"Do you know why that jury was all white, Mr. Carter?"

"'Cause they always is," Papa answered.

Monty grimaced. "Because there are no Negroes registered to vote in Tallahatchie County, Mr. Carter. That's why the jury was all white."

Papa placed his pipe back in his mouth as he considered Monty's words. The only noise in the house at that moment was the distant clanking of pots and pans as Ma Pearl released her fury in the kitchen. Finally a hearty laugh rocked Papa's lanky body. I had never seen him laugh so hard, not even when he occasionally read the funny pages. When he finally composed himself, he asked Monty wearily, "Young man, do you really think they woulda 'lowed a colored man in that jury box?"

"Of course not," Monty answered. "But at least we could have made a case for it."

"Every colored man in the county coulda been on the courthouse reg'stry as voters. Still wouldn'ta made a diff'rence," said Papa.

"Will you even consider it, Mr. Carter?"

"Trying to git on the voting reg'ster?"

"Yes," Monty said, nodding. "Signing up. Registering to vote."

"Son, I have a family to provide for. Gittin' shot down at the courthouse won't put food on the table."

Aunt Belle raised her head slightly. "How can anythinth chane if our people won'th voth?"

As the room went silent, I imagined Papa, aging and hunched over, walking up the courthouse steps in Greenwood. The next thing he knows, a bullet strikes him in the back. Then another. Then another. They keep hitting him, even after he has fallen and tumbled down the stairs.

"When I'm old enough, I'll register to vote," I said. Everyone stared at me, not saying a word. "Papa's right. He has a family to take care of. He can't take chances like that. It's the young folks who have to take a stand while we can. Before we have families depending on us."

When Monty smiled and said, "Good for you, Rose," my heart melted. And it melted for two reasons. One, Monty was handsome and smart, and I was glad he was about to marry my favorite aunt. And two, I thought about Levi Jackson and how, simply because he wanted to vote, he was shot and killed. What if that happened to me and I never got a chance to even vote in the first place? What good was my name on some voters' list if I was dead? Fear rose up in my throat at the thought of something so daring. Now I understood why folks were fleeing to the North rather than staying and fighting. Why die in Mississippi when you could live up north?

But everybody couldn't leave, or wouldn't—like Papa, who seemed to be perfectly content with living and dying in Mississippi. I had never asked him before, but that moment seemed as good as any to pose the question.

"Papa, how come you didn't leave?"

"Mississippi is home, daughter," he said. "I'm a farmer. I loves the land. I loves the fresh air. My animals. The cotton."

"Do you love working for that white man living in his mansion down the road?" Monty asked, his sarcasm lingering in the air again.

"Matter of fact, I do," said Papa. "I loved working for his daddy, too. Every white person ain't full o' evil, son."

I thought about the day after Levi's death, when I went to the Robinsons' and Mr. Robinson was hosting a meeting for the White Citizens' Council. From what Hallelujah had told me about the group, how they wanted to make sure the government didn't interfere with the way things were in Mississippi, I couldn't help but side with Monty.

"I didn't say he was evil," Monty said. "But you have to agree that the living conditions are unfair."

Papa raised his brows. "Who told you life was fair? You think 'cause a man don't live in a mansion he can't be happy?

I never go to bed hungry, son. I ain't never went without clothes on my back. And this roof over my head don't leak. This furniture," he said, gesturing around the room, "I didn't pay a dime for it, but it sets as good as anything you can git in one of them catalogs lying there on the floor."

Monty was silent.

"Mr. Robinson never done me no wrong, son," Papa said quietly. "Neither his father. They were both good to me."

Aunt Belle threw in her garbled two cents. "They oughth thue be. Everythinth they own is becauth of Negroes workin' them fieldths."

"Daughter, I ain't complaining," Papa said. "This is where the good Lord saw fit for Paul Elias Carter to be born, right here in Stillwater, Mississippi. He knowed I'd love the land before I was even here. He shaped me in my mother's womb and fitted me to farm. And with that I'm happy. With that I'm content. Ain't no shame in serving others."

When nobody said anything else, Papa continued. "The minute I saw you," he said to Aunt Belle, smiling, "I knowed you'd be like Isabelle. That's why I wanted to call you Belle. Isabelle was never happy with the land. She hated the outdoors. She hated the fields. She wouldn't even plant a garden or go fishin'. She loved taking care of the house. But she always wanted one of her own. A big one. The first chance she got, she caught that train to Saint Louis and took a job housekeeping for that old white man after his wife died. When he died, his chi'ren give that house to Isabelle. She made herself a living by opening that house up and serving others."

Aunt Belle's face hardened. "Doesth Mama know thath?"

Papa nodded. "She know."

"Humph," Aunt Belle said with a grunt.

This land is your land. This land is my land. Maybe that's why the ninth-grade teacher wanted the class to do a patriotic play and sing that song. Perhaps she, like Papa, considered Mississippi home. This land was her land as much as it was any white person's land. Mississippi. This land was my land too. And I had a right not to let anybody chase me away from it the way they had done Mama and Mr. Pete. All that land. And he sold it to rent something called an apartment.

A battle raged within me. What if I remained in Mississippi and never became more than a field worker or some white woman's maid? What if I never finished school? I admired Papa for his strength. For his contentment. But I couldn't emulate it. I knew I could never be happy living in a shack on some white man's cotton plantation. Nor could I be happy living in a town where I had to look down at the ground whenever I saw a white person approaching. I couldn't be happy living in a place where I was made to feel less than human. Either things had to change in Mississippi, or I had to leave it. Someday.

"What about me, Papa?" I asked. "What did you think when I was born?"

A smile spread across Papa's face. But before he could speak, Aunt Belle chimed in. "I rememberth when thu were born," she said, smiling.

Monty patted her hand and said, "Rest that jaw, baby."

"Soon as old Addie left the room, Belle ran in there to see you. You was as pink as you could be," Papa said, laughing. "Belle begged Anna Mae to call you Rose."

"You did?" I asked Aunt Belle.

She nodded and said, "Rotha. I called you Rotha."

"Rosa?" I asked.

Aunt Belle smiled and nodded.

"How did it get to be Rose?" I asked.

"Pearl," Papa answered briskly. "She said Rosa wadn't a real name." He paused and chuckled. "Old Addie wrote Rosa on the birth record anyway," he said, "no matter how many times Pearl told her your name was Rose."

"She still calls me that," I said. "Hallelujah, too."

"Rosa," Monty piped in. "It's Italian. Comes from Rose of Viterbo, a saint from Italy. But the name also means 'dew.'"

"Like the stuff on the grass in the morning?" I asked.

Monty nodded. "Like the dew in the morning, gently refreshing the earth. The bearers of this name tend to want to analyze and understand the world. They search for deeper truths than simply what's on the surface." He winked at me and said, "Rosa. I like that. A rose by any other name would smell as sweet, right?"

I smiled. Maybe having a walking, talking *Encyclopedia Britannica* as an uncle wouldn't be so bad after all.

Monty turned to Papa. "Mr. Carter, why isn't this girl in school?"

Papa fumbled for words. He removed his pipe from his mouth and, staring at the ceiling, scratched his chin, which I doubted even itched.

During the past three weeks, while I watched Queen and Fred Lee rise and dress for school and I dressed for the field, I had wondered the same thing: Why wasn't Papa fighting for my right to be in school? Why was he allowing Ma Pearl to force me to settle for only a seventh-grade education when he himself had regarded education important enough to teach himself to read and write? I had asked him about it only once, and he'd replied that I was where I was needed most. It turned out he had the same reply for Monty.

"Rose is where I needs her most right now," he said. But then he added, "She'll go to school, soon as the harvest is in."

My eyebrows shot up. "I will?"

Papa nodded and said, "You will."

"I won't have to stay home and help Ma Pearl?"

Papa shook his head. "Pearl'll be a'right. The good Lawd'll send her the help she need."

Tears rushed to my eyes. I was going to school when the cotton was picked. I might be late starting, but at least I was going. I wanted to rush to Papa and hug him. But that was something I'd never done before, and I knew I was too old to start. So I simply whispered a choked "Thank you."

But Monty sat up straight on the sofa. "Mr. Carter, on my many drives throughout this county, I've seen plenty of Negro men who could take Rose's place in that field. These men have nothing better to do than play checkers in front of a country store."

Papa placed his pipe back in his mouth. "Them mens expects to be paid."

"Then pay them," Monty said.

Papa glared at Monty. "I already hired all the extras I could afford. I can't hire no mo'."

"But why Rose and not Fred Lee and Queen?" asked Monty. "Wouldn't you have harvested faster with the extra help?"

"Because Rose is apt," Papa said. "She don't need no school to learn. She'll find a way to get her learning, just like Belle did. Queen and Fret'Lee don't have them kind of smarts. If

I keep them outta school even for the harvest, they'd soon give up. They'd accept that way of life. But not Rose. She know how to make a way outta no way." Papa's expression brightened a bit when he said, "Even now she'll catch up and outrun every child in that school."

"But why now?" asked Monty. "Why have you suddenly decided she should go when the cotton is picked?"

Papa scowled and said, "'Cause a Negro without proper schooling ain't nothing to the white man but a nigger."

Smiling, Monty turned to me and said, "I hear you've been considering a fresh start."

I gave him a questioning stare.

"Saint Louis?" he answered, his brows raised.

"I . . ." was all I could say before the words jumbled up in my mouth and refused to come out. I glanced at Aunt Belle. Like Monty, she was smiling.

"Belle and I have been talking," Monty said. "She told me about your conversation when we were here a few weeks ago."

"Our . . . conversation," I stammered, glancing from Monty to Aunt Belle, then back again.

"I gaith whath you askth me thome thought," Aunt Belle said.

Monty patted her on the knee, reminding her to rest her jaw. "The last time we were here," he said to me, "we weren't prepared to take you back. But after giving your request some thought and talking it over," he said as he glanced lovingly at Aunt Belle, "we'd love to have you in Saint Louis." He nodded at Papa and said, "That is, if it's okay with you, Mr. Carter."

My heart raced. I should have been smiling, leaping for joy at Monty's words, but instead, my stomach churned with nervousness. Since the day Mr. Pete took Mama away in his train of a car, I had wanted nothing more than to go with them. To live a life up north. A life I could experience only from the way colored people from up north dressed, from the way they talked, even down to the way they laughed — which was vastly different from the way things were for colored people in the South. I couldn't believe the door to that good life was suddenly standing open before me. Monty and Aunt Belle were asking me, Rose Lee Carter, to go back to Saint Louis with them.

Like me, Papa seemed to have lost his ability to speak. He sat there, his expression unreadable, staring at Monty. When he didn't respond after what seemed to be more than a minute, Monty spoke. "We'll of course wait till after the harvest, if you'd like." He smiled at me and said, "What do you say to the first week of November, Rose?"

Good thing I was sitting, else I would have hit the floor. Not only were my knees weak, but my whole body seemed to have melted like warmed butter. Here was my chance to leave Mississippi, and my emotions were in a whirlwind.

Especially when I saw the look in Papa's eyes. It was the same look of defeat that held Aunt Belle captive when Roy Bryant and J. W. Milam were set free from the charge of murdering Emmett Till.

"Papa," I said softly. "You want me to go?"

When Papa shook his head and said, "You know the answer to that question is no," my heart took a dive.

But then he said, "But I won't hold you back."

"You won't?" I said, my voice cracking.

Papa's expression brightened. "Not no mo'," he said, shaking his head. "Not no mo'."

Chapter Thirty

SUNDAY, SEPTEMBER 25

★

LET NOT YOUR HEART BE TROUBLED: YE BELIEVE IN *God, believe also in me. In my Father's house are many mansions: if it were not so, I would have told you. I go to prepare a place for you. And if I go and prepare a place for you, I will come again, and receive you unto myself; that where I am, there ye may be also.'"*

For nearly all my life, for as long as I could remember, I had heard those words from John, chapter fourteen, recited by a deacon every Sunday morning that I attended church. But for some reason, hearing them from Papa that morning as I sat on a hard wooden pew in Greater Mount Zion Missionary Baptist Church on the last Sunday in September, right after having watched my own people go through so much change in such a short time, the words had more meaning than usual.

"Let not your heart be troubled: ye believe in God, believe also in me." Jesus spoke those words. I knew that because the words were in red in my Bible. I believed in God even though he didn't answer my prayer and make me pretty like Queen

and Sugar. As I grew older, I realized what a silly prayer it was anyway. God didn't care what I looked like. He didn't care what any of us looked like. According to Reverend Jenkins, John the Baptist looked like a wild man, but God used him anyway. It didn't matter how dark my skin was or how nappy my hair, I was still somebody. I was named after a saint. My name meant "courage." And in one language, my name even meant "dew." And dew is refreshing.

"In my Father's house are many mansions . . ." Papa always said he never needed a mansion on earth because he had one waiting for him in heaven. It was hard for me to picture heaven, or even to believe in it, honestly. When I thought of all the people who had died on earth and all the ones still left to die, the idea of a place in the sky that could house all of us simply made me dizzy and confused. And mansions? Were they real mansions, or did that idea of a mansion represent something else? I didn't know. I couldn't know, which is why it's called faith, as Papa always said.

But one thing I did know as I sat and absorbed those words that Jesus spoke: if there was a heaven, Papa would surely be there. But because I had not "put my trust in Jesus," as Ma Pearl frequently pointed out, I would not. I was destined for hell.

A lump rose in my throat. And before I could retrieve my handkerchief from my dress pocket, tears flowed. As much as I tried to fight them, I couldn't hold back the tears. According to the Bible, Jesus said he was preparing a place for his people so that where he is, there they would be also. People like Papa and Reverend Jenkins believed this. Who was I to deny it simply because I had something to prove to Ma Pearl? I was doing what Papa called cutting off my nose to spite my face, the same thing whites in Tallahatchie County, Mississippi, had done when they set two killers free.

Without my permission, my legs straightened to a standing position and began walking to the front of the church. They were so wobbly I thought I would crumble to the floor any minute. But I didn't. I made it to the front. The look on Papa's face as he stood before the altar podium told me I had made a huge mistake. It was against protocol for anyone to come before the church unless specifically called to the altar. But he didn't chastise me.

When the church completed singing "Pass Me Not," everyone sat except me. I stood there trembling, nervous sweat dripping from my armpits and down my sides. When Papa took his seat among the deacons on the side pews facing the altar, Reverend Jenkins came from the pulpit and stood beside me. He placed his arm around my shoulders and whispered, "What is it, Rose?"

"I want to be baptized," I whispered, my voice shaking. "I want to be saved."

"Have you asked Jesus to be your Lord and Savior?"

"Yes, sir," I choked out. "But I didn't get a sign."

My body couldn't stop shaking. I knew Reverend Jenkins was progressive in his thinking, but I didn't know whether he would accept my confession and allow me to be baptized with the others on the following Sunday, as I hadn't crossed over during revival.

Gently, with his arm still around my shoulders, Reverend Jenkins turned my body to face the congregation. "Our sister Rose," he announced to the congregation, "has confessed her hope in Christ and would like to become a candidate for baptism. Is there a motion?"

When no one spoke, I glanced up. My gaze met Ma Pearl's. Hers was so fierce I thought I would faint. What if I had made a fool of myself? What if no one moved that I become a candidate for baptism, because I hadn't gotten religion during revival like everyone else? I stared down at the floor, too ashamed to face the church. Then, as if in a dream, I heard Papa's voice from the deacon's bench. "I move that Rose Lee Carter become a candidate for baptism."

A moment passed before another deacon said, "I second the motion." My mind was so foggy that I didn't recognize the voice, but a sense of relief washed over me.

"It has been moved that our sister Rose Lee Carter become a candidate for baptism on next Sunday, October second," said Reverend Jenkins, his right hand raised high in the air. "All in favor, say aye."

A hearty "aye" rose from the congregation.

"All opposed, say nay," said Reverend Jenkins.

My heart beat faster with the silence, but no one opposed my baptism.

"It has been motioned and approved by a unanimous vote of yes from the saints that our sister Rose become a candidate for baptism," Reverend Jenkins said. When he smiled and hugged me right in front of all those people, my body melted into sobs.

I stumbled almost blindly back to my seat, feeling free and happy. Surprisingly, Ma Pearl gave me a gentle pat on the knee. Her approval. It didn't bother me one bit that she felt she had something to do with my conversion. I would no longer cut off my nose to spite my face. I would allow her to be proud of what she thought she had accomplished.

I smiled as the church sang, "*'None but the righteous, none but the righteous, none but the righteous shall see God, shall see God. Take me to the water to be baptized. I know I got religion. Yes, I do.'*"

I, Rose Lee Carter, was a candidate for baptism. And when I died, wherever or whatever heaven was, I would be there with Papa and a man named Jesus, who was so important that his words were printed in red in my Bible.

"*Come, we that love the Lord,*'" the choir sang out, "*'and let our joys be known; join in a song with sweet accord, join in a song with sweet accord and thus surround the throne, and thus surround the throne. We're marching to Zion, beautiful, beautiful Zion; we're marching upward to Zion, the beautiful city of God.*'"

Though the choir sang, my mind wandered back to the Scripture Papa had read: "*I go to prepare a place for you. And if I go and prepare a place for you, I will come again, and receive you unto myself; that where I am, there ye may be also.*"

I knew the Scripture was about Jesus going to heaven to prepare a place for his disciples, but I couldn't help but think of Aunt Belle and Monty, who were on their way to Saint Louis — to prepare a place for me. And they would come again in November, and not just receive me, but relieve me from the misery of Mississippi. I couldn't contain my smile. Not only had I "gotten religion" on my own terms as opposed to Ma Pearl's, but I had also finally gotten my chance to fly away, as so many others had done before me.

Chapter Thirty-One

A SCREAM JOLTED ME FROM SLEEP. MOONLIGHT gleamed through the thinly curtained window. The sunlight of Monday morning had not yet arrived. So why was Ma Pearl in our room? And why was she standing next to Queen's bed, yelling for her to get up?

"You ain't 'sleep!" she said. "No sense pretending you is. Wadn't two minutes ago that I just saw you crawl in here."

When a second scream filled the bedroom, my eyes quickly adjusted to the darkness and spotted the black strap of terror. In a perfect arch, it swung and landed *whap* against Queen's curled-up body. And then *whap . . . whap . . . whap . . .* , it lashed Queen, as if it had a mind of its own.

Queen's hands moved in every direction in an attempt to block it. "Ma Pearl, please!" she screamed. "Please, stop!"

"I'm go'n kill you!" Ma Pearl yelled. "I'm go'n kill you!"

I sat straight up in my bed, stunned, only half believing it had taken the changing of the season and nearly a month of watching Queen run outside and vomit every morning for Ma

Pearl to realize there was a baby inside her and not a summer flu.

When Queen noticed me sitting up, she cried, "Help me! Make her stop!"

"Cain't nobody help you but Jesus," Ma Pearl said, pointing toward heaven with one hand while wielding that strap with the other. Her arm rose so high with the strap that it seemed to touch the ceiling. She brought it down with a WHAP against Queen's back. "I told y'all I didn't want to bring up no mo' babies in my house."

When Ma Pearl paused for a moment to catch her breath, Queen uncoiled her body and—still on her bed—fell on her knees. With her hands clasped in a prayer position, she begged Ma Pearl for mercy.

"I ain't the one to forgive you," Ma Pearl said. "That's God's bizness. My bizness is to beat the devil outta you for bringing mo' shame in my house. Sneaking outta here at night like a common tramp."

Dazed by the drama, I hadn't noticed that Queen was fully dressed in a yellow pantsuit.

"Ma Pearl, I'm sorry. I'm so sorry," she said, her head bowed, her body rocking back and forth.

"You ain't sorry," Ma Pearl said, her teeth clenched. "You in trouble. And cain't nobody undo that."

Before Queen could get her hands up to shield her face, the black strap of terror slashed across it. Queen's cry was so loud, it's a wonder it didn't wake the Robinsons up the road.

But it did wake Papa. He came rushing into the room, struggling to pull his britches over his underwear.

"What?" was all he said as his eyes adjusted to the moonlit room.

Ma Pearl turned swiftly toward him. "This gal done gone out and got herself in trouble."

"Queen?" Papa said. His countenance fell as he stared at the sobbing figure on the bed.

Queen lay on her side, her knees pulled up to her chest, her head shielded by her arms, her body worn from Ma Pearl's lashes. "I'm sorry, Papa," she said, whimpering.

"Queen?" Papa said again, as if he somehow expected to get a different answer. "You, Queen?" he said softly.

"Yes, Queen!" Ma Pearl said. She coiled the strap around her thick hand as she stormed toward the doorway. "Ast her who the daddy is."

Papa looked at Queen, then back at Ma Pearl.

"Go on," Ma Pearl said, "ast her."

Papa turned to Queen. "Queen?" he said again. This time his tone was one of inquiry rather than shock.

Queen answered him with heavier sobs.

Ma Pearl folded her arms across her chest. "She was sick too long. I watched her every day. And nothing," she said, scowling. "So I knowed she was leaving at night."

Queen's sobs grew louder.

"Caught her tonight," Ma Pearl said. "Gittin' thowed outta that ol' peckerwood's truck. Jest thowed her out like she was a piece a trash."

"Queen," Papa said, sighing.

Ma Pearl snorted. "Dirn fool like her mama. White man ain't go'n never own up to no colored baby." She stormed out of the room, the sheet serving as a curtain between the two rooms swaying behind her.

"Go on back to sleep," she said when Fred Lee's bed creaked. "Ain't nothing wrong, 'cept Queen done got herself in trouble."

At that, Queen whimpered. And it took only a second for the whimpering to turn into broken sobs.

Queen uncurled her body and reached up. She begged for Papa's embrace. "I'm sorry, Papa," she uttered.

Papa dropped his head. With his shoulders slumped, he turned and left the room.

As Queen curled herself into a ball and wept even louder, I got up and lit the kerosene lamp that sat on the wooden crate that served as a night table between our beds.

At first I didn't speak. Instead, I, the newly saved sinner, knelt beside my bed and offered up a prayer for her, begging God not to allow Ma Pearl to beat her so viciously again. Then I went over to her bed and rubbed her back.

Queen winced.

I could feel the bruises beneath the soft fabric. Dark red seeped through yellow.

"We need to get these clothes off you."

"Okay . . ." Queen whimpered.

But when I began to help her out of her clothes, she wailed. "I just wanna die! Jesus, just let me die!" She curled back into her ball, cringing at every touch.

Tears sprang to my eyes. "It's gonna be all right, Queen," I whispered, my voice choking. I stared at what was once beautiful, almost sand-colored skin. It was now bruised, bloody, and purple.

Staring at Queen's body brought back a memory I didn't know I had. It was a memory of a time before Fred Lee was born—a memory of a night Ma Pearl stormed into that very room Queen and I shared.

Mama and I cuddled in one bed, and Aunt Clara Jean and two-year-old Queen cuddled in the other. The memory was a fog, but I remembered Mama crying and Aunt Clara Jean soothing her with, "Sister, it's go'n be all right."

Tears sprang to my eyes when I thought of Mama possibly getting that kind of beating twice. The memory and the sight of Queen's back made me vow I'd never allow myself to get into that kind of trouble with Ma Pearl.

After helping Queen get out of her blood-soaked clothes, I went to the back room and got the basin of water for morning washing, along with a towel. When I returned, Queen was sitting up, the sheets loosely wrapped around her.

"It hurt so bad," she said when I sat beside her.

"I know," I whispered.

"If you hadna woke up," she said, choking back a sob, "she mighta killed me."

"She wouldn't have killed you," I said softly. "She didn't kill Mama. And she didn't kill Aunt Clara Jean."

"I wish she had. I wish she had killed us both before I was even brought to this miserable world."

"Don't talk like that, Queen. You won't have to stay here forever," I said. "One day you can leave like everyone else. Like me," I added, feeling renewed joy at the thought of going to Saint Louis in November.

"How can I leave?" Queen asked. "Who go'n take me to live with them? I'll have a child attached to my hip." She said that in a tone indicating that the problem was someone else's fault and not her own.

"Mama and Aunt Clara Jean both had babies before they were married," I said. "But they still got husbands. They still left."

"But they didn't get to choose," Queen said bitterly. "What woman would want to spend her life looking at something as big and ugly as Mr. Pete?"

I carefully wiped blood from her shoulder, but said nothing as I considered how small Uncle Ollie seemed compared with the mammoth-size Aunt Clara Jean.

Queen's countenance fell. "He lied to me," she said.

"Who?" I asked.

"Jim," Queen answered.

"Jim who?"

"Robinson."

My eyebrows came together. "Jimmy Robinson?"

Queen nodded.

"What did Jimmy Robinson lie to you about?"

"He said he loved me."

I stopped wiping blood from her delicate skin. I was so confused it seemed cobwebs had cluttered my head. "Why would Jimmy Robinson say he loved you?"

As if the same cobwebs had magically appeared in her head, Queen stared at me blankly. After a moment she flinched. "You thought I was with Ricky Turner?"

I was too confused to answer.

Even in pain, Queen managed a conceited stare. "I got more class than that."

"But Jimmy's only fourteen. The same age as Hallelujah."

Queen stared at me, as if the mention of Hallelujah's name disgusted her. "Jim's more man than that boy will ever be," she said, her nose in the air.

Blood rushed to my head and seemed to pound in my ears.

I didn't know why, but somehow knowing that Queen had gotten in trouble with Jimmy Robinson instead of Ricky Turner appeared frightening. What if Mr. Robinson found out? What would happen to Ma Pearl and Papa? Where would they go if Mr. Robinson ran them off his place because of Queen? Regardless of how good a farmer Papa was, I doubted he wanted to work for anyone other than Mr. Robinson.

My teeth clenched. "How could you do this to them?"

"What?" she said, staring at me as if I had asked her where babies came from in the first place.

"How could you do this to Ma Pearl and Papa?"

Queen rolled her eyes. "I didn't do anything to them. They did this to me." She shifted her weight and moaned in pain. "They lock us up in this house and won't let us go nowhere but church and school."

"That's no reason for you to do what you did," I said.

She rolled her eyes again and said, "When else was I supposed to leave this damn house and have some fun?"

"But with Jimmy Robinson?"

Queen's haughty stare returned. "Why not?" she asked, her tone icy.

"Because he's white, and you're colored."

"I'm as good as any white girl he coulda had," she said, sniffing.

"He told you that?"

"He loves me," Queen said. "I know he do."

I pointed at her stomach. "What'd he say about that?"

As Queen stared at her stomach, tears suddenly flooded her eyes. "He loves me," she insisted, her voice cracking.

I sighed. "But he threw you out of the truck?"

"Ma Pearl lied," she snapped. "He didn't throw me out. I tripped and fell."

I took a deep breath and let it out. But I didn't respond to Queen. I knew for myself how Ma Pearl could dress up a story, but I doubted she was making things up this time. I was sure Jimmy Robinson *had* thrown Queen out of that truck. He had discarded her, just the way his mama discarded the things she no longer wanted. He discarded her and handed her over to Ma Pearl.

October

Chapter Thirty-Two

WADE IN THE WATER. WADE IN THE WATER, CHILDREN. *Wade in the water. God's gonna trouble the waters.'"* The words were meant to comfort the fourteen of us lined up along the sloping path that led to the banks of Stillwater Lake. Mother Edwards, Deacon Edwards's wife, and Ma Pearl had lined us up according to age, with the youngest, nine-year-old Obadiah Malone, leading the way. Queen, being the oldest, as she'd turn sixteen in less than a week, was last. I was in front of her, and Fred Lee stood before me.

The old saying goes that if you aren't truly saved, if your sign was false and you didn't have religion, God would allow you to choke and strangle in the water when the preacher plunged you under. The night before, Queen had confessed to me that she was scared to go down into the water. After Ma Pearl's discovery of her secret, she had said she didn't want to be baptized. But Ma Pearl wasn't hearing it. Queen was already about to bring her enough shame without backing out of her baptism as well. So there she stood behind me, all dressed in white, from the turban wrapped around her head to the thick stockings covering her feet, scared half to death that when she went down into that water, God was going to make it choke her to death.

Reverend Jenkins said that "troubling the waters" referred to a Bible story about a healing pool, where an angel troubled the waters during a certain season and the first person in the pool after the stirring would be healed. But my teacher Miss Johnson said the song was a secret slavery song, directing runaway slaves to wade through water to throw off their scents so dogs couldn't track them. She said God would trouble the waters to keep snakes or alligators from attacking the slaves. I didn't know whose version of the song's story was correct, but I did know that I felt my own knees knock a bit just from the thought of my body being dipped backwards underwater. What if I slipped? What if Reverend Jenkins and Deacon Edwards dropped me? How deep was the water? I couldn't swim, and I doubted whether any of them could either. What if I, like Queen, felt I wasn't truly saved? Would I choke?

"'See that host all dressed in white. God's gonna trouble the water. The leader looks like the Israelite. God's gonna trouble the water.'"

My knees knocked harder as our seemingly fear-free little leader Obadiah waded into the water. He was flanked by his older brothers Abner and Abel, both fifteen and already deacons. All the Malone children had been baptized before they'd reached the age of accountability, but at only nine, Obadiah had outdone them all. I prayed that his conversion was sincere and that he hadn't been like me at that age, confusing the deacons' words, "I move that so-and-so become a candidate for baptism," with "I move that so-and-so receive a box of candy for baptism." I would hate to see him come out of that lake sputtering to catch his breath.

"'If you don't believe I've been redeemed. God's gonna trouble the water. Just follow me down to the Jordan's stream. God's gonna trouble the water.'"

With the water covering the deacons' waists, it nearly swallowed little Obadiah's shoulders, so much so that he could have bent his knees and he would have been baptized as soon as he stepped into the lake.

The little brown face peeking out from all the white of the turban and the baptismal robe didn't look so fear-free once Reverend Jenkins and Deacon Edwards faced him toward the crowd. I was sure Obadiah was about to cry. But when Reverend Jenkins asked him if he believed that Jesus was the son of God, that he died on the cross for our sins, and that he rose again on the third day to conquer death, hell, and the grave, little Obadiah boldly proclaimed, "Yes, sir. I do!"

"Amens" reverberated around the banks of the lake,

after which Reverend Jenkins bent his face toward the sky and belted out, "In obedie-e-e-ence to the great head of the church and upon the profession of your faith, Obadiah Malone, I baptize you in the name of the Father, in the name of the Son, and in the name of the Holy Ghost."

I could feel everyone, including myself, hold their breath as Obadiah was completely immersed in the water and swiftly brought back up.

"'If you don't believe I've been redeemed. God's gonna trouble the water. Just follow me down to the Jordan's stream. God's gonna trouble the water.'"

By the time the line got down to just Fred Lee, me, and Queen, I wasn't as nervous anymore. Maybe that was why they let the younger children go first—to show the older ones that there was nothing to fear. No one had choked or even hiccupped coming out of the water. All eleven of the first candidates had truly been saved.

I held my breath again as Fred Lee was led into the water. He was taller than Reverend Jenkins and Deacon Edwards. What if they dipped him under and couldn't lift him back up, and for that brief moment, he choked? Ma Pearl would have a fit if one of us embarrassed her. *Lord, don't let him choke. Don't let him choke,* I prayed over and over. When Fred Lee was lifted out of the water, I released my breath. Then the nervous feeling that had left me earlier returned. But it didn't come alone. It brought company—a gurgling in my stomach. I suddenly felt like I needed to run to the toilet. *Lord, not now. Not while I'm wearing white.*

When the deacon took my hand, it was shaking. "Don't be afraid, Sister Rose," he said. "If all these little ones can go down to the water, I know you ain't scared."

I got to the edge of the water and froze. My socked feet would not move. Both deacons tugged at my arms, lifting me into the water. I was glad the moment was meant to be an emotional one, as tears were streaming down my face.

The muddy water was still, just as its name implied. Yet I felt as if I were floating, as if I could just float up and float away. When Reverend Jenkins and Deacon Edwards faced me toward the congregants of Greater Mount Zion Missionary Baptist Church, my eyes met Fred Lee's. With a towel draped over his shoulders, his arms crossed over his chest, he smiled reassuringly at me.

Reverend Jenkins spoke. "Rosa Lee Carter, do you believe that Jesus was the son of God . . ." And before I knew it, a toweled hand was cupped over my nose and mouth and I was bent backwards under the water. Ma Pearl had said to make sure we closed our eyes, but I didn't. I knew it was no more than a couple of seconds that I was under there, but it seemed as if I were staring up at that few inches of water covering my face for an eternity. Above the water loomed a clear blue sky, which I took as a sign that one day my life would be as clear and beautiful as it was.

Two days before the baptism, I had asked Ma Pearl to show me my birth certificate. I had never seen it, because she kept it locked away in her chifforobe. I never had a reason to ask for it before, but I wanted to see for myself what name Miss Addie had scribbled there. And just like Papa had said, the name, written in Miss Addie's crooked lettering, was Rosa Lee. So when Reverend Jenkins asked which name I wanted on my baptism record, I told him "Rosa" because that was my name. The name that was recorded upon my birth. Rosa Lee Carter. The name I would carry with me to Saint Louis when I started my new life.

I came up out of the baptismal waters of Stillwater Lake gasping for air. But I hadn't choked. I was happy to feel the warmth of tears rolling down my cheeks, because it was commonly believed that the truly saved would cry after baptism. When I came out of the water, Ma Pearl draped me in towels.

By the time I wiped my face and looked out at the lake, Queen was already in the water and facing the crowd. She looked peaceful rather than afraid. Maybe being the last one was good for her. I just prayed she didn't choke.

And she didn't. She came up out of that water like the queen she was meant to be. Regal and proud, despite the trouble she had gotten herself into.

Chapter Thirty-Three

SUNDAY, OCTOBER 2

After the baptism and the church service that followed, a large gathering of people came over to enjoy Ma Pearl's chicken and dressing. With her having three grandchildren baptized in one day, she was the envy of all the mothers of the church.

Baptism, it seemed, had even changed Queen. Or maybe it was that little issue of the trouble she found herself in that changed her. Either way, she surprised us all by joining Hallelujah, me, and Fred Lee as we sat in the shade of the ancient oak tree in the front yard. Fred Lee, as usual, didn't have much to say. But Hallelujah, in the presence of the Queen, couldn't seem to shut his mouth. And I wanted to punch him in it.

Although he had previously been talking about how colored folks in the South would soon have to stand up for their civil rights, for Queen's entertainment he began to prattle about some up-and-coming rock-and-roll singer he'd heard who was sure to become a favorite of both coloreds and whites.

"Elvis Presley, huh?" Queen said absently as she stared off into the distance.

"Yeah, out of Memphis," Hallelujah said. "Came from Mississippi, though. Tupelo. Just got out of high school a couple of years ago and already got a music contract. Heard he was just up in Clarksdale last month . . ." He babbled on.

Queen nodded but said nothing.

Fred Lee seemed more interested. Staring buck-eyed at Hallelujah, he said, "I didn't know you liked white folks' music."

I held back a chuckle. Hallelujah wasn't any more interested in white folks' music than I was in being Mrs. Robinson's maid.

Hallelujah beamed. "Oh, it ain't just white folks' music Elvis sings. He's got his own style."

Sometimes he sounded like such a fool when he got around Queen. Besides, if this Elvis fellow was on the radio, I was sure Queen had already heard of him, as much as she had her ear pressed to that thing, running down Ma Pearl's "batt'ries."

"I even hear that colored women are starting to name their sons after him," Hallelujah continued. "Can you imagine a colored boy named Elvis?"

Queen snapped her head my way and shot me a dirty look. I shook my head discreetly to let her know that if Hallelujah was throwing any hints her way, it wasn't on account of me. I hadn't told him a thing about her. Oh, I wanted so badly to tell him. To let him know there was no point in trying to impress Queen anymore, as she was already ruined and unfit to marry a preacher's boy. But it wasn't my business to tell. Time and Queen's growing belly would do that eventually.

"That ain't Aunt Ruthie, is it?" Fred Lee said, pointing up the road.

We all leaned forward and peered up the road to the west, in the opposite direction of the Robinsons'. Anybody with eyes could see that it was Aunt Ruthie and her brood of young ones stirring up a small puff of dust on the road.

"I hope she didn't walk seven miles with them chi'ren again," Queen said, leaping up from her chair.

"There's no sign of a car anywhere," I pointed out.

Queen ignored my sarcasm. "I hope Slow John didn't beat her again," she said. Without another word, she stormed across the yard toward the road. Within seconds she had joined Aunt Ruthie and begun gathering the children in her arms. In that instant, I knew, despite all her other shortcomings, she was going to make a fine mother.

When they reached the yard, Aunt Ruthie acknowledged us with a nod. Otherwise she kept her head down. Her right arm was wrapped with one of the baby's diapers, and there was blood on the sleeve of her faded plaid dress.

Out of nowhere, Hallelujah said, "Preacher almost married her."

My head jerked toward him. "Who?"

"Preacher asked your aunt Ruthie to marry him after my mama died."

"Your real mama?"

Still staring at Aunt Ruthie as she ambled across the porch, Hallelujah nodded.

We watched Queen settle on the edge of the porch. Her legs dangled from the solid blue trim of her blue and white checkered skirt, and her forehead wrinkled with concern as she gathered Aunt Ruthie's children on either side of her and cradled the baby in her lap.

"I never knew Reverend Jenkins wanted to marry Aunt Ruthie," I said.

Hallelujah shrugged. "He said she was one of the smartest women he knew."

"Ain't too smart," Fred Lee said, "lettin' Slow John hit her like that."

"Said she used to be one of the prettiest women in Stillwater, too," Hallelujah said.

"Reverend Jenkins said Aunt Ruthie was pretty?" I asked.

"She is pretty," said Hallelujah.

"But she's so d—" I stopped myself when I realized what I was about to imply.

"Dark women is pretty too," Fred Lee said.

"That ain't what I was about to say," I snapped.

"You was," Fred Lee countered.

Fred Lee was right. *I* knew Aunt Ruthie was pretty. So why did I find it hard to believe Reverend Jenkins would find her pretty too? For the same reason I couldn't think of myself as pretty—my own grandmother had made me feel ashamed of my complexion, saying I was as black as midnight without a moon. But I had to remember my own strange words to Hallelujah on the night before the murder trial ended: *stars can't shine without darkness.* And I was determined that one day, instead of fretting over being as dark as midnight without a moon, I would shine as bright as the morning star— which, Reverend Jenkins told us, is the planet Venus and is also a sign of hope.

"How come Reverend Jenkins didn't marry Aunt Ruthie?" I asked Hallelujah.

"Miss Sweet wouldn't let him," he answered.

"Wonder why," I mumbled, staring at the house.

"I wish she had," said Hallelujah. "She's too smart and pretty for a man like John Walker. Preacher said after Miss Sweet wouldn't let her marry him, she ran off with the first thing with legs."

"She'd have been better off marrying a spider," I said.

"I'm glad she didn't marry Preacher," said Fred Lee.

Hallelujah and I stared at him.

"All o' yo' mamas die," Fred Lee said matter-of-factly.

We tried not to, but laughs slipped out of Hallelujah and me anyway.

Yet we knew this was no laughing moment. Here was our aunt, again at her parents' home, again having walked seven miles with her children, again having been beaten by her no-'count husband. And probably would, again, leave the safety of our house and go back to him.

I let my head lean back, and I looked up at the clear blue sky. The evening sun streaming through the leaves warmed my face. October had just begun, so the leaves on the ancient oak towering over me had not changed. They were still full, green, and fluffy. But I knew they would soon change. They would become orange and red and gold; then, eventually, they would fall from the tree. Change was inevitable in nature, as Miss Johnson used to say, but not in people. People had a choice, whereas nature did not.

Reverend Jenkins was sure that a change was coming to Mississippi, that life for the Negro would get better. I had made a promise before the church and before God that I would change, and today my sins had been washed away. Queen and Fred Lee, too, had made that profession of faith to change. And long ago, when she was our age, so had Aunt Ruthie. Now, years later, it seemed she needed to make a commitment to change again. A commitment to permanently walk away from a life where she wasn't really living. I closed my eyes and offered up a prayer for her. Only two people could help my aunt: God and herself.

Change. It's what I had been thinking about since that Monday after the Emmett Till murder trial—the day after Aunt Belle and Monty headed back to Saint Louis. So many thoughts warred against one another in my mind. I thought about what Hallelujah had said on the night before the trial ended, about why folks like Reverend Jenkins and Medgar Evers chose to stay in Mississippi even though they could probably leave, just like Mr. Pete, Mama, and Aunt Belle.

Dreams have more meaning when you have to fight for them, he'd said. And that's why some people chose to stay. They knew they had a right to be there—this land is your land, this land is my land. And they wanted the freedom to do so.

But I also thought about Papa. The thought of leaving him broke my heart. I thought of my own words to Queen when I asked her, "How could you do this to them?" But then I had to ask myself, "How could I do this to Papa?" Especially now that Queen had disappointed him so.

How could I leave Papa? How could I leave Fred Lee? Leaving him would make me as bad as Mama. Who could know what might happen to him if both his mama and his sister left him, not counting the fact that his daddy had never bothered with trying to be a part of his life?

And Hallelujah. Yes, he sat there making a fool of himself over Queen, but he was still *my* best friend. How could I leave him? And what kind of friends would I make in Saint Louis? If any?

My heart ached, both at the thought of leaving and at the thought of staying. Levi had stayed, and he didn't live to see a week over the age of twenty-one. Would that happen to me? I didn't know—couldn't know—but I had to be strong enough to find out. I had to stay—not just for the sake of those I didn't want to leave behind, but for my own sake. I had to know if I could shine in the darkness.

Imagine how bright a star would shine at midnight without a moon!

I had to be bold enough to write to Aunt Belle and let her know my choice. And I had to write that letter without delay —before I had time to change my mind. A chill came over me at the thought. But then, right there, the warmth of the Mississippi sun crossed my face while a single leaf fluttered down and brushed my cheek. I opened my eyes and stared down at the leaf that had landed in my lap. It was still green, with hints of yellow. Yes, a change was coming. And I, Rosa Lee Carter, would be right there to be a part of it.

Acknowledgments

This book would not have happened without . . .

God—who gave me the talent to write and the strength to endure rejection.

The Mississippi Arts Commission—which boosted my confidence with a Literary Artist Fellowship Grant to encourage the completion of the book.

Victoria Marini (Literary Agent Extraordinaire!)—who salvaged my query from the slush and finally gave me the "yes" that changed my life.

Elizabeth Bewley (Super Awesome Ninja Editor!)—who showed me how to make a good story *great*.

Nicole Sclama (Super Awesome Editorial Assistant!)—who double-checked my research to make sure I got the facts straight.

Writer friends—who read various drafts of the manuscript and said, "This is good. Keep going."

The ladies of my Sunday school class at Brown Missionary Baptist Church—who prayed me through a six-year journey to find an agent.

All my family and friends—who believed that one day I would eventually land an agent and a book deal.

And, of course, the wonderful folks at Houghton Mifflin Harcourt Books for Young Readers—who believed this story needed to be shared with children around the world.